ASHA
OF THE AIR

JOHN HUDDLES

NOTABLE
PUBLISHING

Published by
Notable Publishing
ISBN 9781735853529 (Hardcover)
ISBN 9781735853536 (e-pub)

Library of Congress Control Number: 2021951818
Huddles, John
Fiction / Fantasy / Epic Fiction / Literary Fiction / Gothic

Printed in the United States of America.

Notable Publishing
PO 2047, Parker, Colorado, 80134 / 303.840.5787
Cover art by Peter Trimarco / John Huddles ©2022

www.notable-publishing.com

www.johnhuddles.com

To LH AND GH

PART ONE

HERE IN OUR SILVER CITIES above the earth but below the curve of space, where we prefer to live today, we hover eleven miles high. Lifting fields keep us aloft, generated by the immense engines of our particle-spinners. The power of these machines to dilate gravity is staggering, and their effects extend beyond the edges of our cities for a thousand feet in every direction: we can walk through the clouds if we wish, into sheer sky. And where the lifting fields finally decay, electromagnetic markers are in place to nudge us back and keep us from tumbling out of our high home.

We are an engineering society. Those technologies that appeal to us, we excel at. There is a beauty in our science, though also a limitation. Our great flaw, I often find myself thinking, is that we have narrowed our interests too drastically. We are a knowledge-able people, but we are perhaps duller than we might be—a consequence of our address. When residing in a city eleven miles above solid ground, a trillion tons of silver hanging in the troposphere, the practicalities rule. We focus on the physics of things: ultraviolet filters and oxygenation protocols and the brew of isotopes in our particle-spinners. This is not all bad, though, as I've said, it is narrow. For instance: despite the collected documents of eight thousand years in our archives, we are not accomplished historians. We prefer our own lives, our own ventures, our own time.

But I like the past. This comes to me from my mother, who knew the early tales. She recited them to me from the year I turned five. Night after night I listened, drifting to sleep with my mind eleven miles beneath my body. And though I haven't heard my mother's voice in nearly two decades now, lately her stories have been popping into my head again. It's no mystery why: my little girl turns five next month—and bedtime is still story time.

Of course I'll never be as good at the job as my mother was. I have a spotty memory for one thing: I tend to dip into my imagination to fill in the gaps. It seems to me this is a defect in a storyteller, who should be able to receive and transmit without loss of information. My wife disagrees: she says I have a flair for what makes a story worth hearing, which she rates above the data that makes it worth telling. But my wife is kind, and she loves me.

So yes, my mother could have told you this particular story better than I'll be able to, though I think she'd be pleased that I'm going to try to tell it at all. It takes place on the earthtop, some six thousand years ago, near the end of the Age of the Poets, whose own stories and songs, recited from memory, lasted the length of echoes, but no longer. It was a story by the way that my mother believed to be true. Or let's say it was a story she believed in. She called it "Asha of the Air."

i

Shape a palace in your mind. Make it out of spheres and domes and even crescents of white stone, like the waxing and waning of a marble moon. Inlay it with patterns of platinum, and between its colossal orbs and slivers spike white minarets. Let it run an eighth of a mile, end to end. Situate this palace at the southern tip of a polar region, but wedge it within a temperate corridor where a quirk of the earth warms the wind. Along its frontage install gardens of white-rose trees and beyond the gardens plant groves of pine. Become aware that this palace of yours was already an ancient creation by the time your mind arrived at it. Now gloss it with star-light and let your eye fly to the window of its high minaret, where even before we were ready to join her, Asha stood heating a syringe over a candle's flame. She had already tapped at its glass barrel to dislodge clinging air bubbles in the milky liquid it contained; now she was enduring the long minute it would take for the solution to rise to body temperature …

The instant the dava luminesced—"dava" being the word of the ancients for the contents of Asha's syringe—she twisted a cord around her arm to highlight a vein and injected herself. She held her breath until the dava's heat reached her fingertips, then exhaled slowly to settle the rush of nausea that followed every dose. After this she leaned out the minaret's window to take in a riot of starlight moving across the gardens and irradiating the lake. For sixteen generations, Asha's family had ruled this mighty house of Palace Isha and all its surrounding lands. Here in the far north of the raajy, they had been left mostly alone to conduct their own lives and pursue their own fortunes, hearing only rarely from the Shaasak or his government, eight hundred miles to the south. Extreme distance and the brutality of the intervening terrain had made a lonely freedom for them. Asha herself, almost twenty-two years old, had never even been beyond the borders of her own home, which at some forty thousand haiktars of forest and alp isn't quite the same as saying that she hadn't traveled.

Though Asha's family had held legal title to these lands for three hundred and twenty years, Asha was the last of her line. Her father had been an only child, and Asha's one sibling, a brother, had come to them stillborn; so control of the great enterprise of Palace Isha, if not ownership of the vast house itself, had been transferred to Asha's husband, along with authority over the people of the region. This was the answer that Asha herself had settled on.

She blew out her candle now and lingered at the window, silvered by the beams of ten thousand stars. A rising wind stung her cheeks and the tip of her nose, but with the dava in her system she could easily slip between layers of sensation to evade the pain. Outside the moon was scattering its quanta across the tops of the pines and down onto the white-rose trees fronting the house. Asha let the spectacle mesmerize her for several minutes, until with an effort she pushed herself back from the window. After closing the shutters, she climbed down the minaret's stairs and in her bare feet walked the halls between her own marble sphere of Palace Isha and her husband's.

Since her marriage to the Vikaant Cabaan five years earlier, Asha had in fact been the Vikaantee Asha, a title which, while honorable, was something less than the ancient rank of Raajakumaaree that she had been born to as her father's daughter, and which in respect of the law had expired on her wedding day. The reduction in status had never concerned her. Besides, in their remote corner of the raajy titles meant less than in other places: there were so few people here per haiktar that they had always mixed freely, without affectation, and with a sense more of the possibilities of life in one another than the limitations of birth. And whatever Asha's legal status, most people here still considered her Raajakumaaree anyway.

Cabaan's bedroom was shifting with torchlight when Asha

slipped in. She draped her nightsari over the hooped horns of a chair—Cabaan's furniture was carved to resemble the animals he hunted: snow leopard, gazelle, high-altitude ibex—then crossed to join her husband in his bed. Less than two years her senior, Cabaan was in other words not yet twenty-four, though his self-consequence gave him the air of a man a decade older. Any first report of his qualities would also have to include the paradox of his physical form: his face was deceptively beautiful; his hair golden and fiery like a sun god's; his ratio of height to mass and mass to muscle the ideal of his sex. That he was verging on a kind of bodily perfection couldn't be argued, though possibly the most notable reaction to the fact of it was Asha's own: she had never really liked the way he looked. Even his famously mismatched eyes—the one violet, the other pale blue—failed to fascinate her. She knew that Cabaan was pleasing to the senses, but it was more a point of reference than a point of attraction.

Very different was Cabaan's reaction to Asha's own features and physique: the almond complexion of her father's Vaidik line, the dark, gently waved hair that (by embellishment) reflected rather than absorbed light, the bright brown eyes; and from her mother the long legs, high forehead, and full lips, traits of the chronologically distant though genetically remembered hemolactic tribes. While Cabaan's kinship group had originated in the southernmost province of the raajy, issuing from that region's unvaried gene pool, Asha had in her the mix of many, producing a color and form so thrilling that Cabaan not only took pleasure in but frequently commented on his wife's beauty. For a while, early on, Asha had even enjoyed his compliments in this department, until she realized they were less an appreciation than an inventory.

Outside a gale was now whipping the grounds, barbed with ice crystals that the wind had shaved off the glaciers not five miles away. Palace Isha wasn't threatened—even an earthquake couldn't have budged its massive stone domes—but the torches ringing the boundary were blown out. So the house went dark, except for a bright slice of window into Cabaan's bedroom, where, if you could have levitated high enough to look in, you would have witnessed what was called in Bhaashan, or the common language of the era, the "yaun sambandh." While the many-sidedness of desire has always been a feature of human intimacy, Asha's nightly encounters with her husband fell nowhere within the ambit of what for most women would be considered tolerable relations. But the injection that she had prophylactically given herself did its job: each time that Cabaan bruised or cut her as he worked his way ferociously toward completion, her dava came surging into the affected area, mending her chemically and cancelling the pain. It was a powerful cure, and Asha paid heavily for it. And though this may seem a radical accommodation that she had made to the demands of wedlock, Asha had entered into her marriage, if not exactly its consequences, freely. It was, she often reminded herself, the best she could have done.

An hour later she climbed down from Cabaan's bed, leaving him to sleep alone, the way he preferred. She made her way quietly to the ground floor, still in bare feet but having put back on the sheer nightsari striped with platinum thread that made her seem more lunar nymph than girl of flesh and blood. Downstairs she took a hallway through the hidden channels of the house that only she and the oldest retainers at Palace Isha still knew existed: Cabaan was unaware of these passages, and Asha had no intention of ever telling him they were here.

At the end of the hall she bent low to pass through a half-height door that her father had carved with his own hands for her fifth birthday and which she still liked to use when no one would see. This brought her outside, where she found the windstorm dwindled to a gusty aftermath. The heavens, however, were raging. Stars were frantically flashing signals into the unanswering void; Venus was in flames; a red comet came whipping through the solar system and slammed into the moon, leaving a blood-colored crater. If there was some message in this cosmic uproar, Asha couldn't read it: she had no talent at decoding omens and out of long habit tried her best to ignore them. Also she knew that what she was seeing might be a hallucination of the type that the dava every now and then induced. So she continued on to the edge of the western woods, where she came to a protected niche in the base of a redwood. Climbing in, she drew her knees to her chin and closed her eyes. The dava would protect her from frostbite and even hypothermia through the rest of the night, like the magical polypeptides in the blood of a hibernating bear. She could count on it until dawn, and if somehow she slept later than that, her shivering body would shake her out of her dreams before she caught cold. But as she gave in now to the end of another night of damage, her mind nicked itself on the sharp edge of perception, and she saw that even though she had held together one more time, she was still at risk of splitting apart. How much longer she could go on this way, she had no idea.

ii

The shriek of a lemur woke Asha early. She climbed awkwardly out of the redwood, her balance undone by the dava's after-affects. On bad days she had to reach out and steady herself step by step to keep from toppling over; but it was bearable, and the dizziness abated as soon as she forced down a slice of grilled bread. By the time she bathed she was generally herself again.

The morning walk back from the western woods was Asha's favorite piece of the day. Here in the far north of the raajy, tucked between glaciated valleys, they lived in a mild world. The sun lit the green and white panels of their landscape every day of the year; rain fell frequently but fleetingly; and the temperature was almost always just right by midday. The air was crisp and fragrant with pine; the clouds that briskly came and went seemed to Asha the after-images of ships from some bygone Age of Sail, forever plying the dream of an upside-down sea. She often stopped whatever she was in the middle of, to follow them to the horizon.

This morning she made a detour that took her through the pink-mango grove and past the rotunda, that circular pile of blue glass with its copper roof overlooking Palace Isha's lake. Though listed among the real holdings of the palace along with every other significant structure on the property, the rotunda was practically speaking the domain of Asha's last blood relative in the world: her cousin, Omala, who used it as both residence and prayogashaala—or to say it our modern way: her laboratory.

Omala was up early as usual, already bent over the eyepiece of her photoscope: the habit of a vigyaanik with a full day of science ahead of her. Watching through a blue pane without tapping to interrupt, Asha thought to herself that at the age of thirty her cousin now summarized the best qualities of their all-but-defunct family: a certain lively charm, a curiosity about the structures and secrets of the natural world, a rebellious intelligence, a personal conviction about how to live. Asha believed that she had been born with potential of her own in these directions, minus the rebellious intelligence, only the potential hadn't converted. By now the slow poison of despair had seeped into her assessment of herself: she felt that she was on the verge of failing not as her husband's wife, but far more gravely as her parents' child. It was something she hadn't said to Omala or to anyone, though her cousin was her oldest friend and last remaining confidante, because sometime in the previous year Asha had stopped reporting the deep things.

Omala's doings at her photoscope made her observer smile with cousinly pride. Among Omala's innovations was the device she had just reached for: an ebony box that could capture what she had discovered were the acoustic waves of a person's voice. She disliked having to stop to take notes while she worked, so she had devised this unique solution: now she spoke into the horn of the small box as she went about her day's experiments—and her speech was transferred into the specially treated beeswax of a candle held tight at the box's center by magnetized mesh. Later, to review her notes at her leisure and write down those worth keeping, she simply extracted the resulting candle from the box, lit it, and listened to a slightly distant-sounding recording of her own voice released into the air, gone for good once the candle burned to its base, gone like an echo, or like the plot of a dream that dissolves in the moments after waking.

It was the fertility even more than the intensity of Omala's mind that Asha found daunting. She felt no envy of her cousin, only respect, though she did question by way of comparison how she herself had managed to come to nothing so quickly, having started out with so much, whereas Omala had made such wonders from so little.

A compassionate listener might appeal at this point for information on what Asha's allies and well-wishers were thinking as they watched her drift further and more dangerously into a bog of self-doubt, but the prevailing silence in this regard had followed from a perverse truth: Asha's youth and loveliness were natural camouflage for the dark turn that her life had taken within. Also she contained her sorrows extremely well. As we've seen, she had even found a way to hide sorrows within sadnesses, at a kind of costly success. In the eyes of those around her, she was still a beautiful girl. To see her pass by was a small joy of the day, to be spoken to by Asha was a happiness that lasted through the morning or afternoon, to be touched by her on the shoulder or kissed hello on the cheek—though this had been happening less and less in recent months—was a gift. But for the dozens of souls who lived in proximity to her, many of whom had known her since the day she was born, the oddest contradiction of all was this: though Asha believed herself to be locked in a defining if silent battle to become strong, no one around her had ever considered her weak.

iii

It was mid-morning by the time Asha arrived home from the western woods. She bathed slowly, then dressed quickly to make up the time, though no one was clocking her. Stepping out onto a front balcony of the palace's Middle Dome, she found a busy scene below. The staff of the household were carrying tables and chairs into the gardens from the new set of golden bamboo furniture that had been delivered only yesterday for the occasion; they were hanging lanterns of purple glass between the pines, shaping flowers into dense floral balls for centerpieces, and using lifting gas to inflate balloons inside coverings of stitched-together eucalyptus leaves. Tethered by string to stakes in the ground, the floating, silver-green globes made a layer of botanical art between earth and sky, a genre of local invention.

One of Palace Isha's younger handymen, an orphan of twelve by the name of Jothi-Anandan, tied a handful of white roses to a balloon and sent them on a string up to Asha's balcony. Asha plucked the little bouquet out of the air, breathed its sweetness, and blew a kiss down to Jothi-Anandan. The boy waved elaborately, lingering to watch Asha as long as he could before returning to the tube of lifting gas he was charged with operating. Meanwhile Asha stood still for almost a quarter hour, gazing at the decoration in progress. Her mind was not on the purpose of the work: she was enjoying a rare moment of repose, thinking about nothing at all.

Inevitably a twinge of dread obtruded: Asha started up again and turned to go back inside. Bouquet in hand, she moved through the Middle Dome and stepped out onto the opposing balcony overlooking the backlands. Here the so-called "White Forest" of her childhood, a vast field of pines bearing white roses like scoops of snow—her father's forest, hybridized and cultivated over a life-time—was gone. Ripped out in a matter of months and replaced with endless haiktars of kuroop trees. The botanical grotesque of the region, the kuroop was gnarled like a monster of myth, its bark sharp enough to slice skin at a touch, its misshapen branches nearly leafless, since it relied not on photosynthesis for energy but took all it needed from the rich soils of the north. Unlike any other plant in the world, the kuroop could even soak up through its roots the metal wolfram, working it into the low density of its biomolecules. Palace Isha, to complete the picture, sat on the purest veins of wolfram, or what today we call "tungsten," in the whole of the raajy.

When a tract of kuroops reached maturity in its eighteen-month growth cycle, it was promptly dug up and carted off to the mill at the edge of the backlands. Here the trees were sawed and shaped into lumber—blocks and planks of standard dimension—and as a side business carved into kitchen utensils and agricultural implements. Next came the glazery, where the combination of a chemical wash and galvanic current hardened the planks and implements into "wolfram-wood"—light as the wood of the baalsa tree, but strong as metal. In short: the most valuable building material in the world— which Palace Isha now produced in quantity.

There were drawbacks. A kuroop required constant pruning or else such a number of them as were planted here would entwine themselves in a single season into an impenetrable mass, like a jungle of knives. So a labor force of some hundred men was constantly at work: the "aapravaaseen" in Bhaashan (for which no word exists in modern translation), brought in by Cabaan from the distressed lands on the other side of the raajy's western border. Their pay was adequate if nothing more by local standards, but it exceeded by an order of magnitude what they could have earned in the economy of their own realm. They remitted the whole of it to their families at home, though as guest laborers at Palace Isha they were housed and fed free of charge, so they had no expenses to speak of while on the premises. Six of the old domes at the palace extremity had been converted into living space for them and the kitchen in an adjacent seventh dome staffed and supplied to provide them the food and drink of the lands they had left behind. The garments they wore here, woven from the soft hair of the polar goat and warmer than what was needed in the climate they were used to, were given rather than sold to them; and visits from the barber, the dentist, and the physician were all paid for by the palace.

But the work was a torment. Though double-weight gloves were the rule to protect fingers and wrists, kuroop thorns could still puncture if vigilance flagged. Even a speck of wolfram injected into the bloodstream was a poison. Pruners often fell ill. They usually recovered, but were never quite the same.

Reaching for a pair of field glasses, Asha focused on a team at work with shears and loppers. Over their heads, vapors from the glazery yellowed the sky, an outgassing of the chemical wash that hardened the wolfram-wood and locked in its value. In Asha's memory, the White Forest was a rose-scented paradise. Now the air here reminded her of a cookhouse reeking of stale fat. Yet this was not the worst of it. The worst was something unique in the annals of sylviculture so far as she knew: a charge in the air from the glazery's galvanic activity. It buzzed on the skin, especially the earlobes and nape of the neck. For reasons exceeding Asha's grasp of electromagnetism, living tissue was affected most. But the result was clear to all who dwelled here: if you moved too quickly through these backlands, you risked igniting yourself. Every so often a pruner would jerk his arm after being pricked by a kuroop thorn—and his exposed skin would burst into flame like a struck match. Easy enough to put out, if no joy to experience.

Just now Jothi-Anandan's roses slipped from Asha's fingers, falling over the balcony and catching fire in descent. On the ground below, it was Cabaan himself who scooped the little mass of burning petals into his gloved hand and held it up for Asha, forty feet above.

"Dropped something!"

When no reply came, Cabaan tossed the bouquet—more flame

than flower already—onto a heap of potash. He entered the ground floor mud-room, changed out of his boots, climbed the stairs, and came up behind his wife.

"Are you depressed today, Asha?"

"Mutilation has that particular effect on me."

She was still gazing at the backlands, so Cabaan settled in to gaze alongside her. "When I look out this window," he said, "I don't see mutilation, I see money."

"Why did I ever let you do this?"

"To keep you in style."

"What about keeping me in trees?"

"Kuroops *are* trees."

"Are they? I've never been convinced."

"Asha, you're a lovely girl, but there's something of the willful ignoramus about you when it comes to understanding the world the way it really is."

She turned to face him. "There must have been a kinder way of saying that."

"Don't mind the way I say things. They're only words."

Returning to the view, Asha remarked: "My father would not have understood."

"Your father had a genius for landscape while oddly missing the point of having land. He understood how to use all this to his advantage. Yet instead of profiting from it, he covered it with flowers."

"He was an artist. It was his art."

"You and I both know that the true value of Palace Isha is the connection between the wolfram and the kuroop. The kuroop that only grows in profusion in our one region because only our region's soils can nourish it. The kuroop that's the only plant in the world able to incorporate wolfram into its wood, wolfram that our land contains in sufficient purity and quantity to make the whole, implausible, organic-inorganic equation actually *work*. Wolfram-wood, in the amount we can grow and glaze, will make us immensely rich. Your father had this same opportunity his whole life. That he didn't care, you'll pardon me for saying, put his very mentality in question."

"My father knew what he was doing."

"Your father ruined himself and he nearly ruined *you*. I started with nothing and I intend to leave a fortune—your father worked the other way around."

"He had a different ambition than you do."

With this Asha left the balcony; but Cabaan followed her inside, all the way to her writing room in an adjoining section of the dome, carrying on as they went:

"If his ambition was to beggar his family, he succeeded magnificently! You had nothing to offer except your pretty face and a sea of *rose*-trees! You should be grateful that underneath all that 'art' was wolfram. That's why I married you—and that's why you married *me*. Because you knew I'd rip the flowers out and plant kuroops in their place!"

This was not a new conversation. Asha tried putting an end to it by keeping quiet. In her writing room now, she ran a finger along a rose-tree in miniature beautifying her desk: one of her father's ornamentals.

"Why don't you lie down," Cabaan proposed, changing his tone.

"It's eleven in the morning. I'm not tired."

"But I'm tired of talking about this."

"Cabaan, please. I've started to think we're risking something we don't even understand. The Zaabta of Souls won't remember us well if we keep putting our—

"The Zaabta of Souls," Cabaan interrupted, "is a childish superstition. There is no 'cosmic archive' of our lives. We live in a neutral universe that bends to *our* will, Asha. *Our* will. There is no higher law. There is no divine appraisal. There is no Zaabta of Souls. There's only us—we're all there ever was."

Asha had never found a formula to move Cabaan on questions of metaphysics, or "tattvameemaansa," to share the word that her mother's father had taught her for the study of that which exists beyond our direct experience. It wasn't that her counterpoint to Cabaan was deficient, rather that it failed to impress because Cabaan was unshakable in the belief that his own principles were superior to anyone else's. Why shouldn't he have thought so? What he believed had been the battle cry of all his success.

"By the way," he said, "I'll need you to turn over another thousand haiktars."

Asha's heart popped. Losing the White Forest had been a catastrophe; losing the surrounding woods would be a termination.

Cabaan kept talking, to speed ahead of Asha's objections:

"I've had enough of coming to you for fifty haiktars at a time. It's demeaning, I won't do it anymore."

"But Cabaan, a thousand?"

"I need a clear path to the river, to plant over a new vein of wolfram we've identified. It's worth our attention."

"Is it worth a thousand haiktars of forest?"

Cabaan shrugged, as if the simple gesture could delete Asha's concern. "The world needs wolfram-wood," he said. "The Jaanam and her engineers can't get enough of it. And if we manage things well, you and I can produce a thousand maatras a year. Can you really not picture what that means for us?"

"Our marriage contract," Asha said carefully, "gave you half my father's forests, nine thousand haiktars, reserving the other half for my own judgment, which I've been slicing up and handing over for five years. A thousand haiktars is nearly all that's left."

Cabaan snatched a tin of uncut diamonds off Asha's desk. He whipped his wolfram-crush off his belt—a small device used to grind nuggets of ore for analysis—and, filling it with a handful of diamonds, pulverized them. Seizing Asha's wrist, he forced the shattered stones into her hand, pressing shards into skin.

"You wash your hair with diamond dust. The result is worth the trouble, but your jeweler still sends his bills."

"Are you saying *I'm* the reason you need another thousand haiktars? Because I could use well water if we're prioritizing."

"I doubt that, but it's beside the point. I'm saying a comfortable life is what you started with, a comfortable life is what you wished to keep, and a comfortable life is what you've got. But we pay for it by working our land."

"Why don't you take five hundred haiktars. For now."

They eyed each other. Uncharacteristically, Cabaan yielded. "I'll take five hundred. For now. We'll discuss the rest when my men close in on the river."

Though Asha hadn't given up the full thousand, she had still been outmaneuvered. She knew it too as she sat down at her desk and took a blood-thimble from a drawer. This was the implement used throughout the raajy to execute contracts, the way cylinder seals or hieroglyphic stamps were used in other realms. Here a contract carried legal force when signed in the blood of the transacting parties, a vestige of the cult of hemoglobin of the anterior peoples of the region, the hemolactics who had subsisted on blood and milk alone. The present-day thimble was fitted onto the index finger where it punctured the fingertip with its internal pin, causing blood to flow through its stylus. In this way the wearer could use it as a pen.

After Asha put the thimble on, wincing but making no sound, Cabaan produced a sheet of vellum on which Asha was expected to formalize what she had agreed to. "Five hundred haiktars," she confirmed as she wrote. On the leathery document her wet blood shimmered with the chemical residue of the previous night's dava.

"Your blood is tainted," Cabaan said.

"Would you rather I wait until it's clear?"

"I would not."

Asha signed her name. Cabaan thanked her blandly. Asha only nodded in reply: it was the most she could muster. In a conciliatory voice Cabaan said:

"You'll always have your father's ornamentals to look at if you want to see his forest the way it was."

Asha nearly let the conversation die, but then:

"I still don't feel right about what we're doing."

"We're only making money, my love."

"Maybe the money isn't worth the price."

"Try *having* no money, then tell me that."

"Or else we could try having *less* money."

"Now you're being irrational on purpose."

"Cabaan—

"Asha, stop! You have to stop this!"

"Stop *what*, exactly?"

"Stop fighting me! The back of Palace Isha pays for the front! And if you don't like the sight of where our money comes from, then don't look out the wrong window! Look the other way!"

Asha nodded, but seeing he might have gone too far, Cabaan offered compensation:

"Two more days until your birthday. You'll enjoy yourself. I'm going to make it an event for you."

A timid knock behind them ended the discussion: Jothi-Anandan was at the door.

"Raajakumaaree—excuse me, I mean 'Vi*kaan*tee'—sorry to bother you, but your sambharik is here."

Someone calling Asha by her birth title instead of her marriage title would normally have infuriated Cabaan; but he was so glad for an excuse to make his exit that he ignored it, swiftly collecting his document and leaving the room by the back stairs. Asha sat where she was, wondering how this state of things had crept up on her in such tiny steps, then pinned her down all at once.

"Raajakumaaree?" Jothi-Anandan said from the doorway. "Shall I send him up?"

"I'll come down, Jothi. Thank you."

The boy disappeared. Before following him, Asha left her writing room for the dome's main chamber, where she closed and latched the doors to the back balcony, to keep out particulates that would drift in on the afternoon breeze. In a structure of Palace Isha's complexity, it was a chore to keep so many rear doors and windows closed when not in use, and at cross purposes with the natural ventilation of the ancient house to seal off so many rooms in this way; but Asha reminded herself to be grateful at least that the pollution of glazery vapor, floating granules of kuroop bark, and the fumes from a fertilizer made of animal bones treated with sulfuric acid—in combination the miasma that formed each day over the backlands—tended to settle into its own microclimate between the river and the kuroops themselves without jumping the spheres and domes of the palace to the other side. On her way downstairs a moment later, she began to wonder if Cabaan's advice not to look out the wrong window wasn't the sensible thing, after all.

iv

Asha sat examining a tray of vials: infusions that her sambharik had heated over a brazier while waiting for her, so they were already glowing with chemical light in a menu of colors not quite produced by nature.

"I'll need a larger supply of my dava for the month," Asha said, trying for an air of courteous detachment. "I've been finding lately that I need twice the original dose for half the original effect."

"That is, inconveniently, the way of it, Vikaantee."

Self-conscious in the sambharik's presence, Asha made no further comment. It was strange for her to admit to herself that even though she was paying this well-mannered young man a monthly sum exceeding the combined monthly salaries of the staff of the household, she always felt as though she worked for *him* rather than the other way around. How he did this to her she wasn't sure—possibly a technique of manipulation learned in the raajy's lowlands, where he was born and raised. And why he had left home three years earlier to come live so far from everyone he knew, Asha had never asked, sensing that whatever the reason, she wouldn't like it.

She noticed a black-glowing unguent among his vials, and it occurred to her that she hadn't even realized the color black could glow.

"A nepentee, Vikaantee. A remedy of welcome forgetfulness. Drink it and leave behind any sorrow."

Asha picked it up: its black glow spread like spilled ink across her fingertips, fascinating her.

"May I offer you a sample?" the sambharik said.

This startled Asha, which she let show: a rare slip.

"I'm sorry, why would I need a nepentee? I bruise easily—your other cures speed the healing process."

"Certainly, Vikaantee."

"There's nothing I suffer from so painful that I need to for*get*."

"Certainly not, Vikaantee. You're much too young."

She replaced the vial on its tray. "So just my regular dava will be fine for today, thank you."

"Thank *you*."

But knowing she had acted badly, Asha tried making up for it by offering the sambharik a glass of green tea and a bowl of carrot halwa, sitting with him in silence while he sipped and munched. She couldn't have guessed that he despised the taste of carrot halwa or that the quinine in green tea gave him headaches that lasted for days—and no power on earth could have forced him to tell her so.

v

After a quarter hour spent reorganizing her cures on a shelf in her dayroom, Asha was tempted to pop one of the older remedies, just to tide her over until tonight. She eyed the neatly aligned anodynes and soother-tablets that she had given up when switching to the more potent choice of the dava. Reaching for a tablet, she held it over her tongue—but reconsidered and put it back. Instead she lay down on the divan, resting on her side for a view of her favorite rose-tree miniature in its orange-lacquered tray, her father's best ornamental, which always calmed her mind.

vi

In the shadowy dome where the Vikaant liked to dine, Asha and Cabaan sat side by side. Originally a storage area, the dome's prior contents—outmoded furniture and the wardrobes of Asha's ancestors—had been destroyed by fire a century earlier and the dome itself abandoned, its mounds of ash swept out though its charred walls left as they were. But Cabaan found the tenebrosity of the space soothing after a day's exposure in the backlands, especially with the hypnotic qualities of its single light source: a spectacular deepaadhaar. Part candelabrum, part art piece, freestanding, ten feet tall, made of solid platinum and holding thirty-two candles, it was an object commissioned by Asha's great-grandmother for Palace Isha's actual dining room in the Middle Dome, but which Cabaan had ordered moved to its present location when in his second year of residence at the palace he had begun to reshape it, inside as well as out.

Typically for them, Cabaan ate heartily; Asha lightly. For dessert Cabaan put away half a dozen pistachio laddus while Asha spooned at a sugarfoam without once bringing utensil to lips. After a sip of cinnamon tea, she stood, crossed to Cabaan, touched him on the shoulder, and left the room. She thought she would step outside for a breath of air, but passing the entryway to the athainaaium changed her mind and decided to find something to read instead.

Housed in what was once the palace's reception hall, before the vast Gathering Dome was built to accommodate social functions and public events on a larger scale, the athainaaium was paneled in shiny ebony and floored in black marble. Besides the glow from seven fireplaces, the room was lit by hundreds of lightning bugs swirling inside orbs of blown glass hung from the windows. These luminescing beetles weren't trapped—they flew in and out as they pleased—but in their travels they added to the library's mystique by casting their emerald signals along the room's black glaze and across the panoply of its holdings: volumes bound in tree bark that had been treated until it was supple as kidskin, then dyed deep purple, nut brown, burnt gold. It was Asha's grandfather who had built up the athainaaium's collection to its present level of thirty thousand tomes, codices, grammars, encyclopedias, and lexicons, and it was her grandfather's other granddaughter, Omala, who made the most of the books.

Asha was glad to find Omala here tonight, by a fireplace in the corner, burning a white fire from a cord of rare whitewood out of the highlands. She was studying a folio on electromagnetism, which she put down when Asha sat beside her in the fire's snowy field.

"I'm feeling a bit confused tonight," Asha admitted.

"Cousin, you *look* it!"

Asha liked this. She rolled her eyes and sighed, making light of her troubles. Then a glint off Omala's finger caught her attention: a pearly gem—polished but not faceted, like one of Palace Isha's domes—on a leather band.

"I love your new ring. What's the stone?"

"It's wolfram."

"*Wolf*ram? But this is a *gem*stone, wolfram is a metal in a *rock*."

"Not after you cook it in my kiln for a week."

Asha snatched her cousin's hand to examine the ring up close. "I don't be*lieve* it. I've only ever seen pure wolfram made into weapons and tools." She glanced at an antique wolfram firepoker beside them with its pleasant, silvery-black sheen, though otherwise not an object of special beauty, then studied Omala's ring again. "But this is gorgeous!"

"Well, it's no shaanadaar diamond, but it does have its qualities. By super-heating it, I've sensitized it to moonlight, to the point where it reacts by equalizing with its own electromagnetic field."

"*Really?*" (Asha hadn't the slightest idea what her cousin was talking about.)

"This little mass of wolfram on my finger," Omala said, "can now attract any nearby mass of wolfram—even from a distance. It's all about magnetism."

"I *love* magnetism!"

Omala glanced at a window. "The sky's cloudy, so there's no clear path to the moon, but I might be able to get a little demonstration going for you." She stood up, reached for the antique firepoker, gave it to Asha, asked her to take off her scarf and stand on it, positioned her just right, and had her grip the firepoker as tightly as she could, a hand on each end. Next she stepped over to a window some fifty feet away, held up her ring to catch a beam of light as the moon emerged from a cloud, and angled the ring toward Asha across the room.

The firepoker wiggled in Asha's hands. She gasped in delight; but Omala lost the moonbeam behind another cloud: the connection was severed and the firepoker's movement ceased. Omala kept scanning the sky: the obstructing cloud was about to pass, and behind it was a clear patch.

"Hold on, here we go."

This time Omala braced herself against a table. She caught a good beam off the moon and took aim at Asha, locking hard onto the firepoker. The connection yanked the wolfram rod and Asha right along with it in Omala's direction. Asha yelped as a wave of magnetism whisked her fifty feet across the marble floor. The wolfram firepoker in her hands clanged to a halt against the wolfram stone on Omala's ring, sticking there until the cousins pulled themselves apart.

"I—*loved* that!" Asha said. She was laughing and shaking. But then, after a sigh, she told Omala:

"I should've been a vigyaanik too. If I'd only had *half* your mind, I could be spending my life pursuing science alongside you. At the very least I could've been your assistant."

Asha lowered herself onto the bench beneath a window, her thoughts bouncing between gratitude and discontent. She knew that in fact she never could have been a vigyaanik like Omala, if not for lack of intelligence, then inclination. As a child her tutors had offered her all the regular subjects: history, literature, and science too; but as the daughter of two creatives—her father the region's most accomplished botanical artist and her mother a portraitist working in miniatures—it wasn't surprising that Asha had gravitated to the arts herself. In her case the decorative arts: paper craft, calligraphy, the designing of jewelry. She *had* shown an early interest in the philosophical sciences, but her grandfather had died when Asha was only nine, and after that there had been no one at Palace Isha with the expertise in tattvameemaansa to instruct her further.

Shifting from one folded leg to the other on her bench, she confessed:

"I'm feeling, in hindsight, that certain of the bigger decisions I've made in life might have profited from a longer period of deliberation."

"And you're just working that out *now?*"

Asha widened her eyes to emote a shock that she did not feel. "Don't be unkind, Omala. You know what I was trying to do."

"Torment us?"

"*Save* us."

"By marrying a savage?"

Asha pushed the old arguments:

"He made himself rich at fifteen."

Omala shrugged.

"And how you can call a man born a Vikaant a 'savage' I honestly don't understand."

Omala rolled her eyes.

"Do you think *I* could ever have kept us going?" Asha said. "What was *I* raised to do?"

"To be Raajakumaaree of Palace Isha."

"Well, *that* turned out to be worth surprisingly little, didn't it?"

Omala looked up to watch the intersecting shadows of seven fires dance across the curve of the ceiling.

"He saved us from penury," Asha said.

Omala looked down and told Asha eyeball to eyeball:

"It's not enough."

"He kept us from losing our home."

"Still not enough."

"But he's a success! He's a success in a world in which my father, your uncle, as much as we loved him, was not!"

"Yes, Cabaan is your father's opposite!"

Asha put her hand to her neck, to ease a twinge in her throat. "Do you suppose I'm ruined?" she said.

"I think it's never too late to stop making a bad mistake."

But here Asha's moment of courage to be speaking so openly was used up. "Omala," she said, "your hair really is so pretty this length. Don't ever cut it short again. Look at these thick black locks! Girls *pray* for hair like this!"

Omala wasn't having it, so Asha added with a desperate calm:

"I shouldn't have worried you, because the truth is, I really am perfectly well."

"Cousin, you inject a dava into your veins to endure the yaun sambandh with your own husband. And you *still* can't bear sleeping in his bed afterwards. So you sleep in the woods. That is not what 'perfectly well' looks like."

"I enjoy the night air."

Omala shook her head. Asha sighed again, but with a smile. Omala persisted:

"And your husband either doesn't notice where you sleep or doesn't care!"

"We all have our bad points."

"Now you're being ridiculous."

"And you're exaggerating his faults."

"Then go to him tonight without injecting yourself! Just tonight—just one night! Then come back to me and we'll finish this discussion."

vii

Asha stepped into a sunken bath of snow-leopard's milk, piped in hot from Palace Isha's main kitchen, two domes away. Lately she had been deprecating herself for too many hours spent in this dayroom-cum-bathing-chamber, whether soaking or reading or stretching out on the divan staring at the sky through the room's one window; but tonight she needed all of her luxuries to steady her mind in advance of what she intended to do.

She lay perfectly still in the bath for an hour before pushing herself upright in a spurt of determination and reaching for a blue-glazed bottle of shampoo. The blend was her own invention: mint soap, coconut oil, and the colorless, crystalline form of pure carbon: diamonds, ground into dust for this lathering mixture. After washing her hair with it and dipping her head back into the now lukewarm milk, she rose from the bath, powdered herself, and dressed in a nightsari threaded with strips of pink gold. She brushed back her wet hair, glittering from a quantity of diamonds that could have kept an ordinary family going for weeks. Few though would have objected to the expenditure: the combination of Asha's natural appearance and the way in which she adorned herself seemed to others to produce not only a property of matter and radiance that lit her very person, but a condition that prevailed in the space immediately around her. If ever someone's beauty could be felt as a shared experience, so it was with Asha and the people of Palace Isha. They delighted in it as they delighted in her.

Tonight it could also be said that Asha's beauty had risen in inverse proportion to the likelihood of it lasting. Omala's critique had had impact: Asha was not going to inject herself. She had set aside her prepared syringe and was now hardening her mind to meet Cabaan for the first time in many months without the protection of any dava.

In bed with him for the yaun sambandh, she thought at first that she would be all right. He started at her less aggressively than usual. Possibly he was drained from his long day in the backlands for the kuroop harvesting in progress—or possibly, Asha told herself, she had been overreacting all along. But as he worked at her, the same pain in her throat from earlier in the night returned, even before Cabaan reached up to grip her there. Worried suddenly that without the protection of the dava he might accidentally kill her by crushing her windpipe or induce a stroke by causing the blood to clot in one of the vessels of her neck, she pressed her fingers into his rib cage until he realized something was wrong and held still.

Whispering an apology, she undid herself from him a limb at a time, climbed down from the bed, and left the room. She hurried along the halls, through a back passageway, up a flight of stairs, and into her dayroom. Not slowing to light a candle, she fumbled for the prepared syringe on her dressing table and injected herself in the dark to stop the coagulation that she now believed she could feel forming in her throat. Whether the clot was actual or imagined was another matter—and a calculation less important to her than avoiding the result if it proved real.

She knew that taking the dava cold, without warming it first to body temperature, would grind her inside, but only until her blood smoothed out the difference in temperature. The pain came fast, like snake venom raking her veins. She bit hard on her lip, trying not to scream as her organs heaved. Then came the wave of relief. As the chemicals spread through her system, a murky glow seeped from her pores. A moment later she was left in a state of pseudo-calm. Laughing off her little terror, and feeling the clot in her throat melting away, she wet a cloth and pressed it to her forehead before returning to Cabaan.

He was already asleep. Climbing up beside him in his bed, Asha fell asleep too before long. But when the moon edged into the window, she woke up again. She looked down at herself: blood had stained the sheer filament of the nightsari, and she could feel her throat was bruised where Cabaan had held her down. Alarmed that the dava had worn off too soon, she climbed out of bed and hurried back to her dayroom. With unsteady hands, she filled her syringe again, warmed it properly over a candle this time, and injected a second dose.

Nothing happened. Her wounds failed even to shimmer with the subtle radiance of cellular repair, much less disappear altogether. Now she was terrified. She had heard that you could boost the potency of a dava by swallowing it, so long as you could suppress the reflex to vomit. So she broke open a third vial and emptied it into her mouth. The bitterness was indescribable: the dava's acids sizzled in her throat as she gulped over and over to force it down. Her stomach jumped on contact, though she kept from retching. But her wounds remained. Now she panicked. Believing she might truly die at any moment, she resorted to the only thing she could think of. She broke open a fourth vial, filled her syringe, closed her eyes, and stabbed the needle into her breast, its long spike plunging as far as her heart.

The result was instantaneous. The dava's anesthetic effect nullified the extreme pain of the puncturing even as Asha felt a chemical relief washing through her, though at the cost of a short coughing fit when the glut of dava overflowed the tissues of her heart and numbed the edges of her lungs. But her wounds vanished in seconds. This was the physical success of the gamble; mentally Asha was now in a wild state. Possessed by the idea of outrunning the chaos of her thoughts, she hurried to her dressing room, threw on riding clothes and her mother's sable cape, and took the hidden channels of the house underground, emerging minutes later up through the floor of the stable. Here she saddled and mounted her mare, Tapti, and charged off, speeding across the grounds between bolts of moonlight, beyond Palace Isha's boundary and into the western woods.

Sometime later, and quite a distance from where they began, especially for a trip with no destination in the middle of the night, horse and rider were worn out. Asha dismounted by a stream. While Tapti drank, Asha inspected their situation. This seemed as good a place as she was likely to find to spend the night, so she lay down on a plot of moss, made her sable cape into a blanket, and curled up underneath.

viii

A man's singing voice drew Asha back to life. Opening her eyes, she had a view to the canopy of what turned out to be a stand of redwoods, impressive to wake up to, though the moss she had made her bed on was now unpleasantly dewy.

She rose and brushed the leaves from the fur of her cape. The ballad in the air was in an archaic form of Bhaashan: Asha could only pick out a word here and there; but the voice was both bright and warm, worth following to its source.

Taking Tapti's reins, she went along on foot, letting the sequence of notes guide her across a grove fragrant with the morning breeze and down into a dell. Between the trees ahead she could see the ruins of a stone temple, small though charming in decay and overgrown with ivy. On one of its toppled columns sat a young "geetakaar," to say it the way they would have during that long-ago time—a "poetry-singer" in modern translation. Asha's first thought about him was how slight of build he was, and only an inch or so taller than herself, making the heptachord he was playing seem large by comparison. Otherwise he was unremarkable to look at, except for his complexion, nearly as dark as the ebony of his instrument, which Asha could see was fine even from a distance.

She could also tell that he was aware of her before she cleared the trees, though he kept singing as she walked toward him, finishing his song when she passed through the temple's freestanding arch.

She took a last few steps to reach him—and his eye landed on her throat.

"You're hurt," he said.

Asha's hand went to her neck: she felt a swelling from last night's bruises that shouldn't have been there, given the potency of the dava, to say nothing of four doses of it.

The geetakaar stood up, less from delayed courtesy than sudden concern, but Asha assured him she was fine. He reached for her throat anyway—and she flinched. She knew what he saw: that her bruises were the size and shape of a man's fingers. With his hand in the air between them, he asked Asha's permission to touch her. Surprising herself, Asha nodded her consent.

His fingers were warm on her skin despite the morning chill, and as startled as Asha had been when he reached for her, she was sorry when he took his hand away.

"I'm sure it looks worse than it feels," she said.

"If it hurts at all, I imagine that's bad enough."

No evasion took shape in Asha's mind. Instead, for the first time in recent memory, she said what she felt:

"Your voice is beautiful. We haven't had a geetakaar in these woods since I was a girl."

The geetakaar bowed his head.

On the other side of the temple's arch, Tapti was now devouring a patch of hemp. "I think your mare needs a meal," the geetakaar observed. He went over and untangled Tapti's reins, caught in a clump of shrubs, before leading her to a bag of fodder beside his own horse.

"She'll remember you for that," Asha said. "We slept in the woods last night. Unexpectedly."

The geetakaar did not press for details.

Asha looked around the temple's remains. Just enough of its columns remained upright to imply its original design, though its floor had pitched in some preceding eon. "Is this where you live?" she asked.

"For a few days. I'm traveling."

Asha found a way to introduce herself, waiting for the change that her name would bring in the geetakaar's bearing toward her. No change came. He must have been from a distant part not to know who she was. This was no arrogance of Asha's, simply the way things were in their sparsely populated annex of the raajy.

The geetakaar introduced himself as "Ilarô," a name that Asha had never heard in all her life, a rarity in a land where names were ancestral and original ones almost never coined. So both Asha and Ilarô were new to each other, and neither could presume the usual things. Asha was caught off guard, to give one example, by Ilarô's straightforward style. When he invited her almost right away to share his breakfast, she declined politely, by reflex; but this only prompted him to ask if she wasn't a little hungry, because after all it was breakfast time. When she said that she wasn't, he asked if she had already eaten today. When she said no, not yet, he asked if she had brought anything with her to eat later, since she perhaps hadn't thought to pack provisions for an unplanned night in the forest. His questions were entirely sensible, yet Asha resisted giving out even the most innocent details about herself, an odd pattern that she had fallen into lately, details as innocent as: yes, she was a bit hungry for breakfast. It was a kind of neurosis passing as modesty, and she was barely even aware of it; but this is the result of keeping the great secrets: they soon glue to themselves even the smallest truths, until a whole, hidden nature builds up within, and nothing at all of the real person can get out again. Contrary to popular notion, the best disguises are worn on the inside.

"You should share my breakfast," Ilarô said, citing the simple logic that Asha would be hungry sooner or later, and his was the only meal in sight.

An hour from home, Asha knew it would be foolish to ride back that far on an empty stomach. So she agreed.

The breakfast of dates and black walnuts that Ilarô served was modest but, to Asha, delicious, because the fact was that she needed to eat. They sat side by side without speaking through their small meal, a convention Asha was used to from Cabaan, though in this case it was a stillness instead of a silence, drawing her in instead of shutting her out.

Ilarô went to the stream at the edge of the dell and filled his cup to bring Asha a drink, offering it to her with both hands, an ancient courtesy that Asha returned in kind: by accepting the cup the same way.

"It must be pleasant, staying here," she said, taking in the little temple.

Ilarô glanced around, seeing his temporary home through Asha's eyes.

"But it's missing something, I think," Asha ventured.

"Is it?"

"I think so. You have no flowers. You might like to pick some, to brighten the corners."

"I don't know that I have the eye for it. Do you?"

It was in this way that Asha and Ilarô came to spend the rest of the morning walking the dell, gathering bloodroots and marigolds and the occasional gentian. By noon the temple's cracked vases, empty for centuries, were bright again with wildflowers. Since it was still chilly even under the sun, Ilarô built a fire in the stone hearth, and they warmed themselves in this room with no roof, this temple hypaethral, which is a word worth knowing, meaning open to the sky.

Host and guest sat together watching the fire, breathing the sweetness of cedarwood as it cooked. More than once Asha turned from the flame to regard Ilarô beside her; each time he directly met her gaze. Up-close she found his brown eyes no more striking than from a distance, meaning they were perfectly ordinary, which perversely pleased her: Asha still took a youthful pride in her own appearance and comforted herself that however much she might decline in the world or in her own person, and whatever other qualities she might squander or be robbed of or simply lose to the way of things, she would live and die with the dazzling brown eyes of her mother, a feature that she didn't at all mind possessing uniquely.

When her cape slid a bit off her shoulder, Ilarô reached in to straighten it out. When a gust of wind blew her hair over her eyes, Ilarô brushed it back. But during the hour they sat together in front of the fire, Ilarô spoke not a single word. It astonished Asha that a person whose singing voice was so mesmerizing could also hold her spellbound by saying *nothing*. In place of words, he offered something totally unfamiliar to her from her own experience of sitting beside a man: his presence. That she was beginning to love him by the end of this hour should be less surprising than that she admitted it to herself as it happened. But we should try to remember that our few glimpses of Asha so far have not been of Asha as she originally was. The distortions of personality that we've observed—the inner morbidity, the fear of speaking things both trivial and deep, the shutting down to normal involvement—these had all manifested under the pressures of how she now lived at Palace Isha. Here, in the ruins of Ilarô's temple, the pressures lifted, and for a few hours she was herself again.

When Ilarô turned to face her, Asha inopportunely felt the need to yawn. She tried to do it without moving her mouth, let alone opening it—but the unusual expression this produced gave her away.

"I didn't sleep especially well last night," she explained.

"Why don't you lie down then?"

"Right now? In the middle of the day?"

"I'll lend you my bed." He meant his straw mat, unfurled beneath the stone shelter of what a thousand years before this morning was the temple's altar. "Unless the idea of lying in my bed offends you."

"No, no, it's just that yesterday someone suggested I lie down during the day for a somewhat different reason."

"I'm only suggesting it because you've just yawned."

"I don't think I *could* fall asleep during the day. Unless—I don't suppose you happen to have a hypnotic syrup with you ... or a soother-tablet ... or maybe a vial of valerian drops."

"I'm sorry, no. I don't have any of those things."

"Or some sort of calming leaf I could nibble?"

"If I'm not feeling calm, I tend to let myself not feel calm."

"Doesn't that hurt?" Asha asked lightly.

"Often."

"Well, you're stronger than *I* am—I seem to live from cure to cure these days."

"I could sing you to sleep, if you like."

In her mind Asha gasped. Outwardly, after a moment's consideration, she simply offered a diagonal nod.

They crossed to the altar where Asha lay down and let Ilarô cover her with her sable cape, adding his own light blanket for an extra touch of weight and placing his bundle of clothes beneath her head for a pillow. Sitting beside her, he began a lullaby. The melody was traditional, as the best bedtime songs usually are, but the poetry was Ilarô's own. It described a kingdom wedged high between the polar caps, a land of thermal pools and rhododendron fields and clouds of butterflies so thick they brushed your face like sheets of chamois hung from the sky, a realm where even the fearsome snow-bears who came to snatch children out of their beds at night were only white-furred giants wishing to play: they slung girls and boys over their shoulders and carried them off, licking the soles of their bare feet until the skin was too tender to run away on and escape. Back in their dens, children and snowbears played games of chess together and sucked icicles dipped in honey until dawn, when it was time for the white beasts to carry all the land's children home to their beds so they could wake up and start a new day.

Asha was dreaming now. She stood on a front balcony at Palace Isha, warmed by the strong morning light while Ilarô serenaded her not from the garden below, but floating in midair, at eye level. The joy of it was intense, until Cabaan's wet fingers grazed her neck from behind and sent pain streaming into her throat, like the slippery sting of a jellyfish. Ilarô's voice was snuffed out, though his mouth kept moving. Asha had to leave anyway; she followed Cabaan through the Middle Dome and onto a back balcony, where it was midnight. Here Cabaan leapt into the starless sky and vanished, forcing Asha to stay where she was, paralyzed the way it happens in a nightmare.

A red comet came roaring out of space, its gory tail dripping the coagulated blood soaked up from the wounds of many worlds. Aiming straight for Palace Isha, it gained speed and size, looming so large that it cast a shadow over the circle of the earth, darkness upon darkness. It bore down on Asha, but with the roar of death in her ears, at the last instant she ripped herself awake.

She came upright so sharply that Ilarô had to compensate by instantly dipping back to avoid their two foreheads smacking together. It might have been funny, if Asha hadn't been shaking.

"I should leave now," she said.

But neither one of them moved ...

         ...

                ...

                       ...

... until a black butterfly trapped in the sticky pollen of one of the wildflowers that Asha had brought into the temple caught her eye. She rose from Ilarô's bed to go and gently peel back the flower's petals, releasing the butterfly into the breeze. Then she came to sit beside Ilarô again.

"The Zaabta of Souls will add a volume on you for that," Ilarô said.

"Someone insisted to me recently that the Zaabta was a childish superstition."

"Ah. Well. I'm sorry for anyone who would think such a thing."

Asha felt the urge to apologize for Cabaan. She resisted it ... then gave in anyway to the sheer force that her husband exerted upon her even from a distance, as a celestial body succumbs to the pull of a star:

"It really is time for me to go. No one misses me during the day, but at night it's a different matter."

Ilarô accepted this—how could he object?—though Asha could see that he was affected by her reluctance to leave: so unlike

Cabaan, who fended off her states of mind as if they were attacks on his very person.

To the first faint beat of rebellion, Asha mentioned that she and her husband were entertaining guests for a not-so-small event the next day, and she was sure they would be glad if Ilarô came too.

"Thank you, Asha, but I have an engagement to sing tomorrow."

He had called her by name. A simple intimacy, it had a complex effect, the nature of which can only be conveyed by attaching to our account of Asha a fact of some delicacy: during her five years of marriage, with its almost nightly sessions of the yaun sambandh, she had been treated with such neglect on the part of her husband that at the age of nearly twenty-two she was still unfamiliar with the central pleasure of the bodily experience. In recent years she had even wondered if the gratification in question weren't a fantasy, to which she wasn't susceptible, or a privilege, to which she wasn't entitled. Certainly she never imagined that one day she would know the equivalent of it without even being touched. But joy is transmitted in more ways than one, and here it came to Asha on the sound of Ilarô's voice. This was how it happened with them. This was how it began.

ix

Some three hundred visitors were already mingling in Palace Isha's front gardens when Asha came outside. She wore a gleaming silver sarong and her lips were glossed the same color, like a girl stepping down from the stars. She was coasting on memory, greeting her guests warmly but distantly. They couldn't tell; they found her beautiful and polite.

Asha made a point of remembering names and appreciating outfits, even when the choices were dubious, because she was kind by nature, except, as we've seen, to herself. So she praised the women for their saris and their anklets and their scarves and their eyeshadow. One girl had come in a pale pink sari embroidered with white wildflowers, which Asha truly did find pretty and made sure to say. She praised the men too for their colorful sarong-and-jacket pairings and their twilled wolfram bracelets—a recent craze—and for the diamond nose-studs worn on special occasions. Then there was the elderly gentleman who arrived in a bejeweled turban. "What a handsome hat!" Asha shouted into his ear, knowing he was nearly deaf. In reply he asked, due to an impairment of memory, where he could find Asha's father today, but Asha couldn't bear disconcerting him with the news that her father had been buried beside his moon-viewing pavilion for seven years, so she mentioned having seen him by the lake, sending his elderly friend off for a pleasant amble if nothing else.

Making her rounds, she heard rowdy laughter coming from behind the Gathering Dome, where she found Jothi-Anandan and his partner-in-crime, the red-headed vandal, Giribandhava, leaping off the flat roof that ran between a tetrad of the palace's marble orbs, two hundred feet high. The boys were breaking their fall by holding tight to leaves from the chandava trees that adorned the edge of the roof in planters. The distinctive chandava leaf, three feet long by two feet wide, possessed the properties of a natural air-sail, as well as hemp twists on both ends of the frond that made for easy gripping. But wafting earthward holding a chandava leaf over your head didn't mean you could steer: you aimed, you leapt, and you hoped for the best.

The boys touched down inches from the jackal-trap dug alongside a row of Asha's white-rose trees. The narrow trap was Cabaan's solution to the problem of the herbivorous snow-jackals that came down in packs from the polar caps and devoured Asha's flowers in the night: it ran fifty feet from end to end and went ten feet deep, with six-foot wolfram-wood stakes rising up from the bottom.

"Jothi!"

Jothi-Anandan pivoted in alarm. "Raajakumaaree!"

"Jothi, whose *idea* was this?"

"Sorry, Raajakumaaree!" He waited for Asha to say something else, then blurted: "We were only going to jump five or six times!"

"But that's half a dozen chances for catastrophe!"

"But we were being very careful!"

"Jothi, I don't mind you having a little fun, but does it need to be over a *jackal-trap*?"

"But Raajakumaaree, that's *why* it's fun!"

"But if you fell in, you'd be impaled!"

"No, no, Raajakumaaree, we can't fall in, we're too *good*!"

Asha glanced at the roof. "And look at our poor chandava trees! You're plucking them clean! Can't you at least use the leaves more than once?"

"They tear if you jump with them twice!"

"Well, we won't worry about the leaves then, the trees will grow more. But Jothi, we can't grow any more of *you.*"

Jothi-Anandan could see that Asha wasn't angry, only worried for him. "We'll be very, *very* careful, Raajakumaaree," he promised, boyishly sure that he could control his fate, so long as he put his mind into it.

"I'm sorry, Jothi, it's just too dangerous."

Jothi-Anandan crinkled his face into its lopsided frown. "Yes, Raajakumaaree."

"And I'll have to punish you, I think, to make an impression."

Accepting his guilt, Jothi-Anandan waited for Asha to pronounce sentence.

"I want you to march yourself over to the stable right this minute and take the new charger for a substantial outing. Cabaan's horsemaster is busy with our guests, the charger needs to be exercised, and I'm afraid the job now falls to you to stretch his legs."

Jothi-Anandan snapped back to life. He dashed up to Asha and kissed her on the cheek.

"Thank you, Raajakumaaree! Can Giribandhava ride with me too?"

"As long as the two of you don't try riding the charger off the roof!"

Jothi-Anandan grabbed his friend's hand and fled. Watching him go, Asha's memory flared with a random moment two years earlier when, seated in this same garden, she had spotted the then ten-year-old Jothi through a hedge, wandering along, singing to no one in particular:

> *There are leaves growing out of your brain*
> *There are leaves growing out of your brain*
> *I would prefer it if they were on trees!*

Asha projected her dreaming mind ahead to the pleasures of motherhood, the way she used to do, with Jothi-Anandan her idea of a son. But this time her mind played a trick on her: during the few seconds it took for the fantasy of raising a child to play out in her imagination, she entirely forgot that the child's father would have to be Cabaan.

She picked up her rounds inside, waving to people gossiping on sofas in the Gathering Dome, winking at introverts strolling the halls of the house on their own. With so many guests to see to, there wasn't time to stop for conversation, though an exception was made when Asha spotted one of her late mother's friends—"Lady Lotus" her mother used to call her—admiring a miniaturized pomegranate tree in the ground-floor sunroom. The "lotus" sobriquet referred to the impressive lotus sapphire that she wore on her index finger. Never any other piece of jewelry: not a necklace, not a bangle, not a pair of studs in her ears, just the one ring. Seeing it again, it occurred to Asha that if you were going to go through life expressing yourself through a single jewel, you could do worse than a lotus sapphire. The orange-pink brilliance of most lotus stones was rare enough, but the color of this one was truly unique: red as the tiny pomegranates on the miniature tree that Lady Lotus was reaching out to touch, red as blood shimmering with the chemiluminescence of a dava, red as—

—but Asha hadn't stopped to talk about jewelry. She happened to know that Lady Lotus was now living apart from her husband after many years of marriage. They would have dissolved the marriage altogether, except that no such provision existed in the raajy's code of law. Petitioning the Shaasak to grant a divorce by royal prerogative was not beyond the bounds of possibility, though it would have meant a trip of eight hundred miles to the seat of government and back with no guarantee of the desired outcome, too arduous for a couple of a certain age. So they had chosen to separate without any formal change of status between them, unsatisfactory to both though the best that either could think of.

Embracing Lady Lotus with a good squeeze, Asha asked her to please come back soon for lunch, when it would be just the two of them, with time for a nice long talk. After this she continued down the hall, stopping again at a door to the athainaaium: inside Omala was entertaining their community's dozen vigyaanikon by drawing the waves and symbols pertinent to electromagnetism on a slate board set up for that purpose. Except for Omala herself, these scientists were all men, and such was Asha's nature that she prayed for Omala to be loved by one of them. This wish of affection for others came from the most central place in Asha's makeup: it was, to say it another way, her chief reflex, irrespective of the sum of affection in her own life at any given time. When she was loved less than she should have been, she did not rescind her hope of love for those around her in the mistaken belief that more for others meant less for herself; nor when she felt love in some substantial amount from one source or another did she hoard it in the great error of ego that distinguishes between oneself and every other person. Asha's own moments of emotional sufficiency only inspired her to give more of herself away. Today was proof of it: with the thought of Ilarô still brightening her mind, she was concerned, most of all, for Omala. Let's say it plainly then: Asha's kindness was her true inheritance, forty thousand haiktars of forest and highland notwithstanding. And without denying her flaws—of which she would have been the first to admit there were many—it was her kindness that had made her the girl her father had died proud of, her kindness that Ilarô had felt radiating even through her wounds, and her kindness that, if only she could live long enough to recognize its high place on the roster of earthmoving powers, would mean that another great woman had been born into the world, here in this far, forgotten tip of the raajy.

x

Stepping outside again, Asha's eye landed on Cabaan in the open-to-the-air lunch pavilion. He wasn't looking for something to eat, he was basking in the lavishness of the refection: bowls of white radishes, spiced pumpkin and eggplant, green corn curry, gawar with thyme and jaggery, rice in coconut milk, rice with cashews, crispy rice pancakes, spinach kababs, chutneys, raitas, and fruit puddings, a breathtaking fish biryani, peanut curried yoghurt, paper-thin chapati, six types of puri, naan oozing garlic, tandoori pheasant, and a steaming-hot tamarind stew.

Turning away, Asha took a set of outdoor stairs down to her sunken garden, to be alone for a moment, hidden between the garden's high walls. She sat on a bench beside a sundial, put her face in her hands, and shook her head in confusion about the very purpose of her life, a state of mind that had begun to plague her decades before the usual time.

xi

Out of mutual loathing, Omala and Cabaan had for several years done their best never to be in the same room together, though on rare occasions an intersection couldn't be helped. After delivering her group of vigyaanikon into the lunch pavilion and picking up a lachhi for herself, Omala went to look for Asha, whom she hadn't seen all day, but exiting the tent came face-to-face with Cabaan instead. They appraised each other viciously.

"Cabaan."

"Omala."

"Care for a lachhi? It's the last pink mango, but I haven't sipped yet." She held out her glass for him.

"I detest pink mango—and lachhis are not a drink for men."

"In that case …" Omala raised the glass to her lips and drank, taking her time. Unwilling to show his displeasure at being made to wait, Cabaan smiled breezily until the glass was empty, then continued the conversation as if there had been no interruption at all by asking:

"How goes the science?"

"Slow. How goes the planting?"

"Quick."

"As I've always said about you, Cabaan: no one can ruin things faster."

Cabaan felt nothing at being critiqued in this way. But Omala wasn't done with him:

"Careful, Vikaant: you're running the risk of becoming irreversible."

"That sounds to me like a *good* thing."

"Your failure to understand yourself is exactly the trouble."

"I do wonder if you'll ever keep quiet long enough to attract a husband, Omala."

"Still hoping to get me off the premises?"

"I'm only commenting on what I see. You'll be thirty-two this year. Not young anymore."

Omala leaned close to him and said:

"Don't imagine you have the power to bait me. I see you as you are. My cousin may be chemically connected to you, but *my* blood is clear."

"Asha does what she has to, to get by. It's no crime. I admire her for it."

"Why she still admires *you* surpasses my understanding."

"Maybe you're not as smart as we all assume."

"The important question is whether or not I'm smarter than *you* are. Because if I am, you may have more to worry about than you think."

xii

A gong bloomed dully across the grounds. In her sunken garden, Asha touched a wrist to the moist corners of her eyes and examined the sundial: it was midday. She stood, smoothed her sarong, and climbed the stairs back to the garden where Cabaan was already addressing their guests:

"…to Palace Isha, in honor of my wife, the Vikaantee Asha, on this, the occasion of her twenty-second birthday."

Heads turned in every direction before finding Asha by the reflecting pool; applause brought a whispered thank-you to her lips.

"Six months ago," Cabaan said, "the Silent Shaasak allowed his own court singer to leave Aakaash-Nivaas and travel the coast on a tour of the raajy. Today, after giving up his ship for dry land and making the long crossing of the interior, visiting houses great and varied along the way, he's reached Palace Isha, to sing for *us*. The timing is auspicious." Cabaan turned to his wife. "Happy birthday, Asha. I give you the royal geetakaar."

Asha's pulse quickened and her forehead flamed up, but in her mind she stepped back from what was happening: the forces of impossibility and inevitability were working evenly on her, leaving no remainder. She would have to decide for herself how to react.

She watched Ilarô step out from the crowd. Few of her guests had taken notice of him before now: his air was too modest, his height unremarkable, his attire too plain. The darkness of his complexion might have drawn the attention of some, yet his average, even forgettable features counteracted the effect, making him easy to look past.

He took up his position without compromising Asha by glancing her way for more than an instant, but in his concentrated gaze she could read that this was not planned by him.

First he addressed Cabaan, thanking him for the invitation to Palace Isha and the chance to know the polar beauty of the region. He then confessed what he hadn't understood from their correspondence, that the day belonged to the Vikaantee. Cabaan had mentioned neither Asha nor her birthday, so Ilarô was here unprepared, without a song composed for the occasion. He explained this in his straightforward way, expressing regret but not embarrassment. Only a courtier from the Shaasak's high circle would have had the nerve, not to mention the skill, to present himself with such a mix of humility and self-possession.

"If only I'd known my destination better, Vikaant, nothing could have brought me here without a birthday song for your wife."

Cabaan hardly cared, but it didn't matter: the message wasn't for him.

"Whatever you sing today, geetakaar, we'll consider it Asha's."

On this Ilarô and Cabaan agreed completely. They would never agree on a single thing again.

Ilarô began by tuning his heptachord, the favorite stringed instrument of the raajy, with its qualities of both the sitar and the lute.

For a time, between bites of plectrum on string, only the breeze made any sound. Ilarô's audience grew nervous in the absence of either conversation or music; Ilarô remained at ease. That he had come from the sky-lodge of the Shaasak, that fabled palace of petrified wood high on its cliff above the Malachite Sea, was already impressive enough to the men and women gathered here, only a handful of whom would ever visit the seat of the raajy eight hundred miles to the south or even leave their own remote corner of the realm; that Ilarô was also the Shaasak's personal geetakaar, that he had sat at the Shaasak's side, dined at his table, spoken to him about matters large and small and been spoken to in turn, was truly intimidating. They had every reason to think he would sing something memorable for them. They still could not have guessed what was coming.

Ilarô nodded to Cabaan, then to Asha, on opposite sides of the crowd. He knew now what he would perform for them. He might have treated them to something popular, or something pretty, but no simple ballad or impromptu lullaby would be heard today; what Ilarô offered instead was something older, something that had come down out of the ageless past and might even last as long as the unending future. What he proposed was the first canto from the long poem of the Zaabta of Souls. Few geetakaaron still knew this epic song-cycle as late as the age in which these events were taking place; but Ilarô had learned the long poem of the Zaabta as a child, in the classical style, literally backwards and forwards, one sound at a time.

He recited the traditional invocation:

> *All you thought full you'll find empty*
> *all you thought empty is full*
> *Give up your riches for riches*
> *cling tight and you lose to death's pull*

Even his speaking voice threw its spell of sound. His audience shivered with expectation, for now was the moment: Ilarô began to sing.

How or by whom the text of the long poem of the Zaabta had been gleaned out of the mind of time was lost from memory, but those inclined to the mysteries of existence believed its stanzas and tales to be templates of how the acts of our lives would finally be recorded in the annals of the cosmos—and remembered forever. Set to music by the bards of prehistory, the long poem's stories were various in size and style. Many were tales of pairs: the pure and the corrupt, the fleeting and the eternal, the wise who doubted the existence of their own wisdom and the ignorant who doubted the wisdom of everyone else. Others chronicled the lives of the ordinary: actions and intentions, deeds and desires, promises and lies. Set between the stories were pure poetries, the "interstitials." Many of these were well-known, their phrases and rhymes having long ago become proverbs and mottos, however uncredited the source. The most beautiful of them was a song made from a single word: "renounce, renounce, renounce"—its complex syllables in Bhaashan disaggregated melodiously until its meaning wiggled free from the trap of speech and its truth passed back into the listener's intuition. The motif of the interstitials was sacrifice, sacrifice the vast power they revealed. This wasn't so different from the theme of the tales themselves, only seen from another angle.

Ilarô sang for two hours. Even the children in the audience stayed silent, not from politeness, but out of awe. The sweetness of Ilarô's voice against the heptachord's sharp harmonies and even its occasional dissonance made a supreme sound. Ilarô's reserve as a person bore no resemblance to his power as a performer: here he commanded. It was impossible to listen to him and not realize with a slap of awareness that your first impression had been incomplete: this modest traveling singer of gentle disposition and slight build was in fact an artist of the most astounding rank. He was, after all, the royal geetakaar.

From our own vantage point, peering back through six millennia, we can confirm the quantum changes that occurred within those persons who stood before Ilarô listening to his song: then as now molecular biology was subject to the power of sound. But though we can note these changes from a distance, they remain too intricate even today for the brain to sort out—or better said to piece together—and may remain so for daunting eons ahead. Certainly from the perspective of Ilarô's audience there was no understanding of the science of what was happening to them: if they perceived something out of the ordinary, it took shape in their minds as the feeling of dreaming standing up. Moreover it was a shared dream, which is rare, but documented in certain instances of ecstatic reception. In the last minutes of Ilarô's performance, the several hundred in his audience dreamt of rising bodily off the earthtop as a great rupture split the world to pieces beneath them. Ilarô, already floating above them, saved them. He pulled them up, heaving them one at a time off their splintering world and into a green globe of light that was expanding to fit every new person, until the last of them were scrambling up his legs and arms to get over him, and get in, in time, and everyone was included and not a single one left out, not even the corrupt or the cruel. Then the earth crumbled to dust and was blown to the far corners of space while Ilarô's green globe of light crystallized into a new world, precisely where the old one had been and riding its same orbit, and all present felt solid ground beneath their feet again, giving them a second chance of life.

Ilarô ended his song as softly as he could. His performance was over, his concert done. In the dreamy aftermath, no one clapped. Only the breeze made any sound.

xiii

With her guests finishing their katoras of chaay, kofee, sweet mint taak, and a replenished supply of the drink that was, Cabban's dislike of it notwithstanding, the specialty of the house, pink-mango lachhi from the yield of Palace Isha's own grove, Asha stepped away to join Ilarô by the lake. They spoke only a little as they circled its bright water, leaving out altogether the subject of the day's coincidence. Another pair might have done it differently: another Ilarô might have said again that Cabaan's invitation had mentioned no wife, no birthday. This other Ilarô might have pointed out that Asha herself had neglected to mention Cabaan's name or even the place-name of Palace Isha, so he couldn't have known where he was coming today, especially since the far north was terra incognita to the rest of the raajy. Another Asha might have tried to pin down the same facts from the opposite angle, to be sure of things. But this was our Asha, our Ilarô, and we know them well enough by now to understand that Asha had been true to Ilarô and Ilarô to Asha from the first moment: inconsequentialities could not divide them.

Now picture this: a black pane slid across the sky. The children at Palace Isha all shouted in glee; and their parents looked up grinning in shock at the darkening arch over the world. An eclipse wasn't unheard-of at this time of year, though none was forecast in the astronomical tables. Yet here one was. Tongues of fire leapt off the sun's reversed surface; solar winds drove jets of electrons ninety-three million miles in seconds, igniting an aurora in the sky. A pair of incoming comets could now be seen streaking across the cope of space, leaving a purple wake that stayed in place as if drawn by a child's glitter-stick. Adding to the spectacle was a vision of the ringed planet, exotically magnified due to some atmospheric effect, its moons glowing like amethysts and its moonlets like whirling pearls.

Ilarô reached for Asha's hand. Under cover of the blackout, no one could see him raise her fingers to his lips—and kiss her. When the eclipse began to pass a moment later, he lowered her hand just before the sun lit the day again.

—"Vikaantee!"

Four girls ran in, all of them dressed in flowing silk pants and blouses instead of saris, the latest teen fashion. They looped their hostess by the arm, tugging her away from the lake.

"Girls, please! I'm speaking to our guest!"

"Vikaantee, we *need* you!"

Asha glanced backwards at Ilarô as she was dragged off and made to intercede in some romance gone awry. By the time it was settled, she had been drawn back into the duties of her position, and though she looked for Ilarô whenever she could and as inconspicuously as she was able, it was another hour before she caught sight of him again. They met by the stairs to her sunken garden.

"Are you enjoying your birthday, Asha?"

"More than I expected."

Purely by chance, Cabaan appeared on the scene within seconds. The sight of his wife in a tête-à-tête with Ilarô brought no sting of jealousy, no wisp of suspicion, no reaction at all. Cabaan moved through life in the vehicle of his own self-absorption: despite his acumen in matters of agriculture and commerce, in general he was aware of very little. For once Asha was grateful for the flaw.

Now came the appropriate moment for Cabaan to comment in some way on the geetakaar's performance. Knowing what we know of Cabaan, of his tastes and philosophies, we might have expected him to criticize Ilarô's choice of the long poem of the Zaabta of Souls for the day's program; but though he had been present during the performance, he hadn't been listening to the words. Mostly he had used the time to run inventories in his head.

"It was a long song, geetakaar, though well sung. You simply oversupplied us. I would've paid you twice the amount for half the effort."

He took a tin of diamond chips from his pocket—generic currency across the raajy, convenient to have on hand, especially for a traveler—and held it out for Ilarô.

"Thank you, Vikaant, but I'm already well looked-after by the Shaasak."

Realizing the gravity of his error, Cabaan casually slipped the tin back into his pocket. Attempting to pay a royal retainer was tantamount to a breach of etiquette against the Shaasak himself, if it were reported—so he tried canceling it out by pretending it hadn't happened. He thanked Ilarô conventionally for the visit and excused himself to begin seeing off his guests. He took Asha with him. She had no grounds to object.

xiv

Cleared of yesterday's tables and chairs, and the lunch pavilion dismantled and stored away, Palace Isha's frontlands glistened in the dew like a field of sugared violets. Inside, Asha lay asleep along the edge of a divan in her dayroom when a blast nearby flipped her face-first onto the floor.

Righting herself from elbows to knees to feet, she hurried to the window where she saw a green vapor rising into the sky over a newly ruined parcel of forest, its tentacles penetrating clouds on either side. But even more terrifying was the sight of the river: in flames.

She ran downstairs. Outside she charged into the backlands, past four separate groups of aapravaaseen who had stopped their work to watch what was happening.

"Cabaan!" Asha hollered, spotting him high on a platform, forty feet up.

Cabaan rotated in his chair to look down at her. "Asha! I haven't seen you in the backlands in a year!"

"Cabaan, what are you *do*ing?"

"What do you mean? I'm doing what I do. I'm clearing the new parcel you gave me—so I can plant."

"You're clearing it with ex*plo*sives?"

"Are my bombs bothering you, Asha?"

"Half the breakable objects in the house just rattled on their shelves!"

"Half the breakable objects? Really? Did anything actually break?"

"I assume *so*, but that's hardly the measure of the problem!"

"Well, if there's no damage, then why complain?"

"Cabaan, our *river* is on fire!"

Cabaan swiveled for a wider view. "Oh, that's not from the blast, we did that on purpose. We're funneling the runoff from the glazery into the river to dispose of it more efficiently, but I thought it safer to light a controlled burn than let the waste gather and spark on its own. Now *that* could be dangerous."

"Cabaan, children *swim* in that river! We still eat *fish* out of that river! That river feeds half the highlands!"

"Everything will be fine."

He had said this warmly, as if truly wanting to reassure her. This reduced Asha's indignance but increased her astonishment. Again Cabaan had left her with nowhere to go. She didn't understand how he kept neutralizing her in this way. Starving for insight, and operating on only a sliver of intuition, she knew she had to do something differently.

"Cabaan, put the fire out."

"Pardon me?"

"I said put the fire *out*! I want you to stop our river from burning! Right now!"

Cabaan turned a dial on his small panel of controls. This lowered a secondary platform to the ground. He gestured for Asha to step onto it, and when she did, he raised her up beside him.

"Touch this," he said, indicating a silver switch on his panel.

"Why? To set off another bomb?"

"It shuts off the pipe from the glazery. The combustible waste will stop flowing—and the river will stop burning."

Asha touched the switch, triggering an explosion in the distance and sending a second green mass into the sky. The shockwave was so intense that the earth itself came rippling towards them: striking their platform it knocked Asha to her knees, though Cabaan, strapped to his chair, remained in place.

Asha struggled to her feet. "That was unkind," she said in a small voice.

"I was only having a little fun. And I thought you might like to feel the power of it. Do you know how much land you've just cleared?"

"I neither know nor wish to know."

"Oh, Asha, *please* stop taking it all so seriously. Why don't you go open your birthday presents. We'll look through them together after dinner."

⋅⋅⋅
⋅⋅⋅
⋅⋅⋅

At the rotunda, Asha found Omala taking apart her photoscope.

"I've scratched a lens. I'm going to see if I can polish it; otherwise I'll have to grind a new one, which is three weeks' work."

Asha watched in silence for a full minute before admitting:

"I'm thinking of taking a short trip."

"To see the geetakaar?"

"What?!"

"Oh! You mean you're going to see someone else?"

"No! But how could you possibly *know* that?"

"I'm a vigyaanik, I observe. The two of you were communicating from opposite sides of the gardens yesterday. It was fascinating."

"Well, I'm not sure I'm going *any*where yet, I'm only considering it. I may not go at all."

"Cousin, here's a simple law of physics: if you don't change your direction, you'll end up where you're heading. Is where you're currently heading where you'd like to end up? If not, take the trip."

❖

❖

❖

Asha made her way into the backlands for a second time in the same day after having avoided these grounds for even longer than Cabaan had remembered, nearly fifteen months. She skirted a tract of forest churned up like ground meat; she hurried past a team of aapravaaseen working a mature parcel of kuroops. Up ahead, Cabaan was having a word with one of his managers at the riverbank. Spotting her, he was good enough to meet her halfway.

"I'm going away for a few days," she said. "To see a friend."

"You know I don't like the house empty."

Asha knew no such thing, but she wasn't about to let it stop her:

"I can't stay here while you're bombing the place."

"Let's consider the situation. You want to go and I prefer that you to stay. So what you need to do is incentivize me to change my mind."

"Incentivize you how?"

"Asha, don't look so pained. You always miss the sport in things. You should learn to negotiate for what you want."

"Honestly, I've never understood the point of negotiations. Why give a person something only so you can take something else away?"

"Try it."

"I won't."

"Then I'll do it for you. Every night you're gone will cost you a hundred haiktars. You have five hundred haiktars left. You can buy yourself a nice little break."

✧

✧

✧

Wearing her sable cape and a scarf of pale-green silk knotted at the throat, Asha left Palace Isha on horseback; but cantering past the rotunda had a thought and stopped in to see Omala first. Omala wasn't there—most likely she was asleep on a sofa in the athainaaium, where she tended to nod off when reading into the early hours. Even so, Asha left the rotunda having borrowed a certain device that would change her fate in ways more intricate than she could ever have imagined. She had only thought of it in a moment's inspiration as something that Ilarô might find amusing—and expected to return it to its owner soon enough. She left a note saying as much, hoping her cousin wouldn't mind; then she wrapped the device in her own scarf to protect it and placed it carefully into Tapti's pannier for the trip to the dell.

The western woods were still jacketed in frost when Asha rode up.

A polar wind crisped the air.

The golden chips of the aspen trees glistened with rime.

Tapti's hooves cracked patches of ice on the forest floor.

Arriving at the outer boundary of Ilarô's temple, Asha dismounted, but in touching ground felt all the weight of her body shoot up from her feet into her head, as if the force of nature that attracts a quantity of matter toward the center of the earth had suddenly reversed its force and was trying to fling her up and off the very planet on which she stood. It was, needless to say, no actual inversion of gravity, only an inversion of mind, the result of what Asha saw: an empty space ahead.

Ilarô was gone. Why would he have stayed? They had made no plan to meet again. He knew now that she was married. He had met Cabaan, he had seen her at home. Of *course* he had gone. She had traded away five hundred haiktars, the end of her inheritance and her father's final gift to her, for a ride through the woods.

—"Asha."

Ilarô stepped through the temple's rear archway, arms loaded with kindling. He had wanted to build a fire for Asha before she came.

He stepped forward and kissed her lightly on the cheek. She thought she might not hold together: she was fighting urges to burst out laughing, burst out crying, and collapse to the ground. But she only smiled delicately, a testament to her skill at self-containment, itself the result of much recent practice. Had she known Ilarô even slightly better, she might even have let herself collapse. Ilarô would have preferred it.

"I've brought breakfast," she said.

Ilarô declared himself famished. So from Tapti's pannier Asha produced a meal of sweet rice and tangerines, which she served in platinum bowls along with pear nectar from a matching platinum tharamas. They sat on a toppled column to eat. Afterwards they walked the length of the dell, taking in views of the temple from every different angle, imagining who might have stayed here through the centuries—and why.

That night they lay beside the hearth, wrapped in Asha's sable cape and flecked by frozen crystals drifting down from a single circling cloud. They stayed this way for hours in their temple hypaethral, under the stars, pointing out their favorite constellations, describing their childhoods, naming the songs and poems they had read from year to year, until something happened beyond imagining: the sun flew up from behind the mountain in the distance, stationing itself beside the moon—an eruption of beauty from the alp of the earth into the night sky.

"What *is* it?" Asha whispered.

"A midnight sun," Ilarô said.

"A midnight sun? I've never *heard* of such a thing."

"The early geetakaaron used to sing about it."

Reaching deep into the storehouse of memory, Ilarô retrieved a fragment of verse and tone:

> *A midnight sun will warm someone*
> *once in a thousand years*
> *A midnight sun for some love comes*
> *once every thousand years*

Asha tilted her head to warm her face alongside Ilarô's. The rays of this midnight sun shot between snowflakes until the whole sky glimmered with gold and ice. Water co-mingled with fire, night with day, solar with lunar, making a throng of opposites into a single spectacle that dispelled, at least momentarily, the dividing lines of the universe. Those misguided philosophers who insisted to us, who nearly convinced us, that a thing was either one way or the other—up or down, hot or cold, good or evil, friend or foe—were well-meaning intellectually but so violently naive. Each thing contains it all! How often do we forget that the sun and moon sit permanently together in the heavens: only the eye fails to perceive their concurrence, and the mind follows the eye's lead. But occasionally, as on this night, reality declares itself.

A minute after it rose up, the sun dropped down again into the waiting mountain—and the night's starry scenery reappeared.

"How long can you stay with me?" Ilarô whispered.

"Five days. I can afford five days."

They fell asleep in each other's arms. In the morning they rose lightly and walked the forest. During his few days here, Ilarô had discovered many distinctions of the woods surrounding the dell of the temple. He took Asha now through the hidden features of his little realm, including a grove of coconut trees that was home to a lemur colony, then down to a miniature glacier in a glade frozen by some subterranean link to the polar fields. Here he cupped water from an icy stream and offered it to Asha: she drank from his hands.

They circled the glacier. Behind it coexisted a thermal lagoon, bubbling with chemical light.

"A remedy pool!" Asha said. "I thought they'd all dried up years ago!"

"I've seen more than one in your woods."

"Have you? I don't be*lieve* it! We used to have a remedy pool in the backlands. If I sneezed even once, my mother had me soaking for an hour!"

Ilarô loved hearing this. Asha's delight fueled his delight. He noticed that her best moments came when she was surprised by something she hadn't known, or when she realized she was wrong about some long-held idea or another; and it pleased him to see her discard an old assumption as easily as she tossed aside her sable cape in the midday sun.

❖

❖

❖

That evening they lay beneath another astronomical sky, ruminating on the planets and their moons, Asha's hand resting on Ilarô's cheek before dropping to his neck, where she felt a choker beneath his shirt.

"Are you wearing a necklace?"

Ilarô reached behind his collar to unhook a choker of beads held together with a thin filament of platinum. These were shaanadaar diamonds: orbed rather than faceted, black yet glistering; so priceless that they were to other jewels as other jewels were to seashells.

"How fabulous!" Asha said. "I thought only the Shaasak was allowed to wear shaanadaar diamonds!"

"Or whoever he gives them to."

Asha was well aware of the legend: it was said that if you crushed a shaanadaar diamond at night, starlight trapped inside the stone would be released, rocketing back into the firmament. Omala had explained once that if the concept of "trapped starlight" was understood as poetic license, then the science behind the legend wasn't *entirely* impossible. The glistering center of a shaanadaar diamond, she said, might contain zinc oxide which, if exposed to and photocatalyzed by the elements of the air, would luminesce. The ancient miners who dug for these stones, having accidentally crushed one, would have been dazzled by what they saw, embellishing the experience at storytime with tales of the black diamonds beaming their strands of starlight back into the patterns of the cosmos.

But even this was only a theory sprung from a legend that was likely a myth, because no one within living memory ever *had* crushed a shaanadaar diamond. The stones were simply too valuable to destroy. Asha imagined that a necklace of the quality she now held in her hand and made from such a number of perfectly matched shaanadaar stones as these might have been worth as much as a year's profit from Cabaan's wolfram-wood enterprise. It was incredible that Ilarô should be wearing it.

She let the black beads fall between the curves of her fingers while asking him:

"How long have you lived at the sky-lodge?"

"I've never lived anywhere else. I was born there."

"And how long have you been the royal geetakaar?"

"I've sung for the Shaasak since I was eight."

By all accounts the Silent Shaasak was a good-natured man. He was also among the most powerful persons on earth; he had no need to give gifts unless the giving meant something to him, and of those gifts he did give, few could be the equal of a necklace of shaanadaar diamonds. It was reasonable to expect that such an individual should respond to Ilarô's particular qualities; but in a world that often ruined the talented and punished the kind, Asha was thrilled to realize that, in this case at least, a person of the Shaasak's standing knew perfectly well what his geetakaar was worth.

Ilarô took his necklace from Asha's fingers and fitted it around her neck, locking its hidden clasp. But when he looked at her again, he saw that she was struggling to hide something.

"What *is* it? Asha, what's wrong?"

"Nothing. It's nothing. I was thinking of my father."

"Was he unkind to you?"

"Oh, no—I adored him. But lately, when I think of him, I have to fight tears."

"*Fight* them? Why?"

"I've been training myself not to cry."

"But … how excruciating for you!"

"Well, it's time I made myself stronger."

"Is it? For what reason?"

"Because I've been terribly weak. If I can train myself not to cry, at least I'll be moving in the right direction."

Ilarô's face was burning at the very thought of it. "I'm sorry, I don't understand that at *all*," he said. "You miss your father. How is that not sad? And why *shouldn't* you cry?"

Asha was unable to answer; she had lost the logic of it.

"If you train yourself not to cry," Ilarô said, "what comes next? Will you train yourself not to laugh? Or eat? Or sleep?" He waited for her to say something. "Or have you done those things already?"

Asha was beginning to pick up the rhythms of Ilarô's beliefs. He numbed himself to nothing, insisting on feeling every emotion that came to him, including every pain. Asha herself had learned mere tricks of emotional reception instead. For instance: folding up incoming feelings and dropping them down the slots of her mind. The result was a tidy mental housekeeping, but otherwise she couldn't recommend it. She promised herself now that during these five days with Ilarô that she had bought with the end of her inheritance, she would work to learn something of his talent for living. But so much of Ilarô's talent derived from his willingness to forgive himself his faults, and here Asha's way was blocked. Side by side with Ilarô, the comparisons between his self-regard and hers were unavoidable, and she began to see that the loneliness of recent years, which she had refused to admit, had been differentiating inside of her into a hostility toward her own person. It was the side effect not so much of her time with Cabaan but of the horrendous decision to marry him in the first place.

In the weeks leading up to the wedding, Asha had congratulated herself for bringing it about, thinking herself quite mature for having faced the fact of her dwindling resources and embracing an opportunity to restore her fortunes. In reality she was only clinging to what she had been raised with and felt she could not go forward without. She hadn't yet learned that precept of the ancients: better to need less than to want more. The wisdom of it was reported everywhere, even in the long poem of the Zaabta of Souls, in a ballad that Asha knew well. Better to need less than to want more: a guiding principle that might still fix her in her future, though it would have helped her already in her past. Ignoring it, as most young persons do, the damage that Asha had done to herself, though not irreparable, not yet, went deep.

Meanwhile, at least, she could enjoy Ilarô's company. He was less serene than she had realized at first, more jolly. He had an excellent sense of humor: he loved pointing out the comic effects of being alive. He reveled in the contradictions of the people he met, and though he never once in Asha's time with him laughed at the expense of another human being, he frequently laughed at humanity in general and at himself in particular. Also he was a brilliant mimic, the voices of the animal kingdom being his specialty. Birds, monkeys, even noisy insects formed the core of his repertoire. He wasn't much for telling funny stories, though he frequently lay in wait to execute a wordless joke: Asha might be napping and wake to see him sitting on the other side of the temple, reading a book upside-down, eyes covered with slices of boiled egg from breakfast.

Apropos another aspect of his personality, Asha had understood him perfectly from the first moment: he was the most affectionate man she had ever met. He often smiled at her for no reason whatsoever, not even for reassurance. He kissed her many times an hour: on the cheek, on the lips, on the nose. Once he left the woodpile he was working at and crossed to where Asha was seated—some forty feet away—to press his lips to her kneecap before turning right around and going back to his chopping. At least twice a day he took Asha's hand and simply held it to his heart.

After her third night with Ilarô, Asha woke up startled by his very body: his limbs paired with hers, his lips in contact with her back. Many listeners will know this simple pleasure from their own lives; Asha did not. Even after five years of marriage, she had never slept with a man through the night.

She turned to face him and for half an hour watched the movements of his closed eyelids, trying to pick up the signal of his dreams. She also tried imagining what his life must be like in the Shaasak's sky-lodge, and in his own apartment there, taking up two or three of the palace's legendary eight thousand rooms. She pictured him looking down through open windows, a breeze on his face, foamy whitecaps below detonating across green sheets of sea.

Ilarô opened his eyes. The edges of his lips quivered, forming a sleepy smile at the sight of Asha examining him from the distance of ten inches. Overacting, he moaned:

"Kiss me or I think I'll die."

Asha made no move. She wasn't teasing him, she was lost in the sound of his voice. Even this single sentence from him was enough to send her mind flying. Ilarô's speaking voice was nearly the equal of his singing voice in the way it worked beyond the reach of language. Asha reacted so strongly to the flow and inflections of his signature in sound that frequently she had to guide her mind back to conscious interpretation of what he was saying, reminding herself that he was actually talking to her and expecting a reply.

Groggily Ilarô asked again for his kiss. This time Asha kissed him. But afterwards he wanted more: instead of struggling to his feet and into the day, he pulled Asha in and asked her to kiss him again. She kissed him again, and together they slipped back into a velvet trance, Ilarô's cheek coming to rest on Asha's shoulder, his arm over her hip and his hand around hers. This was typically the moment for Asha, which is to say the moment between the suspension of consciousness and dreaming, when she had such insights as her nature and circumstances allowed, though she invariably lost them to the filter of sleep; but what came to her this time, not so much inspired by the press of Ilarô's body against hers as *activated* by it, was a realization so sharp that it etched itself into the crystalline structures of memory then and there: love was not the displacement of hatred, love was the rejection of fear.

❖

❖

❖

On their fourth day together, Ilarô proposed a "vrddhi," or what we today might call a hike, to explore the headwaters of the dell. Asha, who loved a good walk, was only too happy to go. So after a breakfast of yam cakes with sage—prepared by Ilarô, the one true cook between them—they set off. It was another chilly morning; Asha found herself shivering after a minute away from the hearth, but soon there was slanted uphill climbing through a grove of eucalyptus and then a mile-long stretch across a sunny flat of wildflowers, so the explorers quickly warmed up. At the end of their vrddhi, they came to another out-of-place glacier rising a hundred feet in walls of cerulean ice. It was Ilarô who was cold now: he was a little too lean for the bite in the air; so Asha placed her sable cape on his shoulders. A small gesture, made on instinct, but a fundamental moment; because through some flash of insight that may remain forever opaque to followers of Asha's story, but which flared from nothing into Asha's own consciousness the way existence itself burst into being ex nihilo, placing her cape on Ilarô's shoulders was the moment that she would forever after consider to be the very first act of her adult life.

They spent their five days together doing things in this way. Not having had the advantage of romantic contact before now, Asha was flooded with its array of benefits. Emotional, biochemical, psychotherapeutic, dermatological: everything improved. What's more, she became aware of these many changes in herself as they happened. It might have gone another way: she might have been overwhelmed by the largeness of the experience, blinded to the details; but even though Omala was the family's woman of science, Asha too, when her blood was clear, could anatomize phenomena with precision, if in her own manner. On the question of love, what surprised her most was discovering the ingenuity of its mechanism: designed to stop time, void the past, and make the present moment the sum of existence.

As if mind-reading, Ilarô said:

"Explain to me then, Asha, why you keep punishing yourself for the mistakes you say you made before we met."

It won't reflect well on Asha to tell what came next: a flash of anger. All because Ilarô had flatly asked her to tell the truth about herself. But why not ask her to jump off the little glacier they had returned to and were now seated atop, to see if she could fly? Impressive if she succeeded, but more likely to end in shattered bones and burst organs.

She imagined answering with a storm of sound, demolishing the forest below them and clearing the land for her to go and stand in, alone. An overreaction—and of a piece with Asha's recent states of mind. The question before her though was to what extent she would let an overreaction control her *now*. If she could not produce a true storm of sound, she could at least voice her displeasure. Or, having observed Ilarô's practice of noting his own emotions one at a time before letting them recede into the void they had sprung from, she might try copying the process: she could note the anger gushing out of her brain—then watch it evaporate.

She did neither. She raised a finger to signal that she needed a moment to think, trying to come up with a way to be acceptably incensed. Still, she had no intention of answering honestly: naming her failures out loud was something she had done more than enough lately, in her dayroom or in the minarets of Palace Isha, pacing in circles and insulting herself like a person unleashed from her reason. But after a moment's consideration, she changed her mind: she might take a step off this ice-cliff after all. As Ilarô himself had said of her, she had a flair for throwing off her opinions when the time was right. Yes, on second thought, she *would* step forward. Slamming into the earth below and destroying herself was maybe even preferable to any more hesitation at this cliff's edge. So she gave Ilarô his answer, admitting the details of her bad decisions, confessing how she had come to be where she was in the world, spitting it out as fast as she could. It was not a pleasant confession, because in the telling there was no more denying. Hard to pretend a thing hasn't happened when stating exactly how it took place.

Afterwards she expected Ilarô to comfort her. He did not. Wise enough not to pick up denying Asha's problems where Asha had left off, he sat quietly beside her instead … until she carried on of her own accord. She was suffering when she told him:

"I have to stop Cabaan. I can't let him pull us down any deeper. I do understand that. And I know I can't expect help from anyone else. We succeed or we fail on our own."

Ilarô rose up in shock, not at Asha, but at all the lies she had learned:

"That's quite wrong, Asha! It's a mistake you risk never recovering from, this idea that your strength is your virtue and the stronger you are on your own, the better! Whoever's been telling you that we don't have a right to expect help from one another, to *depend* on one another, hasn't been telling you what's true! You think you can survive the hardest parts of your life by yourself? Well, I promise you, it can't be done! But I can *carry* you, and you can carry *me*!"

Ilarô wasn't saying he could save her, only that he could help her save herself. Hearing it, Asha shivered with a premonition of the difference between life and death.

❖

❖

❖

What hasn't yet been mentioned about Asha's time with Ilarô was the one thing we might have expected to hear about first—and the last thing that Asha would take with her out of these five days away from Palace Isha: Ilarô's songs. At last she asked him to sing for her. He was happy to do it, and he sang for some time—because Asha kept begging him not to stop—offering her at least one of every type of song that he knew. Airs and lays, ballads and descants: all the forms of madhuratshruti—translated as "euphonies" in the ancient-to-modern wordbooks—that were loved in the raajy. After these he performed the so-called "cosmic sequences," sound-shapes without words, for Ilarô was a student of the Dhvani ka Gyaan, the original body of sonic knowledge that had once been the basis of every geetakaar's training, and he could duplicate a portion of the primal tone from which the universe itself was said to spring. The universe being an utterance, not a place—though some understand it best as an announcement. Finally he sang a lay that he had composed himself that very morning, just for Asha. Listening to it all, to Ilarô's interpretations of madhuratshruti, Asha was fully exposed to the scope and depth of his gift. Nothing in what she knew or even imagined had prepared her for such an experience: these were dimensions of time and beauty that Ilarô conjured and offered, worlds of purpose and solace whose existence Asha had never guessed at.

She could also now consider the more superficial effects on her person of Ilarô's voice. Though Asha did not see herself as an intellectual, still her mind had been working intensely on the matter, and she came to conclusions proving once and for all that her own powers of perception, together with her stamina for mental exploration, were not so modest as she insisted. Apropos the constant question of how even the sound of Ilarô's speaking voice could transcend the limits of language, how the things he said reached further into her than the codes of words should have been able to go, Asha realized with a leap of intuition that his speaking voice indeed *borrowed* from his singing voice in the faintest units of melody—as imperceptible but real as the microscopic flow of solid glass in the direction of gravity—to the point where his words became music too. This joining of song and speech was almost certainly unconscious on Ilarô's part—Asha doubted he was aware of it at all—but its power was indisputable: it deepened and lightened the listener at the same time.

—"Oh, no!" Asha cried, jumping up and cutting off Ilarô's song in mid verse. "No, no, no, no, *no!*"

"Asha, my god, what *is* it?"

"I've forgotten to give you your present!"

She ran to Tapti. From the horse's pannier she carefully extracted that inspired afterthought of her departure from Palace Isha: Omala's ebony box that could capture the waves of a person's voice in its magnetized mesh and transfer the sound into the specially treated wax of a candle.

Ilarô, you'll need to know, as early as adolescence had formed a powerful distaste for extra possessions, especially any that he had to carry. His apartment in the sky-lodge, one of the finest outside the wing belonging to the Shaasak and Jaanam themselves, would have bewildered Asha: it was nearly empty. A bed, a desk, a table, a shelf of books, a series of stringed instruments hanging from hooks. Its walls paneled in ivory, its view of the Malachite Sea, and its balcony high over the water were exceptional, but as for the decor: austere. Ilarô was denying himself nothing, he had simply grown up needing less rather than wanting more, which becomes an aesthetic as well as a moral preference over time. The occasional gift of a rare heptachord still tempted him, but otherwise he was disinclined to accumulate, sincerely preferring not to be given gifts. He almost never said so, out of courtesy, and it was a good thing too, because it might have prevented Asha from surprising him now with a device that, in a matter of seconds, he would not have known how to live without ever again.

She showed him how it worked. Taking a candle out of the bundle of twelve that she had brought from the rotunda, she inserted it into the box's metal mesh, replacing the partially used candle that had been left there by Omala. She snapped the box shut, flipped its jade handle, and spoke into the small horn attached to its side:

"Greetings, royal geetakaar. This is the voice of Asha, recording a message for you by means of a magnetizing box that she wishes you to have, but which she can only lend you at present, since it belongs not to her but to her cousin. Nevertheless, if you enjoy the use of it, Asha promises to have another made for you exactly like this one before she sees you next."

She pulled down the jade handle, opened the box, took out the candle, lit it, and heard her words repeated back to her with only the slightest distortion as the wind caused the candle's flame to flicker:

"Greetings, royal geetakaar, this is the voice of Asha, recording a message for you by means of a magnetizing box that she wishes you to have ... "

Ilarô shook with ecstasy. He had lived in the sky-lodge all his life and had seen every innovation that had made its way to the Shaasak's mat in the last twenty years, but never, ever anything like this.

"Omala uses it to take notes while she works," Asha said, "but I thought, why couldn't you make candles out of your songs? You could leave them with friends in distant places, so on lonely midwinter nights they can light them and listen to you sing. Anyway, it's quite a clever invention, don't you think?"

Ilarô couldn't speak. Seeing him this way, like a boy on his birthday, Asha's satisfaction was profound. It said something larger about her than the conventional compliment of it suggests that, although she was not a person who minded finding herself on the receiving end of a gift, she preferred *giving* a gift even more. When Asha focused her mind on pleasing someone in this way, she would cogitate at length on the tastes and desires of the intended recipient. She could easily devote a week to a selection, or on landmark occasions a month. Whether the diamond hunting knife carved out of a single monstrous stone that she had presented to Cabaan in a scabbard of platinum mesh the day they were married ... or the two-person gubbaara for Omala's thirtieth birthday ... or today's gift-on-loan to Ilarô of the magnetizing candle-box: Asha's achievements in the art of generosity were considerable.

The gubbaara had been a special success. Then as now people liked to say "it's the thought that counts," but sometimes, Asha knew, it was the money. Without cash to spend, and lots *of* it, she could never have commissioned the little airship. In essence a sailboat of the sky, the simplicity of a gubbaara's function belied the sophistication of its design. First a vast silk balloon, an "envelope" in engineering parlance, was meticulously woven and inflated by lifting gas. From the envelope was suspended a basket made of the braided vines and stems of the black rattan, large enough for a pilot to stand in and work a small rigging of sails fitted onto the side of the craft, at minimum a large sail for propulsion and two small ones for navigation. A hand-cranked propeller was sometimes added for impetus during windless spells. The body of knowledge to turn out these components with the precision required to make the sum of them fly was closely held by the materials scientists of the raajy's southernmost province: a cooperative of sky-wrights. Their understanding of the tolerances of fibers and fronds for atmospheric currents, velocity, rains, and even the odd electrical storm on an ill-timed trip was the only safeguard against the dangers inherent in journey by air. And the black rattan, uniquely sturdy among the climbing palms, was endemic to the raajy's lowest latitude, where the sky-wrights made their home and where they bred in secret the genus of silkworm whose thread best withstood the rigors of flight.

A monopoly, they could charge what they liked for their work and take only as many commissions as suited them. In the last several years, for reasons unexplained, they had been accepting even fewer orders than usual, all of which meant that buying a gubbaara, not to mention having it transported from the far south to the far north, entailed a fantastic amount of cash. This being the one area of Asha's current circumstances in which she was not constrained, and having set her heart on an airship for her cousin's birthday surprise, the item was ordered, the purchase made, the craft constructed, and the gift delivered on time. Omala's rapture at the sight of the fully inflated gubbaara once her blindfold was removed was so intense that, after kissing Asha, she even mouthed a spontaneous "thank you" to Cabaan. Since then not a week had gone by without her sailing above Palace Isha's forty thousand haiktars, mapping its features the way she loved to do in her capacity as the region's official cartographer.

On the subject of Asha's talent in the kindred art of gift-presentation, it may be enough to say that she had the eye of a girl raised by artists of the most cultivated taste and the purse of the richest person you know. A delivery from Palace Isha might come in a box sheathed in platinum foil, if an outer gleam fit the gift inside. A trove of white linens that Asha once gave for a wedding present was sent in a cylindrical chest of rare whitewood, inlaid with mosaics of onyx in which the names of the bride and groom were intertwined in stylized glyphs. Even simple bouquets of flowers sent by Asha were wrapped in leaves embossed with images of the flowers they contained, hand-stamped by Asha using the stamps that her mother, an adept at woodblock and intaglio, had carved. Asha boxed and wrapped each gift at her own desk, never passing the job to anyone else, another way to imbue the things that traveled from her hands to someone else's with a bit of herself.

Have we laid to rest the unoriginal thought that children without siblings grow up disinclined to share? Asha had demonstrated the opposite tendency from the earliest age: her parents' influence; though eventually, as she settled into life with Cabaan and fell back from the life that had preceded him, the ever-multiplying number of gifts that flowed from her paper-craft room, which doubled as a wrapping station, paradoxically threw into relief how Asha was beginning to *fail* in what would otherwise be face-to-face connections with the world—and its people—around her.

Today, with Ilarô, her connection was complete. But like so

many highpoints in life, it had its context. For now, and no later, these five days with the geetakaar that Asha had exchanged for the end of her inheritance were used up. It was time for her to return to Palace Isha. A talented procrastinator, she could think of no way to delay.

xv

Asha and Cabaan sat finishing a late dinner. The sweet course was pink-mango sugarfoam, a dessert that never would have been served under normal circumstances; but the kitchen was in turmoil after the sudden passing of Palace Isha's longtime cook, and her replacement was not yet versed in Cabaan's every partiality and aversion.

They ate in silence. Asha's eyes were on her plate, as they had been through the meal: she was afraid that if she looked at Cabaan directly, she would burst out laughing. Having managed not to lose control of herself so far by biting down hard on the inside of her cheek, the taste of blood was now mingling in her mouth with seasoning from the aloo gobi, nobody's favorite vegetable dish of spiced cauliflower.

"This sugarfoam is luscious!" she blurted, though really she was only speaking to release the pressure building inside of her toward a blast of hilarity.

"If you'd be very kind," Cabaan said, "and instruct the new cook never again to serve anything pink-mango-related, I'd be terribly grateful."

The courtesy with which Cabaan often spoke was not meant to disguise but rather to accentuate the contempt he frequently wished to communicate.

Asha reached for the serving bowl. "Well, if you dislike it *that* much, I'm taking the rest to Omala."

Cabaan smiled meaninglessly. "See you soon," he said.

A quarter hour later, the cousins were lounging outside the rotunda, enjoying a view of Palace Isha's starglazed lake through a gap in the pines.

"How has it been here since I left?" Asha asked casually.

"Loud. Your husband keeps bombing things."

"My *hus*band?" Asha thought, shifting in her seat. The unchanged fact that the man she had just dined with was her legal spouse had actually jarred her.

"I don't know how much wolfram-wood he's aiming to produce next year," Omala said, "but it seems to me that *attacking* the land as a way to cultivate it is an idea of unverified merit."

"Well … I'm sorry for the noise."

Omala dismissed Cabaan with a sweep of her hand. "And with you?" she said. "How has it been with *you* lately?"

No sentimentalist, Asha abridged what was rightly an epic of the emotions to a somewhat shorter version:

"Better."

Omala set the bowl of sugarfoam on the ground, leaned back, and demanded to be told everything. Asha had no intention of *telling* everything, but she didn't mind telling *some*. The account that she now gave describing the intimate link that had formed between Ilarô and herself was discreet yet vivid.

"So when will you see him again?" Omala said.

"I'm not sure yet."

"But you will *see* him again."

Asha nodded slowly before adding: "Though I don't know how I'm going to get the time away from Cabaan."

"I'll take care of Cabaan for you—with a hatchet."

"Omala, that isn't helpful."

"Anyway, how did you leave it with Ilarô? What is he expecting you to do?"

"He's expecting me to make up my own mind."

"Ah. Now I like him even more."

"I need a few days to think it through. In the meantime, I did want to send him something. A note—or a gift."

"Why not a book? He's alone in the woods, he has plenty of time to read."

Omala's idea of gift-giving always began and ended with a book, but in this instance she was on the mark, so they left the rotunda for the athainaaium and its thirty thousand tomes. An hour later they were still there, on the floor beside a fireplace burning a cord of the costliest whitewood in the raajy, a luxury that was becoming Omala's routine indulgence. Surrounding them were dozens of rejected options, while from a fresh stack Omala was reading titles aloud for Asha's consideration:

"*A Compendium of Extinct but Significant Flowers … Hieroglyphic Medical Riddles … A Picture-Book of the Great Glaciers of the World … Ziqqurats and their Architectural Descendants …*"

"All fine ideas," Asha said, "but none say 'Ilarô.'"

"Here's a good one: *A Manual on the Correct Methodology of Volcanic Research and Lava Collection.* Who wouldn't love a good book on lava?"

Asha had just found something more suitable: a history of stringed instruments. She passed it to Omala who paged through its illustrations in diamond-flecked ink of chordophones through the ages: the lute, the oud, the veena, the lyre, including a chapter on renowned heptachords and their sobriquets:

The Traveler,

The Sorcerer,

The Expressionist …

… and others named for their illustrious owners of the past or the famous players they had once belonged to:

The Dharmaraaj,

The Aakanksh,

The Chandravadan,

The Mahaprajapati.

"Perfect," Omala said. She passed Asha a pen to inscribe the flyleaf.

Placing the book on her knees, Asha conjured the memory of lying with Ilarô beneath their midnight sun, golden snowflakes landing without melting on his black curls.

She inscribed the book with an intimate message; but before she had put down her pen, Giribandhava was pounding desperately on the open door.

"Vikaantee, we have an emergency! Please hurry—it's Jothi!"

The cousins jumped up and ran outside to the site of the trouble: the long roof between the palace's tetrad of colossal orbs. Jothi-Anandan and Giribandhava had been leaping again in a midnight air-sailing adventure, using leaves from the chandava trees. But Jothi-Anandan's shirt had caught in descent on the high branch of a pine: he was dangling upside-down over the jackal-trap in the gardens below. If his shirt tore, he would plunge onto the trap's wolfram-wood stakes.

"Jothi, stop wriggling!" Asha shouted. "Just hold still until I get there!" She tore her sarong at the thigh for flexibility and pulled herself into the tree over Omala's protests:

"Wait for someone to bring a ladder! You'll kill yourself!"

This was no overreaction: Asha might easily have slipped and been impaled along with the boy she was trying to save.

She inched up the pine. Above her, one of Jothi-Anandan's shoes slipped off his foot, grazing Asha's ear along its eighty-foot drop into the jackal-trap, where it was pierced at the heel by a spike. The blood was rushing to Jothi-Anandan's head by this time; he was starting to shake.

Asha reached him. His arms had been pinned back by the awkward angle of the collision, so all he really needed was careful unhooking, a limb at a time. This Asha did for him fairly easily.

Text

[1]RFID 3M

FIC HUDDLES

Asha of the air /
R0700156524

R0700156524

Restored to his boyish powers, he whipped himself upright and launched into promises about better behavior starting next week. (Not starting right now, Asha was amused to hear, not starting tomorrow morning, but starting next week.)

From below, Omala shouted up:

"Jothi, you can tell us how sorry you are later! Just get Asha down from there!"

The boy obeyed. When he and Asha reached the ground, scraped but safe, he started again on his apology, but Asha threw her arms around him and squeezed so hard that not only did he stop speaking, he started to cough. By now twenty of the staff of the household had left the warmth of their beds and made their way outside. Asha's after-surge of emotion had taken hold of her as she called out to them:

"I'd like this trap covered over first thing tomorrow morning, please! Let the snow-jackals eat my roses, I don't care anymore! Let's give the roses up! Let's cut down the rest of our rose trees and leave a trail of petals all the way to the foothills!"

Hearing this, Omala's mind jumped and her relief of a moment earlier vanished. Asha wasn't sounding *entirely* like a maniac, though she wasn't sounding much like herself either.

"Asha, let's go in. I think what we all need is a nice hot mug of masala chai."

They headed for the athainaaium, intending to straighten up the clutter they had left behind and collect their things before going over to the kitchen. Instead they stopped short in the doorway at the sight of Cabaan reading Asha's inscription in the book for Ilarô.

He looked up—and whipped the book at Asha. It flew across the room, struck her weakly on the stomach, fell to the floor. Asha turned and walked out.

"Asha!" Cabaan barked.

Asha ran. She went through the long hall, out the door, down into the sunken garden. Unsure what to do next, she waited a moment, then reversed course. She went back up and through to the athainaaium using a side entrance, to retrieve the book for Ilarô. But Cabaan hadn't left the room.

"Asha!"

"Stay away from me!"

She fled into the Gathering Dome—and from there into the hidden channels of the palace, knowing Cabaan would find them out now. She ran along an underground passage, she scaled an uneven staircase, she darted through a series of obscure rooms. Cabaan was following, but ignorant of which egress to take where there were options, he was too slow to catch up. Reaching her own marble dome, Asha exited a secret corridor and came into the gallery of her father's ornamentals. Here she kept his botanical artwork on permanent display: living compositions of foot-tall trees, many bearing his signature white roses, blooms reduced to the size of buttons. It was the most important room in the house.

Asha slid the bolt and waited. In a minute Cabaan was on the other side of the door, hammering it with his fist. But even with an axe this door could not have been penetrated, because it was made of solid wolfram-wood. How this had come to be was down to Cabaan himself. A year earlier he had pulled half the aapravaaseen from the backlands and into the palace for a week of work removing every door in the house—numbering some nine hundred and forty-three once tallied—and switching them out with wolfram-wood replacements. He had come to hate the centuries-old hardwood originals, finding them not only out of fashion with their carved calligraphic designs, but needlessly heavy, and as such irritating to be constantly opening and closing in the course of the day. The new doors were light, strong, unadorned, and had the special wolfram-wood sheen: an improvement all around. For her part Asha had always taken pleasure in the great weight of Palace Isha's old doors. As a child, having to put her muscle into pushing them open and pulling them closed gave her a secret feeling of mightiness. When Cabaan had begun to complain about them after eighteen months of living here, it had seemed to Asha an odd objection for someone of his height and strength. Now she realized it had been just another way to dominate his environment, by putting his controlling touch even on how one could pass into or out from a room.

With Cabaan still demanding to be let in, Asha slipped out of the gallery through a back stairwell and made her way into the short hall leading to her dayroom. Again she locked herself in before Cabaan came shouting and pounding, but the door to the dayroom was now made of wolfram-wood too.

The pounding stopped. Asha sank to the floor, asking herself how, after her beautiful childhood in this same palace, in this very *room*, could such a thing be happening here? Against the din in her mind, she failed to hear an unusual sound nearby, like the exaggerated thrashing of a flame. When it finally registered, she stood and went to the window—and this is what she saw: Cabaan had the staff of the household dropping her father's ornamentals off the large fourth-floor balcony. The staff were in tears—but how could they refuse him? One after the other the miniature rose-trees ignited as they fell through the strange vapors of the backlands.

Asha's insides seized up, as if her organs had all jammed and their functionings ceased. Her temples hot with terror, she knew she had to do something quickly …

… but with a jolt her organs started up again—and she reversed herself:

"Let them burn then," she said out loud to no one. "Let the ornamentals burn. This is no longer my father's house, this is no longer *my* house. We own nothing here, not even ourselves. Let Cabaan destroy all of it—it tells of what we've come to."

The White Forest was gone: Asha would no longer delude

herself to the contrary by admiring its image in miniature. At least Cabaan was telling the truth about the state of things. If rose-cultivation refined the personality, as her father used to say, let rose-obliteration savage them all, let them admit the new rule of how they lived at Palace Isha!

But the staff of the household couldn't know what Asha was thinking, they only knew they were cutting her off from her father by destroying his artwork, his miniaturized rose-trees that could have outlived them all, lived for hundreds of years. And the worst was still coming: Jothi-Anandan, wearing only one shoe in the aftermath of the jackal-trap incident, was guarding the ornamental that he knew Asha loved best, the one she kept by her daybed, the rose-tree miniature in the orange-lacquered tray. It would have been in the gallery for tomorrow's pruning when Cabaan thundered in—and was now in the possession of Cabaan's littlest foe. Jothi-Anandan was clutching the miniature in folded arms, refusing to throw it off the balcony. So Cabaan scooped him up and flipped him upside-down, holding him by an ankle over the edge. Shaking him, he commanded the boy to let the rose-tree go. But the boy refused.

"Let go of it!" Asha whispered from her window. "Jothi, let go! Let *go!*"

She imagined him drowning in terror, his poor heart about to explode. But what couldn't be seen from the vantage point of Asha's window was how large Jothi-Anandan felt in his smallness against Cabaan, how strong he felt in his weakness.

Unbolting the door, Asha ran into the hall. She was quick to reach Cabaan's supply room, to get hold of a particular weapon … and just as quick to run across to the gallery, where:

—"If you hurt that boy, Cabaan, I will kill you where you stand!"

Cabaan whirled to face the door. Asha was there, gripping the diamond hunting knife she had given him the day they were married.

"I will *kill* you, Cabaan! Decide!"

Possibly it was the incongruity of seeing his wife wielding a weapon or possibly it was the surprise of the weapon she had chosen to wield—whatever the reason, Cabaan put the boy down. He held Asha's gaze—until she dropped the diamond blade and ran. He went after her, but Asha kept ahead of him long enough to escape the fourth floor and climb a staircase to the roof.

She exited onto a windy field of stone supported by four marble moons. No actual moon shone overhead due to an encroachment of clouds, though an eerie glow filtered through, lighting Asha's head and the leaves circling Cabaan's legs as he ran after her.

Asha stopped short, spinning to face him.

"Stop following me! I'm leaving Palace Isha! I'm *giving* it to you. Take it and leave me alone!"

"Palace Isha hasn't been yours to give in anything but name for quite some time."

"Then enjoy it without me, because I'm going!"

"Of course you're *not* going. But why you would think you want to is the question. Because of an infatuation with a wandering poet?"

"Because I'm not becoming myself here, I'm becoming *you*!"

"Ah. I see now. This is a medical condition. You need to take a dava and calm yourself."

"I don't need a dava! I need to leave!"

As Asha's vehemence rose, Cabaan's anger died down. "Please calm yourself," he said with the same, softly modulated voice that he used to defeat occasional outbursts of misery from the aapravaaseen.

"I'm leaving, Cabaan."

"Kindly stop saying that."

"I'm leaving, and you mustn't try to—

He smacked her face with enough force to snap the neck of a small dog.

Asha touched her bloody lip, then examined the dark dot it

made on her finger.

"You're my wife, Asha. That's who you've become. And despite whatever you've done outside this house in the last five days, you won't see your geetakaar again."

"Please listen to me. It's no infatuation."

"How obscene of you to say so. I repeat: you will never see him again."

"I *will* see him! Because I understand the world better with Ilarô than without him! With you it's all chaos!"

Again Cabaan smacked her. This time she hardly reacted; but Omala, watching from the door to the stairs, felt the blow from a distance. It was too much. She wanted to run in and attack, but knew she lacked the physical strength to stop Cabaan on her own—and Asha would be horrified if any of the staff of the household were put in harm's way on her behalf. There was, however, one other person in the vicinity who could be called on.

Hurrying down five flights, Omala ran across the grounds, past the rotunda, and into the little airhouse. Moments later the structure's tin roof rolled open on its pulleys, and a gubbaara rose into the night sky. At two hundred feet, Omala worked the craft's side-sail, sending her little ship over the tips of the pines, toward the western woods. Just six minutes after taking off, she spotted a fire burning in the hearth of a ruined temple that she had heard so much about earlier in the night.

Ilarô crossed to meet the descending vessel as it touched down at the edge of the dell.

"Asha is in trouble," Omala said.

Ilarô stepped into the basket of the gubbaara, securing its movable panel behind him. In minutes he and Omala were hurtling on a gale over the dark forest. The wind was with them now, so they reached the boundary of the palace in half the time it had taken to go the other way, though the gubbaara itself, built for the patient gliding of scientific observation, was shaking at the speed they were demanding of it. A hundred yards ahead of them and fifty yards down, Cabaan and Asha were locked in the end of an ugliness. Asha had been forced to the roof's edge, Cabaan's hand around her neck.

"He's strangling her," Ilarô whispered.

"Worse," Omala said.

Ilarô looked again: but Cabaan stopped himself when the white blur of the gubbaara dropped into his peripheral vision. He stepped back from Asha to prepare for whoever was coming.

The small ship rushed down on a wave of wind, landing roughly. Cabaan glared at Omala as she stepped out, before his eye shifted to Ilarô. Ilarô barely noticed him, he was already onto Asha:

"Are you hurt?"

Asha shook her head.

Now Ilarô took up the matter of Cabaan, addressing him in a voice that was low and grave:

"Vikaant Cabaan, I inform you by dictum of law that you are from this moment forbidden to touch Asha again, on pain of shaashvat dand."

Cabaan moved forward, right up to Ilarô … and spat on Ilarô's hands, saliva sticking to skin like the secretion of an insect.

"When you say 'dictum of law,' geetakaar, what questionable ordinance do you imagine I'll believe?"

But here Cabaan's presumptions were defective. Ilarô had been tutored in the house of the Shaasak and knew things which in the distant regions were long forgotten. By ancient statute, deriving from an adherence to the moral impulse of the long poem of the Zaabta of Souls, a feature of the raajy's legal code that had never been rescinded however little remembered it was today, Ilarô had not only the authority but indeed the obligation to confront Cabaan. The authors of the long poem had seen fit to include not one, not two, but three different tales of sexual violence against women and a fourth such offense against a girl. Varying in plot and setting, the import of all four stories was the same: this was a crime to be dealt with immediately upon discovery and the circumstances that had allowed it made impossible ever again. Ilarô said as much now, in language so sharp that no one could have misunderstood him.

Through a wisp of collective memory, and with the sacred-sounding formula, "on pain of shaashvat dand"—in today's words, "on pain of eternal punishment"—having its belated effect, it dawned on Cabaan that Ilarô was telling the truth. This didn't stop him from trying to beat Ilarô down:

"The last time we saw you here, geetakaar, you were a performer under the shield of the raajy, this time you're a common trespasser. I offer you one chance to leave on your own."

The two men clashed. Cabaan thundered without a word, Ilarô merely stood still. Cabaan's malign logic had no chance to prevail; he was neutralized, though at the cost of enraging him:

"Geetakaar, I will kill you if I don't see you starting to move!"

Ilarô turned to Asha. "Come back with me. It's not safe for you here."

"I'll be all right if you go," Asha said. "But if you stay, he *will* kill you."

"That doesn't frighten me."

"But it frightens *me*! Ilarô, please! You have to go!"

"Take the gubbaara," Cabaan said in disgust. "I'll gladly buy Omala a replacement if giving this one up means getting you away from me any faster."

Ilarô still did not move. Asha had to put her hand on his back to compel him into the little airship. She reached in herself to throw the lever releasing the craft, sending it up to dark treetops and the breadth of night beyond.

xvi

The storm began.

Hail shredded the tight turf fronting Palace Isha. It pelted the rotunda, cracking a dozen blue panes. It churned the lake and stunned a school of fish. Lightning struck an ancient pine. The stately beauty had lived for three hundred years, now it burned to the ground in an hour, branches flailing like arms, ice-balls piling around its charred trunk. No one at the palace saw it happen: they were all hiding inside.

Asha had barricaded herself behind the wolfram-wood door of her dayroom, which had easily withstood Cabaan's hourly assaults. She paced the room in confusion, eyeing her array of cures. Even the vials themselves—even the *empty* vials—triggered her craving. She reached for a syringe, but stopped herself. She exhaled, thinking the danger had passed. Then her hand twisted itself free from the grip of her mind, and she saw her fingers snatch a vial of hazy liquid from a shelf. The syringe was swiftly filled and its point swiveled for injection. Only with the most extreme effort did Asha regain her volition, flinging vial and syringe into the stone bath.

Pinpricks rolled across her cheeks and chest: she felt as if she were being mummified while wasps stung her through the bandages. In unprecedented pain, she threw vial after vial into the bath, smashing them. She struck a match and tossed it into the heap of glass and fluid, igniting a fire the color of phlegm that jumped so high it scorched the field of grasshoppers painted onto the ceiling tiles by Asha's mother a generation earlier. Asha stood hypnotized before the strange flame, wondering if this was what all the old omens had been predicting, that she would end up here, barricaded in, alone. It was a stab of self-loathing so vicious that in the brain of its victim it cut her apart even from Ilarô. For this was the awful moment in which Asha realized that it wasn't Cabaan she hated, it was herself. She projected her mind along the arc of her life and saw herself and those depending on her herded into ever smaller spaces at Palace Isha, until they were boxed in tight and there wasn't enough room left even to fill lungs with the air needed to speak.

But if she had put herself in this position, could she not now do the opposite? There must be *some* way to fix her situation, as Omala had more or less said. A vigyaanik would not be wrong about the science of cause and effect.

After a burst of optimism, Asha sank down again. It went this way for an hour: grit, fear, conviction, dread, until eventually, watching her glowing cures burn the stone of the tub, she made use of a moment of hope by rummaging in a cabinet for a scrap of paper to write on. She composed a note, then went to unlock the door to the hall. Swinging outward on its hinge, the door pressed against a soft obstacle after only an inch. Asha guessed that Cabaan had wedged her in with a stuffed chair, but looking down through the crack, she saw Jothi-Anandan curled on the floor, asleep, presumably there to guard her.

She whispered his name. He came to life slowly, like a flower unfurling in the sun, until realizing where he was and who stood over him he shook himself awake.

"Raajakumaaree! Are you still alive?!"

The depravity of circumstances that had produced such a question set against the purity of heart with which the question had been asked seemed to Asha to describe a distance as great as the long length of the galaxy itself and all its outspread worlds. Like a tale from the long poem, it spoke to her of how far she still needed to go if she intended making her way out from this nightmare.

"I'm still alive, Jothi, but I may need your help to stay that way."

The boy was ready to do anything for her. First Asha told him to sit still. She went back into her dayroom, returning with a damp washcloth and a brush. She wiped Jothi-Anandan's forehead and brushed out his hair, still encrusted with the sweat and blood of events of the previous night and sticking in clumps over his eyes.

After she finished tidying him, Jothi-Anandan said:

"When my mother was dying, Raajakumaaree, I was always sad, and I felt sick to my stomach every day; and also I slept a lot. Then one morning she came into my room and lay down next to me and said there was nothing wrong with me that a little love and happiness wouldn't cure, and there was plenty of both in every direction, so long as I was willing to look. May I say the same to you, Raajakumaaree?"

Asha tried—and failed—to defend herself against a rush of tears.

Jothi-Anandan offered her back her washcloth. "Now, Raaja-kumaaree, tell me what you need."

Asha dabbed her eyes, wiped her nose, and handed over her note, to be delivered to Omala.

"But Jothi, you absolutely must not let Cabaan see you with this, for your own safety. If you can help it, you must never let him see you again."

Jothi-Anandan put the note in his pocket and darted off. Minutes later he reached a rear window of the rotunda and tapped at a blue pane.

Omala came out from the kitchen. She opened the window, found Jothi-Anandan crouching in the starless night, accepted his note, gave him the rest of her pink-mango lachhi to drink, and sent him to bed. At her worktable she opened the sealed letter.

O—

Cabaan was right about one thing: I've been willfully ignorant. I intend to put an end to that, but I'll need another day to arrange things. If I work it well, he won't guess in time to stop me.

Would you take a message to Ilarô? I'll leave
here tomorrow night after Cabaan has his
dinner. I'll go directly to the remedy pool east
of the temple. Ilarô will know where I mean.
I'll send word to you as soon as I can after that.

I adore you, my brilliant cousin, and I thank you.

—a

xvii

Omala left minutes before dawn, pausing at the smoldering
husk of an ancient pine. Her mind was on her mission, but no one
could have passed a loss as great as this without stopping to pay her
respects.

She had no trouble making her way: the ground had dried
from yesterday's hailstorm, the sky had emptied of clouds, and there
was a lavender light to see by, and even a bright crescent moon. She
rode fast. Her focus was so tight that she failed to notice Cabaan out
for an early hunt, on foot in a glade beside the forest path. Cabaan,
however, noticed *her*. He was on his charger in seconds, bandook
tucked under his belt, huntsack looped around his saddle.

Omala's mare was faster than Cabaan had remembered, and
there was a moment when it seemed horse and rider might escape
him. So he unclipped a wolfram-wood throwing blade from his belt
and threw it hard. The sharp edge sliced straight through a fetlock of
Omala's mare, separating the animal from a hoof. The mare tumbled;
Omala was flung onto the path. Cabaan shot past her, turned around,
and guided his charger close to Omala's head. He dismounted without offering Omala any assistance, shadowing her with his bulk.

"What's the purpose of this outing?" he said.

"Don't demand things of me. You have no right to anything of
mine."

"That's the problem with you, Omala, you're so frequently wrong. What a painful defect it must be in a vigyaanik."

"Well, if we're really going to have a talk about defects, let me say that *you* exhibit no less than a—

"You're already boring me," Cabaan interrupted. "Tell me why you're heading west."

"I won't let you hurt my cousin again."

"Tell me where you're going or I'll shoot you dead."

"Try it."

He reached for his bandook, a small, expensive firearm; but Omala snatched a fallen branch off the ground beside her and smacked the weapon from his hand.

They both scrambled for it. Omala was there first: she jerked around and fired with Cabaan lunging at her. Struck full in the chest, he fell backwards, but stayed on his feet. He grinned—and Omala dropped the bandook in shock.

Cabaan reclaimed the weapon, then took off his coat to reveal a webbing around his chest.

"Wolfram-wood mesh. I wear it when I hunt. Sometimes the animals don't like dying right away and try fighting back."

He plucked out the pellet that Omala had shot into him and flicked it into the woods. Omala used the time to get to her feet and brush herself off.

"How did you go so wrong, Cabaan? I don't remember you quite this way in the beginning. Don't misunderstand: I disliked you intensely from the day we met, but I didn't fully *despise* you yet. If only you'd become someone better instead of someone worse, Asha might even have found a way to love you."

Cabaan shrugged.

"Did you ever love *her*?" Omala said.

"She takes up too much of my time for me to love her. I'd have preferred someone more like *you*, as a matter of fact, with a life of her own. But then I would've needed you to be pretty too, and we can't claim that for you. Not with a face like yours."

As a rule Omala was little susceptible to insult; such was the power of objectivity that a life of science afforded. And in truth an insult from Cabaan was more bracing to her than painful, like the burn of a health tonic going down the throat.

"My cousin's great misconception," she said, "was believing you were a success. But I know your secret, Vikaant: you're just a failure in a very good disguise."

"I return the compliment." He smiled—then punched Omala in the face.

Her legs buckled. Stunned on the ground, she was unable to stop Cabaan from rifling through her coat.

He found Asha's note to Ilarô, read it, mounted his charger, and started in the direction of the western woods.

Omala struggled to stand while Cabaan rode off with information he should never have been allowed to possess. The morning moon's silver wedge lit the forest ahead of him, and there was nothing left to stop him from committing the high crime he was surely rousing himself for. Nothing except the branch of science concerned with the properties of energy and matter—and the woman who, more than anyone living in or around the lands of Palace Isha for a hundred years, had dedicated her life to its understanding.

Anchoring herself in place by horizontally extending another fallen branch between two pine trees and standing behind it, Omala rubbed her wolfram ring against her coat to clean the stone, lifted her hand, caught a shaft of moonlight, angled it at Cabaan's charger some forty yards off, and cast a beam directly at his back. She had never tried electromagnetically connecting the ring to wolfram-wood rather than pure wolfram, let alone connecting to the interlaced structure of a wolfram-wood mesh, but sometimes the moment to test a hypothesis chooses *itself*.

Cabaan felt an invisible force clamp onto him. Mystified, he tried brushing it off, though this was like trying to brush off moonlight. The beam tugged at him, pulling his bottom up the cantle of his saddle. But just before he was dragged from his horse, the beam broke off.

Omala fell backwards on disconnection, into the detritus of the forest floor. She pushed herself up again to study the moon's position for better hand-to-eye coordination, because what she was endeavoring to do was as much sport as science: the way she worked her wrist would relate to a successful outcome no less than the underlying physics.

She caught another shaft of moonlight, angling it at Cabaan, some eighty yards away now. This time the streak off her ring locked solidly onto his webbing and yanked him straight off the charger. He was dragged down the forest path, tumbling over himself for fifty feet until he managed to work himself upright even as he was being whipped along, his heels digging into the dirt, sending up streams of earth. He was facing Omala as her beam whisked him towards her at an accelerating rate that even she could not control.

She readied herself for contact with his onrushing mass. In the last instant, she clenched her fist hard, and Cabaan's jaw collided with the stone on her finger.

This time it was Cabaan who buckled. Spread on the ground, he seemed to be unconscious, possibly dead. Omala reached down to check for a throb in his neck when his leg shot up between her thighs and flipped her over. She was on her back as his fist came at her face again—and there the continuity of her awareness ended.

Cabaan stood up wiping his chin where Omala's ring had gashed him. He booted her in the chest, sending blood into her lungs. Still using his foot, he rolled her off the path. Had Asha been there as witness, she would have concluded that even an emotion as base as the urge to murder could not be countered by force of intellect. Omala had been lost to the experiment. To stop Cabaan, some way outside of mind would have to be found.

xviii

Ilarô had just finished restringing his heptachord when Cabaan appeared on horseback at the temple's boundary. Neither man reacted to the sight of the other: Cabaan because the encounter with Omala had burned through his actual rage and he was advancing now on a cold line of inertia; Ilarô because his reactions ran level with his thoughts.

After dismounting and tying his charger to a pine, Cabaan followed the mossy path to the temple's entrance while Ilarô put his instrument in its case. The ancient archway was too low for someone of Cabaan's height, so to set foot inside the sanctum itself he was forced to bow. He could have stepped around the freestanding arch altogether and climbed over a mound of rubble, but he was a person disinclined to alternatives once his objective was fixed.

Coming to the center of the roofless room, he stopped a few feet from where Ilarô was seated and said:

"My wife was going to leave Palace Isha tonight, to be with you. I'm going to kill you instead."

"Killing me won't help your cause, Vikaant."

"But think of the satisfaction I'll have watching you die."

"If I die gladly, will you still enjoy it?"

This confused Cabaan, who had shaped his mind into a key that fit a single lock on a solitary door—though life, as the long poem of the Zaabta advises, is a house of countless rooms.

"You should let Asha go," Ilarô said. "Her time is coming. Stepping aside is your one chance."

Cabaan lunged at him. In a flash he had his hands around Ilarô's neck; but Ilarô was stronger than he seemed: he pried back the tips of Cabaan's fingers, keeping the two of them in stalemate.

"If you die for me, geetakaar, I'll let Asha live! If you keep fighting, I'll take her from the world tonight!"

Of all the poems and lays that Ilarô knew, all the fragments of early verse and the epics of day-long length, all the morning songs and evening songs, the love songs, dance songs, and ancient battle songs, the songs of arrival and songs of departure, the songs for babies born and the songs for parents lost, the songs of indignation, the songs of apology, the challenge songs that were really songs of sport and the songs that posed riddles for the listener to solve, the songs in the form of rhyming debates between two, three, or even four voices, the songs of waiting impatiently for a beloved to appear and the songs of lament for a beloved's death, the political songs, the satirical songs, the duets written as letters between partners who never imagined that their emotions would live on as countermelodies a thousand years after their bodies were dust, of all the poetries and sentiments and exhortations and stories set to music and bequeathed by the eons, a single piece came into Ilarô's mind: "The Cloud-Messenger." In it, a young man separated by a great distance from the young woman he loves persuades a cloud to take a message to her, the young man describing as inducement all the beautiful sights of the world below that the cloud will see along the way: lush jungles and sparkling rivers, snow-glazed mountains, flocks of birds like flying rainbows, magnificent temples and processions of monks in flaming-orange robes, children at play in the sunshine, and of course mighty elephants and their young wallowing in mud baths. It was the original and most famous example of a bygone genre, the messenger-poem, in which a young man—or every so often a young woman—implores a cloud or a hawk or occasionally a butterfly to carry an intimate word to someone far-off. On his back now, with Cabaan's massive hands strangling him, Ilarô could see to the top of the trees: it was an uncommonly sunny day for the region, not a cloud in the sky. Even if there had been one, he thought, it would be difficult speaking to it with Cabaan's thumbs pressing into his throat all the way to his spine. He wouldn't be able to get out the words to convince the cloud to fly to Asha, with an escort of lightning on either side, and deliver to her the message of his indestructible love. But it was a perfect way to die to realize that Asha already knew.

Let there be no wrong impression: Ilarô would have preferred to live. Understanding, though, that Asha's own death would be the price, and believing that Cabaan meant it when he said he would kill her that same night, there was no hesitation. Some may feel Ilarô should have fought on, unlikely as it was that he could prevail over Cabaan by force; but despite being young, Ilarô had already learned to live in true-time. He did in the moment what he would have wished to do looking back.

Cabaan felt his rival's fingers loosen. Keeping one hand tight around Ilarô's throat, he reached down to his own belt, pulled up his bandook, and shot Ilarô in the head.

Blood squirted onto the temple floor. Cabaan watched—and waited—until there was no chance Ilarô would get up again. Then he lifted the body onto the room's marble altar where he used his diamond hunting knife to stab Ilarô's chest, cutting the heart from the hot corpse. He stuffed it into his huntsack before dragging Ilarô's remains into the hearth.

The wind picked up sharply, which we might like to believe was a kind of cosmic reply to the evil that had just been done here, though in fact it was the result of the morning spike in barometric pressure characteristic of this small valley. Cabaan's charger was spooked any-way and resisted being mounted. It only caused a short delay. On his way out, Cabaan glanced back at the ruins, glowing with reflected fire. Easy to think that a hearth consuming a butchered corpse would spark crudely and stream the stench of death, but it was a smooth flame that lit the toppled columns of Ilarô's temple, and the air of his dell was already filling with the scent of butterscotch and vanilla from the pinewood that Ilarô himself had laid into the hearth only minutes earlier.

xix

Asha was packing a satchel to fit into Tapti's pannier, taking as many small items of tradable value as she could squeeze in: her mother's ruby rings; a chain-link necklace of platinum, easy to snip into sections should the need arise to make payments worth less than the whole; four tubes of loose diamonds; a pair of yellow opal earrings; six polished stones of red beryl acquired for a bracelet that she had been contemplating; a sculpted jadeite rabbit: antique, only three inches long but worth a considerable sum; and a lotus sapphire pendant, the stone asymmetrically cut to best reveal its orange-pink brilliance, or in some light its pink-orange—a gift from Cabaan on their first anniversary. She was hoping she wouldn't have to trade away absolutely *all* of these pieces for ready cash wherever she lived next, because the lotus sapphire went so well with her skin tone, and it only made sense to have a few jewelry options on hand, to keep one's looks fresh. But these were matters for another day.

She hesitated over an emerald pillbox, knowing it was still filled with soother-tablets, only a mild pick-me-up though nothing she wanted Ilarô to see her relying on. She slipped it into a green kidskin glove anyway, put the pair of gloves into the satchel, changed her mind, took the pillbox out, emptied the soother-tablets into a sink, started to put the empty pillbox into the satchel, but then replaced it on its shelf.

Downstairs, in the mud-room, she selected a pair of comfortable riding boots and a thick cape, stowing them in a corner cabinet and hiding her satchel underneath.

She joined Cabaan for dinner at ten o'clock, the hour he liked, seating herself next to instead of across from him, the arrangement he preferred. She worked hard through the meal not to alert him to any change in her manner, feigning submission to the state of things, which, with the exception of recent days, he was used to from her. He seemed not to suspect it was a trick. On the other hand he was paying unusual attention to what Asha ate. He watched her slice her food, he kept his eye on her as she chewed and swallowed, he signaled for a second helping to be served to her when she finished her first. They enacted the meal with the dignity of ritual, in a silence so sharp that each incidental sound, as from a knife scraping a plate through a slice of meat, grated.

Asha finished first. After a spoonful of dessert, she said:

"I'm not feeling perfectly well. It may be a slight fever. You won't mind if I don't come to you tonight."

"If you're not feeling perfectly well."

"No, I'm really not. I'm sure I'll be fine in the morning, but tonight I suppose I should rest."

"Rest then."

She smiled warmly for him—even after all of it, she felt he should have at least this from her to last him the rest of his life—then stood to leave. It was an effort to take her time stepping unhurried from table to exit and not tear out the door …

In the mud-room she snatched her gear and flew. Only ten minutes later she burst from the stable riding Tapti. With a glance back at the array of domes and globes that made up the white immensity of Palace Isha, she cried:

"Goodbye, my old home! I've loved you very much, and someday I'll come back to you!"

She raced for the western woods, crazed with hope. She didn't even mind cutting her hand on the tip of a misjudged branch: the blood on her fingers felt cool and wonderful. Nothing was an obstacle now, everything a point along a path. Asha had launched herself into freedom, and only minutes into the decision she wondered why it had taken her so long.

At the remedy pool east of the temple, she dismounted and spun around searching in every direction, expecting Ilarô to step out from behind a tree to meet her. It took a dispiriting hour to conclude he wasn't coming. She rode on to the temple itself, finding Ilarô's few possessions, but not Ilarô. Turning Tapti around, she sped off. Her trip backwards to Palace Isha was the vilest passage of her life. She knew something had gone wrong, though the extent of it was beyond her power to imagine. After five years of life with Cabaan, Asha still could not work her mind to picture the things he was capable of.

Jothi-Anandan ran out in a panic to meet her.

"Raajakumaaree, what's happened?!"

"He wasn't there! Is he *here*?"

The boy shook his head, mirroring Asha's alarm without knowing why. Asha herself was still looking for scraps of hope:

"Has any note come for me since I left?"

"No, Raajakumaaree!"

"No message of any kind?"

"No, Raajakumaaree!"

"Not even from Omala?"

"Your cousin rode off with *your* note before dawn and hasn't been back."

"Hasn't been back at *all*?"

"No, Raajakumaaree!"

"Jothi, are you sure?

"I *think* so, Raajakumaaree!"

Asha's plans burned in her head. Handing Tapti's reins to Jothi-Anandan, she ran to the rotunda; but not finding Omala she hurried next to the athainaaium. She scanned the dark room three times, though seven cold fireplaces made clear that no one had been

here all day. With a sickness spreading inside of her, Asha went up to
Cabaan's bedroom, where she had never expected to step foot again
during his lifetime.

Despite the hour, Cabaan was working at his desk. He looked
up at Asha with no special expression.

"Where are they?" she said.

"Omala is lying just off the low path to the western woods,
possibly alive though most likely dead. And I've converted your
geetakaar to a pile of soot in the hearth of his ridiculous abode. You
ate his roast heart for dinner. You had a good appetite tonight, which
isn't faintly like you. But you were getting ready for a trip."

Asha stood still until Cabaan looked down at his work again.
Then she stepped backwards into the hall, closing the door quietly
behind her. She swallowed a lump of mucous in her throat: first
sign of a cold coming on, she noted, wondering if there was any
sealroot in the house to crush into a glass of warm water and gargle
before bed. Her reason hadn't ruptured; she was under the spell of
denial. For half a minute the spell worked, protecting Asha with its
thin shield—until she shivered violently. This was only a foretaste
of what was coming. There was enough time to walk downstairs
and out through the gardens before it happened again. Now she
began to shudder. All the warmth poured out of her and in its place
the sharpest chill rushed back in. Her lungs seemed to freeze solid,
she couldn't suck any air through the ice. She felt her brain harden
inside her skull—then heard it crack. Her motor functions ceased;
her arms and legs stopped working. She fell down onto her back.
Paralyzed, she could still see: in the night sky above, the stars began
to shift, rearranging themselves into perfect rows, which every person in her right mind knows should never happen. Next came the
bombardment: a volley of starry missiles shooting down to earth.
Perfectly targeted, they exploded up and down the length of Asha's
body, delivering pain to every piece of her. It was all taking place in

her imagination, but we mustn't mistake this to mean that it hurt her any less. A hammer to her kneecaps would have been kinder. She hardly cared: she was doing it to herself. Asha could no longer bear to be in the world and was calling on every force of nature to smash her out of it. If she could have annihilated herself in actuality, she would have done it, but if she could have gouged a chunk out of the timeline of history on either side of her own birth, even better. Asha didn't want to die nearly so much as she wanted never to have lived. In her mind she begged the pain to destroy her.

xx

Four days later, on a bench in her father's moon-viewing pavilion, Asha lay in the dark, rolling her fingers over Ilarô's black-diamond choker around her neck. She had sent the palace horsemaster and his grooms to search the paths into and out from the western woods, to find Omala. After three days with no result, it had been hard to conclude anything but that, whether living or dead at the time, Omala had been dragged off by an animal and was lost to them.

The staff of the household had come into the pavilion to do what they could, bringing Asha food and drink, blankets and pillows. No one had been able to help her; and Cabaan hadn't tried. Desperate to be useful, the staff had carried out Asha's last instructions before events had overtaken her, covering over the jackal-trap along her gardens with planks of whitewood, though quietly declining to cut down the rose trees or leave the flowers in bouquets for the snow-jackals.

Asha was unaware of their work. She hadn't left the pavilion since going in, nor moved from the bench she lay on in half as long. Here the fear of losing her mind came rushing into her again, shocking her with the speed at which she could relapse toward what she

assumed would be psychosis. What was she supposed to do now? Go
back to the way things had been? The question itself was insane. She
couldn't imagine how she would make her body move again, much
less go about any of the old chores. Maybe it was time to swallow a
jarful of soother-tablets, enough to ease her out of the world not just
tonight, but forever. The thought of never having to wake up again
was the one idea left that appealed. And really, who would it hurt?
Cabaan would be outwardly embarrassed, but privately relieved. The
people who knew her would mourn her, but only for a while. If they
could see into her now, see her scorched brain and charred heart,
they would open their own medicine chests and contribute to the
cause. She would be free, and the world would go on. It was a good
plan—until she thought of her father, which ended the fantasy. Asha
could not bear the thought of the Zaabta of Souls listing her as a
daughter who had failed her parents. So she would have to live on,
in this trap.

Jothi-Anandan knocked. He was carrying a pink-mango lachhi
and a bowl of pistachios. Asha glanced at him before looking away
again.

"Raajakumaaree, please."

In a daze, Asha said: "Jothi, how do you suppose all this happened to us? Do you think I caused it? Because if I'm not an evil
person, how did so much evil find me? I must be a *little* evil, don't
you think? Otherwise I can't make sense of it. Would you have any
other idea how this could have happened?"

Jothi-Anandan might have had something sensible to say
about this, but there wouldn't be time for it, because as soon as he
opened his mouth to speak, a quake shook the room, sending vases
to the floor and cracking the pavilion's glass roof. Jothi-Anandan fell
too, cutting both knees. This activated Asha for the first time in days:
she sprang off her bench, pulled Jothi-Anandan up by the elbows,
and carried him outside between aftershocks. Here she plucked

the sticky shards from his kneecaps, then together they ran toward the source of the disturbance, on the other side of the house, in the backlands.

Cabaan and his men were detonating shudder-bombs along a ridge leading to the river. These were specialized explosives that could shake the earth apart lengthwise instead of straight down. The ridge itself now resembled no landscape in nature.

Cabaan saw Asha coming. He knew she was here for an explanation, so he gave it to her without playing games:

"We're using shudder-bombs to move the dirt. That's why you felt it in the house. It's nothing to worry about. We have to shift enough earth to dam the river. We've found a massive bed of wolfram just under the water line; we need to expose it horizontally for another planting."

"But if you dam the river, you'll choke the woods for miles!"

"Oh, Asha, we're not going to start all that again, are we?"

Roused from her days of stupor by an outrage so ferocious that it displaced momentarily every other thought in her head, she excoriated Cabaan. If her words could have skinned him alive, she would have let them. She railed at him uninterrupted for more than a minute before concluding:

"There are thousands of creatures living in those woods! Are they all supposed to lie down and *die* for you?!"

"I'm not asking them to die. When they get thirsty, they can drink somewhere else."

"But why should they *have* to? For more wolfram-wood? So it takes a little longer to plant more kuroops if you have to go around the river! You'll still get what you need in the end! Isn't that enough?"

"I've never understood the theory of 'enough.' Enough for who? Enough for what?"

"Enough to suffice!"

The tautology evoked from Cabaan a look of gentle amusement.

A person meeting him for the first time might have been beguiled into an appreciation of such expressiveness by the sheer appeal of the features out of which it was composed; but Asha herself, after five years of exposure to Cabaan's looks, found it infuriating that his physical beauty seemed to endow every face he made with more importance than it deserved.

"I suppose it's only fair to tell you," he said, "that when I put our estimate at a thousand maatras a year, I meant our *official* estimate."

"*Official* estimate? You mean the official is different than the actual?"

"We have twenty times the official estimate of pure wolfram beneath our feet. From which I can produce at least ten times more wolfram-wood per year than I've said."

Even to someone as generally apathetic to mathematics as Asha, the figures were stunning. "But what's the point of it?" she whispered.

"Think, Asha."

She did as he asked, trying to conceive of it as he would, to understand what he meant by it all—to understand *him*.

"You're inflating the price," she said. "You keep the cost high by exaggerating the scarcity of the supply. As long as your middlemen and buyers don't all talk to one another, which the distances between them make unlikely, no one can catch you."

"Nicely done."

For nearly the length of her marriage Asha had been uneasy at the things about herself that Cabaan chose to praise; now her stomach turned at any hint of approval from him whatsoever.

"But why is this *nec*essary?" she said.

"Because it will make us an order of magnitude richer than we would've been otherwise. Tell me I'm not a miracle."

"You don't know what you're doing. That's what's wrong here: you just don't know what you're doing. You *tell* yourself you do, you tell *me* that you do, but in reality you have no idea."

"Well, I'm sorry if that's how you feel. You should've thought of it before you traded away your last five hundred haiktars. I couldn't have reached the river without them."

Asha's mind flew along the timeline of Cabaan's intentions: in the western woods she saw dead lemurs heaped in their colony, dead fish lining the forest's desiccated pools, frogs' carcasses hardening on crusty moss, the icy glades melted, the dell of Ilarô's temple withered brown.

"You can still enjoy the river for a good while," Cabaan said. "We're only just getting started. We'll be working it for months."

He returned to his team, terminating the discussion. Asha couldn't have said much more anyway: her fury-charged spurt was used up. With her eyelids already sinking, and wondering how she would walk all the way back to the house under her own power, she made the most hopeless decision of her life:

"Jothi, run ahead and send for my sambharik."

"Yes, Raajakumaaree."

"And Jothi, tell him to bring his nepentee."

"Sorry, Raajakumaaree?"

"His remedy of forgetfulness. Tell him I'm ready for it now."

xxi

The vial of black solution threw an inky glow into the curves between Asha's fingers before moving up her arm all the way to the elbow, like a spreading infection.

For the first time she paid the sambharik herself, out of her own monies, instead of referring the bill to Cabaan. She no longer had any reason to distance herself from her circumstances. She had just bought the strongest cure on earth: she expected to be using it for the rest of her life.

In a small voice she asked the sambharik what exactly the nepentee was made from. He gave the appalling information with his eyes on the floor:

"The glands of cadavers, Vikaantee."

"And the glands of cadavers can do for me what I need?"

"Yes, Vikaantee."

"And I take it how often?"

"You inject yourself morning and night. The nepentee is potent, but its duration is brief."

"But it *will* work for me? You know this to be true?"

"Yes, Vikaantee, with one condition: the nepentee works broadly. Along with what you wish to forget may pass from your mind what you wish to remember."

Taking possession of the case of six vials, Asha stood and left the room without offering a word of appreciation or even a simple goodbye.

xxii

The injection was painless. Asha felt nothing at all, not even the sting of the needle. For a moment she wondered if she might be immune to the nepentee's particular effect, but its effect was the subtraction of awareness, and it was working the way it was meant to. Had Asha been standing in front of a mirror, she would have had exotic proof. In seconds she began to glow with a black light out of her pores. Then she vanished completely, a complex effect relating to the new wavelength of light that her body was emitting and its correspondence to the light naturally lost along her skin from absorption. She reappeared a moment later, her body adjusting, but a subtle black radiance would persist as long as the cure was present in her bloodstream.

When she stepped outside, she suffered one of the nepentee's unique side effects: the sky and everything under it went several shades darker, as if a circular pane of tinted glass had been slid around the world. But Asha lacked perspective: it wasn't the world that had been enclosed, it was herself. She couldn't tell as she moved through her white gardens that her body was emanating a portable prison of black light.

At night this made it impossible for her to see the stars: the nepentee's tinting effect against the black of space blocked them out. Asha noticed it right away, though it didn't bother her: along with the stars, the nepentee had blocked the disappointment of not being able to see them anymore. Really she had nothing to complain about. She couldn't even remember why she should care.

On that first night she bathed the way she liked, in steaming snow-leopard's milk, washing her hair with a shampoo of coconut oils and diamond dust. At her dressing table she injected the nepentee's second dose, seeing in the mirror that the first dose, as a bonus effect, had already restored the whites of her eyes, subtracting the red of recent days and accentuating the bright brown of the irises. After this she completed herself elegantly in a pale green sarong, though she entered the Dining Dome barefoot, a strangeness which Cabaan chose not to comment on. Eating in a mild mood, she glanced pleasantly at her tablemate several times. Cabaan found this almost too peculiar not to express an opinion about, but in the end reserved judgment.

Over the next ten days, at nine in the morning and eleven at night, Asha tapped the vein in her arm and injected herself with a punctuality that was nowhere in her natural character. The new behavior extended to other activities. After breakfast each day she went directly to her gardens, pruning and planting straight through to lunch. When lunch was done, she went to her dayroom and napped for half an hour. At four each afternoon she walked to the lake and circled it eleven times, a shimmering black figure exercising her body if never achieving the neurological re-set that is the usual gift of a stroll in nature. Once, on her way back, she crossed paths with Jothi-Anandan who had spotted her from a window of the house and dashed out to bump into her. Seeing her up close, in her trance, he wanted to shake her until she remembered what had happened. He was about to do it too, but Asha smiled at him and moved along before he could work up the nerve.

In bed she accepted Cabaan without objection, though her body no longer moved beneath him the way it used to. After a week and a half of it, Cabaan pulled back.

"Asha, I don't like you this way! What is *wrong* with you? Are you taking your nepentee?"

"I haven't missed an injection."

"Well, maybe you're taking too much! Or maybe you're not taking *enough*. You should double the dose!"

He left the bed in disgust and stood by a window looking onto the backlands. Moonlight in its pure form was deflected by the miasma hanging over the fields, but an eerie sheen still filtered to the ground. Not pretty, though enough to see by at night.

"Why don't you go riding tomorrow," he said. "That should perk you up. You won't want to be here anyway, we'll be detonating close to the fault line all day. The aftershocks might be too much for you."

xxiii

Asha left on horseback. By the time she entered the western woods, she had closed her eyes and laid her head on Tapti's neck, letting the animal take her where it liked. But falling asleep on a moving horse is not necessarily a sign of exhaustion: as cold is the privation of heat, fatigue may be the privation of purpose. Apart from the rote of bathing and breakfasting and gardening, Asha had simply lost touch with the purpose of staying awake.

Eventually horse and rider came to the ruins of a stone temple, overgrown with ivy and scattered with dried wildflowers. Here Tapti stopped, the cessation of motion rousing Asha from her blankness.

She didn't know where she was. Her sambharik, had he been asked, might have explained this obliquely, saying that the nepentee had turned her blood black, the way a cadaver's blood turns, and that the black blood of a cadaver carries no memory of time or place. Perhaps best though to describe the literal mechanism of forgetfulness in this instance: stepping through the little temple, the residua of Asha's experiences here did try to penetrate her awareness, but among the nepentee's other effects, the black field of bioelectric force that it cast from her person into the space around her repelled any catalyst of recollection. In the threads and fibers of Asha's mind, past and present could no longer find one another, leaving her body in a state of meaningless nowness.

She spent half an hour cleaning crumbled flowers out of stone vases, for no reason except that it seemed to her that this needed to be done. Afterwards, to sweep out the heaps of leaves in the corners of the roofless room, she was about to use a branch for a broom when she heard an explosion in the distance. The forest went silent, staying that way for several seconds. Then a tremor shook the dell. In the backlands of Palace Isha, one of Cabaan's shudder-bombs had struck the fault line that ran into the highlands by way of these western woods. The initial shiver had been deceptive: a full-blown earthquake now struck the dell. Slabs of stone that had fallen to the temple's floor in centuries past popped up again, their enormous weight cancelled by the surge of energy out of the ground. Asha was lucky not to be pinned underneath any of them as they came back down patternlessly; but what happened next was the greater danger. Its effects magnified by the dell's barometric anomaly, the quake precipitated a windstorm that quickly gathered into a localized tornado. A colony of rabbits was yanked into the sky and asphyxiated; trees were ripped from the ground, leaving upended roots exposed and trembling; sheets of nettles were flung from one side of the dell to the other.

Asha pulled Tapti behind the temple's half-sheltering back wall, then hid herself beneath the stone altar. She stayed here for an hour until the vortex dissipated. But her head was throbbing and she was shivering. It seemed the nepentee gave no physical protection like the dava.

Even more important than getting home now was getting warm, so Asha thought to build a fire in the hearth. The wind had thrown plenty of kindling her way, and half a cord of pine was available to her, stored inside the hearth's stone vault. By dusk she had a fire going and was warming herself and Tapti against its pink flame. The fragrance was especially sweet, even for the sweet pine of the region. What Asha could not know was that she was also inhaling the ash of Ilarô's body, or that the quantum mingling between Ilarô and herself was having its effect. The nepentee had nearly worn off by this time too, waning with the waning of the day. Not having planned to be out this long, Asha had brought no evening dose to inject.

As the black light out of her pores dimmed and the dark bubble she moved in decayed, she felt her exhaustion. During the tornado she had found a mat under the altar, so she went to lie down on it. She closed her eyes, and here her original mind took over. She was less than awake though unaware that she was dreaming when she heard a man singing in the distance. His song was an ancient air: melancholy, but the voice was very fine.

She went to investigate. She had to walk a while before she found him: a geetakaar on a floating ice temple, anchored in a not quite frozen river between the walls of a glacier. He was seated on a bench at the temple's entrance, though facing away from her.

When she reached the riverbank, he stopped singing. Setting

down his heptachord on a mound of eucalyptus leaves, he turned around: it *was* Ilarô. Almost. Ilarô but altered, his features faintly scrambled, his hair too long.

"Please keep singing!" Asha shouted across the water.

As if to do as she asked, he picked up his heptachord by its neck …

… then swung it down hard against a wedge of ice, splitting it open.

Out of its broken pieces he withdrew a syringe, primed with solution and glowing black. Asha watched him raise it to his mouth and inject into his tongue what could only have been a nepentee. He vanished for an instant before reappearing inside a flickering black bubble.

Asha called out in alarm:

"But can you still sing?!"

"I don't think so—I've forgotten all the words."

He had somehow made himself heard without raising his voice, even at a distance.

"Try to remember!" Asha shouted.

He hesitated, but eventually opened his mouth and began:

> *A midnight sun will …*
> *A midnight sun …*
> *A midnight—*

He stopped.

"Remind me please what a midnight sun will do?" he said.

Asha gasped, not from the question but because a second heartbeat had just started up in her chest. The sensation was so strange that it shocked and annoyed her at the same time. But forcing herself to think past it, she shouted:

"Please try again!"

This time, instead of singing, the geetakaar used his hands, communicating by a system of gestures and signs. Now Asha was completely at a loss.

"I don't understand what that means! What are you telling me?!"

He picked up the broken-off neck of his heptachord and plucked a series of notes from its strings, sending a sonic energy onto the surface of the eucalyptus leaves at his feet, inscribing them the way a stylus would.

He reached down, scooped the leaves up, and cast them across the water toward Asha.

She had to step into the river to retrieve them, stinging her feet in the gelid shallows. Five of the leaves came into her possession, each inscribed with a single word:

* More
* Time
* Even
* Not
* One

On the icy riverbank she laid the leaves out and switched them around until she worked out their intended order and read the message they contained:

Not—Even—One—Time—More.

She looked up to say she understood—but the geetakaar was gone. With a direct line of sight now to the frozen door of the ice temple, she could see only herself reflected. Which is the truth of all dreams in the end, is it not?

Just now the propulsion of blood through her arteries syncopated so sharply that it jerked her awake.

It was morning. Asha had slept for thirteen hours. The quakes and the storms were done, the nepentee's black bubble gone.

She stayed where she was, under the altar, for several minutes, integrating herself. The winds of the previous day had pushed mounds of leaves into her little compartment, but in the shifting of things, Ilarô's pack had also been uncovered, though it was pinned down by a small altar stone fallen in the earthquake. Asha recognized the pack right away—her hands dove to pull it free. Inside it she found Omala's magnetizing box, crushed from the fallen stone, but the bundle of candles that Asha had left with Ilarô the last time she saw him was intact. And the clear wax on all twelve candles had gone opaque, the way it did when magnetized. Every one of the candles was opaque. Ilarô had recorded on them! Asha would hear Ilarô's voice again! She would hear his voice!

Climbing out from the altar she stepped across the rubble to find Tapti, who had come through the night with only a mane full of leaves and was now feasting on a windfall of acorns.

Asha tucked Ilarô's candles into her satchel. They were so precious to her that the shadowy form of a man coming up behind her caused her to spin around ready to strike him dead if need be, to defeat any theft. But the shadowy form was only the shadow of a boy.

"Jothi-Anandan!"

"Raajakumaaree!"

Her heart beating so hard that she could feel the blood pulsing in her throat, Asha laughed in relief.

"Jothi, how are you possibly *here*?"

"Raajakumaaree, you looked so *sleepy* when you left yesterday! I was afraid you would fall off Tapti and hurt yourself! I took a courser and followed you—we spent the night in the woods. Are you all right?"

"I'm fine. Are *you* all right?"

The boy nodded, blurting: "Didn't you love that tornado?!"

Asha pulled him in and hugged him. Crushed in her embrace, he said: "Raajakumaaree, are you ready to come home now?"

She let go of him. "No, Jothi, not yet. I have a trip to make first."

"Where to?"

"To Aakaash-Nivaas. To the sky-lodge."

"The *sky*-lodge? But that'll take months!"

"Which I can't let stop me from going."

"But Raajakumaaree, do you even know the way?"

"I'll find it."

"Could I come with you?"

"I would love that, Jothi, but I should probably make this trip alone. And who would Giribandhava have to wreak havoc with if you were gone that long? You should go home and stay out of Cabaan's way until I'm back. That's what you can do to help me."

"But Raajakumaaree, *why* are you going to the sky-lodge?"

"Because I have business with the Shaasak."

Not knowing what to say to this but flooded with feeling about it nonetheless, the boy pressed his tharamas into Asha's hands, insisting she take it to carry extra water. Then he promised to go home and stay alive until she came back. Considering the state of things at Palace Isha, it was a substantial offer.

—*I'm sorry, but I'll need to stop here. My daughter will be home from school any minute. She'll be wearing her white cape and the green hat she loves when she steps off the hyperpath that whisks us from point to point around the city—and I like being at the door to let her in. Her mother does the same when she can, but my wife is away this week on municipal business, in another of our floating cities, halfway around the planet.*

It's hard on my daughter, as I imagine it must be hard on any girl of five, to be without her mother even for a week and not able to speak with her during that time. This is the side effect of the lifting fields that dilate gravity around us and hold us eleven miles high: we are unable to project signals through the air. Or, to be accurate, we can project them, but they rot to static en route. The trade-off for living as we do. An inconvenience, without question; though there have been unexpected benefits. We've learned to speak properly to one another again. We make trips to see one another now, and we are no longer quite so indifferent to one another's needs. It's hard to be indifferent after traveling half a mile across the city or twenty thousand miles around the equator to deliver a note. Six millennia after Asha's day, we can only communicate face-to-face or by handwritten message, the way she did. The twist of the timeline. We are advanced, but we are ancient again: our peculiar atavism.

We are ancient again in other ways too. Three millennia ago, during the Age of the Explorers, we began to leave the earth and for a thousand years sent our navigators into space. They traveled in immense starcraft that tunneled through the cosmic deep on engines running off the torque of super-strings, our men and women armed with atom-hammers to generate localized energy—and even to defend themselves, God forbid—once they reached some new world orbiting some new sun. But we never heard back from them. Not a single time. We do not know if they lived or died, thrived or were annihilated. So after a thousand years of sending and hoping and waiting, we settled back into our own world and inevitably lost our taste and then even our capacity for space travel. We let the requisite technologies lapse. Honestly, we have enough trouble raising our children. Perhaps hurling ourselves to the stars was beyond our power in the first place.

There's my daughter at the door. I'm going to go see how her day went. Then I'll cook her dinner, give her a bath, and put her to bed. After that I'll be back. I'm not sure how well or poorly I've been doing with Asha's story so far, but I still have more to tell, if you still have the patience to listen.

I won't be long.

PART TWO

MY DAUGHTER is finally asleep. Some nights take longer than others; you can never predict which. Tonight, she was worried about her bed falling through the floor and dropping into the sky. I used to have my own fears of falling at her age, so I could sympathize. Though I admit, I didn't like hearing an echo of those old nightmares coming out of my daughter's mouth—until I realized she wasn't describing a nightmare, but a dream.

I'd misunderstood: she was saying she wished her bed would fall *through the floor and into the sky some night, so she could fly in it over the earthtop, where things aren't always silver but come in her favorite colors: turquoise and purple. Turns out she'd like to float down on her bed and collect various leaves from an assortment of trees. And I'm happy to report that, after a little fatherly probing, I've realized she has no fear of heights whatsoever. You have to listen to your children fairly closely to really know what they're saying. It's been my experience that they're almost never saying what you think.*

Anyway, she's sleeping now, so I have a few hours to offer the rest of Asha's story, as best I can and as close to the way my mother used to tell it as I'm able ...

i

The ancient word "yaatra" will prove a term of special significance to us. In the vocabulary of Asha's day it was a noun meaning "travel" or "journey"—or sometimes "passage" or "iteration." But the meaning we're most interested in is "trek." (Bhaashan was not a tonal language that depended on the use of pitch to distinguish between lexical or grammatical categories, though no one could say its word-stock was wanting in subtlety.)

In fact we'll have two yaatras to discuss, one in motion, which we'll come to in a moment, the other stationary, which we'll refer to first. We'll need to reverse course to look into the latter, returning to that grim showdown between Cabaan and Omala on the path to the western woods, at the conclusion of which Cabaan booted his cousin-in-law's lifeless body into the forest. Cabaan himself went on to find Ilarô, but Omala, it seemed, wasn't going anywhere ever again.

This isn't exactly what happened. Omala lay face down on the forest floor for three hours, nearly dead, but not quite. Leaves blew across her back. Beetles invaded her hair. The trickle from a nearby source wet her clothes and reached her mouth. And here things took a turn, because this wasn't ordinary water, but rare. It flowed from a remedy pool, whose corrective properties, even in miniscule amounts, were the salutary inverse of those extreme venoms you hear about, even an iota of which can fell an elephant.

Omala came to. Weak but alive, she ran through her senses one at a time: she felt the creeping of insects under her blouse; she sniffed a mineral reek; she heard the gurgling of water; she tasted the flavor of disinfectant on her lips—and she grasped her good luck. She should have died, but the runoff from a remedy pool had saved her.

She raised herself on elbows and began to crawl. A poison vine caught her arms, lacerating the skin and raising boils in seconds, but this hardly mattered: if she found the remedy pool, the poison would be neutralized along with the rest of her ills, if she didn't find the pool, she would be dead in an hour no matter what.

She found it: not only a remedy pool, but a thermal remedy pool, percolating just above body temperature. She lowered herself in, laying her head back against a shelf of mud that was cool on the nape of her neck. She let her burning arms sink into the water. The pool's high level of lithium soothed on contact, while its fungal symbionts went to work almost as fast, infusing this battered bather not only with bioticides to kill her infections, but leukocytes and theriac serums that could regenerate compromised tissues, even ones on the verge of necrosis.

Omala's bruises and cuts would be repaired in a matter of days, this was nothing overly magical given her envelopment in liquid antigens. The damage to her internal organs, however, to her lungs especially, was severe. So Omala's long journey without motion began. The distance she would have to travel was punishing—all the way back from the border of death—and the time it would take could not be calculated in days or even weeks. But she could survive now as long as it took to recover. These waters contained broad-spectrum nutrients; they would feed her their constituent superfood of violet algae by osmotic process, directly through the skin and into the bloodstream. How the presence of such beneficial reservoirs fit into the macro-biology of the earth itself as a single living organism, or even less grandly into the workings of these local woods, no one knew enough to explain; but as Omala closed her eyes and slipped into a nurturing repose surpassed in finesse only by the supremacy of the womb itself, the embarrassingly unscientific notion entered her head that these pools were simply here to dole out prescriptions of planetary love. Before she could even laugh at herself, the pool's bubbling warmth lulled her to sleep.

ii

Sometimes stationary yaatras, especially ones as extreme as Omala's, can exceed by sheer internal magnitude the overall dimensions even of their counterparts in motion. Not this time. Omala's journey would at best save a life; Asha's might make one.

She left the western woods with Ilarô's few belongings: his sleeping mat, his thermal pants and sweater, his gloves which still carried the scent of his skin, his collapsible drinking cup and his simple cooking tools. She would have taken his horse too, but it had fled in the hour of his death. Her own mare was inclined to disobey, and though Asha admired the creature's vitality, horse and rider had never been an ideal fit. Nevertheless, for the long journey ahead of them, Tapti would be Asha's sole companion and Asha Tapti's only hope. Both went out of their way to make the arrangement work.

For three days they moved easily through the forests Asha knew, passing stands of cedar, sleeping in groves of fir and on carpets of yellow moss. When they came to foothills studded with hyacinths, they began to climb. They rose ten thousand feet to the timberline, and for short stretches above it, into a land of alpine tundra, a delicate world of short grasses which themselves came to a halt at fourteen thousand feet, where only lichen grew, clinging to granite cliffs as if in a dried-up sea at the top of the world.

Sloping down again a day later, they spent half a week in the stark terrain left by the retreat of prehistoric glaciers. They skirted a chain of high-altitude lakes and stepped carefully up one side of a mountain of loose rock and even more carefully back down the other. Asha had been here once before, as a girl, on an expedition with her father to sketch pictures of all this jagged beauty. They had come then with a team of fifty: guides, porters, cooks, men to build and un-build tents, even a geetakaar to sing them to sleep. A different time.

Nine days out from the dell of the temple, Asha's familiarity with her surroundings came to an end. Now she and Tapti were in the wild. The glacial peaks and airy pines of their original region were replaced by silver-white forests reflecting light so glaringly that, without her riding goggles, Asha was reduced to tearing a strip of gauze from her under-sari and tying it around her eyes as a protective filter, letting Tapti guide them for long stretches. Still, the lack of eyewear was distressing, though with plenty of time both to contemplate her own mind and to let her mind drift, it eventually occurred to Asha that if she kept wishing for every accoutrement she was used to, gloss for her lips and cream for her knees, a pair of goggles to counter the glare and a pair of field glasses to see long distances, her heliotrope perfume to make her feel distinctive and her diamond-dust shampoo to make her feel beautiful and the mint-scented powders that she liked to step on after she bathed in the morning to make her feel complete—the secret baseline of her day—then this trip would swiftly deteriorate into an ordeal. So she forced herself for a while to wish for nothing at all.

Ilarô had indicated, but not until now did Asha really begin to see, that the states of the mind were surprisingly flimsy. For Asha this was practical information: with nothing to do but think for hours on end, she had the first extended interval in her adult life to monitor her own mind minus the mixing stimulus of anyone else to corrupt the observations, and she found the stream of her feelings rather laughable. If she let her mind go where it liked, she could be furious and subdued, thrilled and morose, hopeful and destroyed, a scholar and a psychotic all in the space of six minutes. But if her emotions were this shifting, were any of them real?

The features of Asha's external world were coming at her in pairs of extremes too. The blinding gleam of those silver-white woods was soon counterposed by a forest so densely packed with trees of slick black bark that from a distance Asha thought she was looking at a solid wall. Even up close, it seemed impenetrable. Tapti refused to go forward. Asha had to dismount and tug the resisting

mare into the narrowest passage any horse ever got through. They
squeezed along for a mile. It was a dry forest inside, and unnaturally
quiet, except for acorns the size of fists dropping down in startling
bomblets.

They came out the other side of this block of trees onto the
high ridge over a canyon system. Asha surveyed the landscape: the
fissure below snaked for what might have been ten miles to the horizon. If we separate ourselves momentarily from our subject and rise
a thousand feet over her head, we can see that the true distance was
triple Asha's estimate: she was as an atom at the edge of a cosmos.
But let's not look too far forward, we'll learn more by dropping back
down and settling in again with Asha herself, who knew only that
she had a long way to go. She mounted Tapti, took a tight grip on
her reins, and began the descent.

For eight days horse and rider moved through a slot canyon
wedged between walls of orange dolomite. Occasionally the path
opened into wider vistas where the flow of prehistoric waters and
three hundred million years of erosion had left behind cities of
stone. Letting Tapti move at a leisurely pace, Asha passed a rocky
arch with a ten-ton boulder perched atop its center of gravity; she
sidestepped colossal blocks in a canyon courtyard, like the toys in a
playground for the children of giants; she circled a rock tower two
hundred feet tall; she looked down into the inky crevices of a ravine
where iron and manganese deposits had produced purple pictures in
white limestone.

Succulents grew in the nooks of these rocks, including many
flowering species and several bearing edible fruit or protein-rich
nuts. Asha easily found enough to feed herself and Tapti. She also
stored provisions in her satchel against the threat of future shortage.
Herbs and wildflowers grew here too. Amateur botanist that she was,
Asha knew the fundamentals of plant life and assigned herself the
task of collecting items of medicinal value: the leaves of the sorrel, a

tastily sour source of antioxidants; houseleek, to ease inflammation; horehound, which when made into an infusion or a throat lozenge could relieve discomfort in the chest or even full-fledged bronchitis; fraxinella, for fevers, though also good for a refreshing lemonade; calendula, made into tinctures to prevent cuts from going gangrenous and sprinkled by advanced cooks into sophisticated stews; and of course valerian, the most common of the naturally occurring sedatives. In the end her pharmacopeia included several plants with properties less benign than the aforementioned: a hemp and a germicide, two anesthetics and a purgative, a somnifacient, an opiate, a hallucinogenic, and a weed that could make you vomit from just one lick.

She was testing herself. Given her habit of recent years, not to mention her touch of hypochondria, she could have conjured any number of pains requiring the medicines in her pocket to cure, but she wanted to see if she could reach for precisely none of them. This was Asha's chance to redirect herself after the long chemical detour. For the first time in three years she went without tablet, dava, nepentee, or cure of any kind. The pangs of withdrawal hurt less than expected, and after a while Asha could feel her senses inching back, then flooding into her out of the shadow-death of narcosis, like the painful-but-welcome prickle of shaking a limb back to life after sleeping on it badly. Soon even the pain in her throat that had been plaguing her for months, and which she secretly assumed was a cancer that would one day bulge into a tumor and kill her, receded—and vanished. There had not been any cancer after all, only the threat of it, which in certain cases can precede the disease itself with a foretaste of the agony to come, warning the sufferer less of inevitability than opportunity. As Omala liked to advise: change your direction or you'll end up where you're heading.

At night, instead of the injections of recent months, Asha stargazed. To begin with, she could *see* the stars again, so the delights of metagalactic space all came back to her. In her imagination she stood on the icy crown of a comet—as if standing upright on Tapti transformed—and gripping reins of light raced between the planets and wove around their moons, outrunning riderless comets on either side of her, speeding through clouds of stellar glitter before banking back around and coasting home.

To keep herself warm while she slept, each evening she built fires burning the juniper wood that she collected during the day. Before closing her eyes, she would spend an hour watching the canyon's fauna make their appearances: furry voles darting between rocks; bioluminescent frogs hopping into the open, turning the chalky canyon floor electric orange beneath their glowing bellies; rare nocturnal hawks diving and rising and mating in freefall; and schools of flying fish whizzing overhead, presumably moving between hidden bodies of water, additional evidence of which included the chain of rivulets that Asha herself had been drinking from. But no large animals dwelled here, and the terrain was not arable enough ever to have attracted human habitation. Even the anterior tribes of the raajy, the fierce hemolactics who had subsisted on a diet of blood and milk alone and had been able to set up their outposts anywhere, had failed to find these canyons inviting enough to spend time in. Even they had shunned this place. This no-person's-land had kept the northern annex of the raajy sealed off for a chiliad. Asha, however, felt fine here.

iii

During the first third of her yaatra, Asha had been putting off something that not many could have resisted. Finally, on a windless night when even Tapti wished to be left alone, Asha installed herself under a shelf of dolomite, opened her satchel, and took out the first of a dozen candles. She struck a match and touched it to the wick. And though she knew that she was about to hear a recording, when it began she jerked her head around to look for Ilarô behind her, just to be sure—so real was the sound of his voice released from the altered wax and the effect of its echo into this snug chamber of rock.

Illarô mentioned a song that he had composed only minutes earlier. If we pause to recall the order of events relating to Asha's gift of the ebony box to Ilarô and Ilarô's untimely death, we'll understand that Asha hadn't heard this song before now, nor even known it existed.

Ilarô said that he thought Asha might just like this particular melody, with its superterrestrial motif. There was as little possibility of Asha *not* liking it as there was of her listening calmly. Halfway through the song's second verse, she had to bite hard on her lip to stop sobbing over the words, which could never be heard again once the candle burned down, after this single re-playing. Her thoughts were fluctuating wildly between wanting to bask in the music itself and wanting to lock her mind onto the lyrics, between turning her mind off to luxuriate in Ilarô's voice this first of twelve last times and turning her mind on high to try memorizing his words before they were gone forever.

It was too much: she snuffed the candle out. She would light it again later and hear the rest when she could bear it, after deciding which way to listen. But having heard Ilarô's voice again even for half a minute was enough to whisk her into the open sea of memory, where she was subject to every wind and wave. She soon drifted in a familiar direction ...

How, she asked herself, had she failed so completely at the business not so much of living but of life? After all, Cabaan was only the effect of her troubles, hardly the cause. The deformity of his ambition had not deformed her in turn: she had invited *him* into Palace Isha. So to blame him now would be absurd. Was it not even her own ambition that had caused *Cabaan*?

The blast of accountability made it hard for her to breathe, more so as she grasped its consequence: so long as she imagined her husband to be the holder of her freedom, she could never take her freedom back. Though she hadn't said so to anyone, and had even protested to the contrary to herself, for more than two years she had cherished the idea that Cabaan not only owned her, but had ruined her. It now seemed obvious that this was an evasion within an escape. The idea of something outside of herself that could control her so utterly was the great lie that her mind had made to cover up her own mistakes.

But if Cabaan was not her captor, neither was Ilarô her liberator. Two ways of thinking she had indulged in, both quite wrong. Like a character in a tale out of the long poem of the Zaabta, Asha suddenly wondered if Ilarô and Cabaan were not even two manifestations of the same potentiality—her own. This was truly something that a sage might have glimpsed, sprung from the heart of a young woman who was not even yet an adult. Because despite her outward form, Asha knew that inwardly she was in a state of suspension, that time itself had divided its effect on her, and that if ever she managed to go forward again in body united with being, a single question would remain to be answered: who did she intend to become?

Now a last echo of obsession: for a long time Asha had imagined some great pivot in her future, or occasionally some momentous event, or, as she ultimately pictured it, some beautiful new place, in the passing through of which, like the result of a lever thrown, she would be both restored to her original nature and transformed into the person that she was expecting of herself. In this place of her desperate mind, disguised as a yearning fantasy, she had believed she would be deserving of the life that her parents had tried to make for her. Ilarô, having gleaned Asha's fantasy out of something touching on it that she had once mentioned, had told her: "That place is here, Asha, that moment is now; you yourself are the pivot, and the lever is love. Wait to become perfect before you begin to live and you'll die wishing for all your hours back."

It would not be unfair of a listener to ask: why had Asha come to this crossroads in the first place? Why *had* she made her alliance with Cabaan? *Why* had she invited him into Palace Isha and married him? Was it really for the money? We've certainly seen, and Asha herself had never tried to hide, her requirement of comfort, but did that explain everything? The answer, of course, is no. She had done it for her father. The vast enterprise of Palace Isha, that white world of marble moons with its ancient importance, its forty thousand haiktars of forest and highland, and its hundreds of living dependents, at the time of the marriage in question was nearing financial ruin. Asha's father had been dead a year, her mother was dying and would be gone within the month. At seventeen, Asha herself had lacked any resource apart from the patterns of her character, which she was already beginning to discount. But if Palace Isha had been lost, all her father's goodness would have come to nothing. This Asha could never have allowed.

Not that she hadn't also been thinking of snow-leopard's milk. (A misnomer by the way: the milky solution that Asha bathed in was a plant juice, an extract of the rare polar licorice that was the snow-leopard's favorite treat.) Asha had never been interested in trading luxury for penury or taking baths in well water as if she were a child again—and would not have denied it if asked. But defending her father's reputation was more than anything what drove her. The urgency to preserve Palace Isha in his memory was only sharpened by the guilt she felt at lacking the means to do it on her own. Cabaan, by fifteen, had already made himself rich. By nineteen he seemed capable of anything. So Asha had invited him in. She hadn't fooled herself into thinking it was a perfect plan: on this point she had harbored doubts from the start, despite what she said to Omala in subsequent years, a late reiteration of which we heard ourselves during that first night we watched the cousins together in their grandfather's athainaaium. But Asha hadn't been looking for a perfect plan at the moment of her marriage, only a plan that would work. And no one could say that she hadn't succeeded at keeping Palace Isha intact.

For a while afterwards she used to wonder why life had been made to trap her. Her conclusion, that somehow she must have deserved it, turned her against herself, convinced her she might have found a way to avoid the trap entirely, that a smarter girl would have seen how to work it, but that she had been too stupid, her age and inexperience no excuse. It was the first step along a dark road. Without the counsel of those who love you, your life can come undone as easily as that.

With an after-flash of perception Asha saw that, in fact, she *had* fooled herself—and that her plan had been defective from the start. Even while fighting Cabaan in words, she had been absorbing his lies for years, not only adopting but participating in his view of the world. She had even started to believe him when he referred to her father's incompetence, when he made himself large by making her father small. What a catastrophe! To be drained of one's energy by a misguided plan was bad enough, but to be stripped of one's very senses?

No more. She would go forward and die if dying was the result of moving in the direction she had settled on, but she would never, ever go back. In her mind a new plan began to take shape, an opposite to the original, to the one that had come so close to destroying her. This new plan would be costly, it might take from her everything she possessed, even the very palace of her ancestors. But if she aspired to freedom, perhaps this was its price. The one obstacle she faced was the old guilt at the thought of losing her parents' home. Could she really trade it away? Could that truly be right?

The answer came to her in a dream. That night while she slept, she drank spiced chai with her father beneath the glass roof of his moon-viewing pavilion, their faces alive with lunar sparkle. Her mother sat across from them, painting Asha's portrait. This much was an insertion into the dreamscape of something real: Asha's mother *had* painted this same portrait in this very spot when Asha was fifteen, imagining her daughter seven years in the future and titling the work accordingly: *Asha At Twenty-Two*. Though her specialty was the art of painting in miniature and her usual medium enamel, on occasion she had worked in oils and on canvas if it suited the need. In the time of the dream she had been exploring a new style altogether: portraiture that, tricking the eye, looked like mosaic. Each tiny brushstroke of *Asha At Twenty-Two* resembled a tessera of ruby, gold, dark purple, or pitch-black, for a configuration of painted tiles adding up to the face of its subject. Asha felt immense joy to be sitting for her mother again—until her father dropped his cup of chai to the slate floor, where it shattered.

Asha gasped.

Her mother put down her brush.

Her father looked up as if Asha had announced something terrifying, though she hadn't said a thing. Nevertheless a question had run between father and daughter with the sting of an electric current. How and where Asha would live by the time she reached her age in the portrait, and whether by then she must still be holding onto Palace Isha itself at any cost, was what had been wordlessly asked. And here is the answer with which Asha's father now replied:

"Daughter, this was *never* what we intended for you. Give it up, our darling! Give it all up! It means nothing to us, and we would trade away not only palaces but all the riches of our line to give you the chance of happiness! Remember this above all else: *you* are our one concern!"

Now we know that our parents, after they die, are gone, never to come back again. When they speak to us in our dreams, we understand that their words are issuing out of our own minds, yet this hardly lessens the truth of what they have to say. All that our parents

lacked during their lives vanishes in the end. Their flaws cannot out-
last the brief incarnation that gave them bodies to make mistakes in.
But their gifts to us live on. Asha knew that her parents were wise,
and she knew that they were right. She would do as her father had
told her, she would give up everything. This time she would obey her
parents verbatim. It was, it turned out, the only way.

iv

A month had passed since exiting the arid world of the canyons.
Asha could have plotted a less arduous course, via the trade route
down to the Malachite Sea that the merchants used, including
Cabaan's chain of middlemen transacting their consignments of
wolfram-wood along the way. That route at least was flat, the better
to haul goods. But it would have added hundreds of miles and an
unknown number of weeks to Asha's journey. Anyway, the path she
was on had begun to offer certain compensations for the trouble,
yielding dabs of lime and myrtle … unscrolling ribbons of jade and
aquamarine … revealing strokes of olive with flashes of emerald …
until lush sums of viridescence were bursting from the earth, more
art-form than plant-life, at least to Asha's eye.

When the pigments and shapes of the terrain gathered into
an elevation that was something less than a mountain if more than
a mound, Asha left Tapti to drink at a stream and set out on a side
trip. She climbed a slope scattered with dried branches, white from
weathering and twisted in bizarre corkscrews and curls, like antlers
off the heads of mythical beasts. At the summit she picked a spray
of orange daisies from the wildflowers at her feet before watching an
osprey glide into the wind and come to stop, floating there fixed in
midair, staring back at eye level.

Asha sat down and opened her satchel. She had decided in the
weeks since snuffing out Ilarô's candle that trying to memorize his

words while he sang would not only fail, it would miss the point of
the music. Better to listen the regular way.

She struck her match, touched it to the wick, and felt herself
start to shake at the tones of Ilarô's voice. But the music quickly took
hold, steadying as much as entrancing her. This would become the
pattern of the next twelve days. Each afternoon Asha would stop her
yaatra, go where she liked for an hour, light a candle, listen to Ilarô,
and work at the riddle of why we live and die. On the last of these
dozen days she rode Tapti through a bamboo forest, coming out
into a field of high grass bordered on three sides by the white walls
of what this time was a proper mountain, rising several thousand
feet. The air was thin here, and much cooler than it had been on the
other side of the bamboo, and a light wind blew. In the middle of
the field Asha came to a clear, fishless lake. She sat at its edge as the
sun and surface flashed signals back and forth like communicating
minds. Here she lit the last of Ilarô's candles; but his voice warbled
each time the wind blew, and then the wind put the candle out.
Lighting it a second time brought no different result: the gusts were
too strong. So Asha put the candle back in her satchel and returned
to the protection of the bamboo forest, where the wick lit easily.

Between songs on these recordings, Ilarô would occasionally
speak to Asha directly, and by chance, on this candle that Asha had
chosen in no particular order to listen to last, there had been a good
length of extra wax left after Ilarô had sung his last note. Rather than
waste the time recording nothing, he had spoken off the top of his
head for close to twenty minutes, telling Asha embarrassing anec-
dotes out of his life's large supply. He described slicing his finger on
a string of his heptachord in the middle of a concert for the Jaanam's
birthday the year he turned eleven, and the Jaanam herself having
to bandage him in front of six hundred guests. He described nearly
drowning after a collision with a seal in the Malachite Sea: falling off
his surfplank, dazed in the waves. He described the girl from whom

he had caught the chhotee maata at the late age of thirteen—and the precocious manner of transmission. To Asha every word was a treasure. But it was the very last thing he mentioned that would stay with her the longest, which is to say until the day she died. Hearing it, she assumed that Ilarô was quoting, or paraphrasing at least, from the long poem of the Zaabta of Souls, though she would realize on reflection that he was giving voice to what he had never read anywhere:

"The subtraction of love brings madness, Asha. But add love back and you'll heal."

The candle went out, its charred wick releasing a black loop. Asha packed her things, took Tapti's reins, and hiked on into the now windless night. Normally her head would have been storming with echoes of Ilarô's songs and stories, but instead she went along as quietly within as without, in part because she had come up against that notorious limit of language that all the sages warn of. Also she was trying not to fall. She had been on a rough downhill slope for several minutes and had to concentrate on where she walked. The rocky undergrowth of this bamboo forest had turned treacherous, so Asha remained on foot, leading Tapti to keep her from twisting a hoof. Once Asha did slip and fall, but her reflexes were sharper than they used to be, so she only scraped her palms.

Over the next week, she rounded the edge of a rose-red sea. Its size was unexpected, its pink waves and coral foams issuing from what seemed an ocean instead of any large lake, though Asha had never heard of such a body of water between the regions of the north and the seat of the raajy. It was, moreover, salt water, supporting her maritime suspicions; but in confirming it, she realized this might mean no drinking water for days.

She was right. She went eighty hours before finding another freshwater spring, coming to the very edge of her body's resolve and well beyond Tapti's usual tolerance. Only the extra water in

Jothi-Anandan's tharamas saved them. Asha's chest went heavy thinking of him. She offered a wordless prayer, hoping he had managed to keep out of harm's way. In Cabaan's fury over her disappearance, he might lash out at anyone, Jothi-Anandan being the obvious victim. She wondered if she should have brought him along after all.

Let's follow Asha's progress now as she descends the impact crater of an ancient meteorite, then scales the other side. The sweat on her forehead and cheeks has given her a salty glaze. Where her arms are bare from having ripped the sleeves off her shirt, new muscles flex. Her nails are no longer lacquered with a polish of crushed opals, but the caked-on remains of digging fingers into dirt for edible roots. No diamond dust refracts the light in her hair. No gloss connects her lips to the sun. It's nothing like the look that she was used to composing in her bathing chamber each morning or with a change of dress and adornment before dinner, but when she caught a glimpse of herself in the shine of Jothi-Anandan's tharamas, she was not entirely averse to what she saw.

v

The ground beneath Tapti's hooves was black glass: a layer of obsidian topped the terrain here. Not so easy for a horse to walk across, but at a turtle's pace it worked. Then the weather turned. What began as a refreshing breeze rose to a gale. Asha had to lean forward on Tapti's mane, holding her hands over the mare's eyes to protect her against flying debris. When the temperature dropped, an ice storm broke loose. Freezing rain on glass-like ground made progress impossible. Asha spotted the mouth of a cave and aimed them for shelter.

They spent an hour beneath the cave's rocky hood. The storm wasn't going away anytime soon, so Asha turned into the cave and lit the quarter candle that she had been keeping in her pocket for

emergency light, because Ilarô had stopped recording on it before
the wax was done. But after a moment's flickering silence, Ilarô's
voice picked up again! He hadn't stopped recording before the end
of the wax, there had been some sort of technical interruption! He
was in the middle of a lullaby now, which calmed Asha and Tapti
too as they stepped into the unknown, guided by candlesound on
top of candlelight. Soon they were into a strange world of rocky
punctuation, stalactites and stalagmites around which Ilarô's golden
voice darted and flowed, and into whose shadows his candle sent its
dancing flare. Where the waters of an underground lake had receded
millennia ago, mineral dust glittered as if the cavern's walls had been
painted with crushed gemstones.

They came to the vestige of the lake itself. Overhead a colony
of bats hung in slumber. Stiffening at the sight of them, Asha managed to give her mind back to Ilarô's lullaby. Tapti was tugging at
her reins, wishing to drink from the little pool, so Asha let her go
before kneeling to fill her own tharamas. As she leaned toward the
ancient lake's rim, a red piranha shot out of the shallows, triangles of
teeth visible until they clamped onto Asha's thumb. Asha stumbled
backwards shrieking and whipping her arm around; but the bite of
the red piranha was strongest of all vertebrates in the biology of the
raajy. Examples of these tiny monsters skeletonizing a human body
in seconds were perhaps rarer in nature than in storytelling, though
the discrepancy was of no comfort to Asha in the moment.

Forcing herself to stand still despite the firing of every
terror-transmitting nerve in her body, she raised the piranha to
her own mouth and bit down hard. It worked. The piranha's mouth
unlocked; it dropped to the cavern floor, flapping back into water.
Asha retched from fish blood on her tongue and spat ten times to
clear the taste. Then she snatched Tapti's reins and fled.

They slept poorly. In the morning they left as early as they
could, and by late day they were into another terrain altogether.

These weren't microclimates of the type Asha knew from the lands surrounding Palace Isha, they were macrosystems, large and self-contained. The white world she now entered was made of gleaming gypsum dunes. Oases dotted the landscape. At one of them, Asha came upon a mob of dromedaries licking at pockets of surface water. These harbors in the sand offered food as well as drink: Asha made a tasty meal of dates and nuts before building a fire to push back the desert cold that would descend on them at sundown. For the next week she and Tapti moved along in much the same way, methodically mounting dunes, sleeping beneath the incandescent objects of the universe, exploring slopes and springs.

Finally the sands dwindled to dirt: they had reached the white desert's end. Ahead of them a gorge sliced the land in two; beyond it, a snowcapped range rose fifteen thousand feet in a patchwork of purple and ivory, on the far side of which, Asha believed, lay the Malachite Sea. This meant Aakaash-Nivaas was within striking distance, somewhere between the northern face of these mountains and the southern. The severed pieces of a hanging bridge that had once spanned the gorge suggested as much, or at least suggested human activity in the recent past. The gorge itself was some hundred feet across and a thousand feet deep: there would be no casual crossing.

Asha dismounted and looked for another way. But the gorge stretched as far as she could see in both directions: going around might take weeks. Climbing down into it and back up the other side seemed the sensible thing—until the howl of a jackal below reduced the appeal. Scanning the terrain for ideas, Asha's eye landed on a patch of vegetation growing along the edge of the gorge. As she stepped toward it, the patch sharpened into a single chandava tree that was in fact growing up from, and even more precisely *out* of, the vertical wall of the gorge itself. But the tree was out of season, its leaves either already dropped off or browning on their stems, with only a single greenish leaf remaining. A modest tug from Asha detached it, a sure sign of cellular decay. She whirled it overhead anyway, to test it the way the boys did. Certainly it was not as safe to use as it would have been even a week earlier, but it might just be safe enough.

Few travelers nearing the end of a yaatra such as this would have considered leaping across a thousand-foot drop on a trajectory of a hundred feet using only the questionable power of a leaf for lift, fewer still using a leaf threatening to shred apart at any moment. But despite the various challenges of mentality that Asha had contended with so far in life and would have to contend with further if and as life continued, she was possessed of a certain mental strength that hasn't yet been commented on: no fear of heights. As a child she had been such a *lover* of heights, such a climber of trees and runner along rooves, that her father had dubbed her "Asha of the Air." On balance Asha's mind was largely un-phobic and actually rather sturdy. Which is not to say that flying over a canyon hanging from a leaf is something other than a contest with death.

Asha's preference was to live: she wished to stay in the world as long as it took to set right what she had let go wrong. She had a debt to pay her late parents, an implied promise to keep to Ilarô, and a responsibility to Jothi-Anandan and the hundreds of others living in and around Palace Isha. She also had something of a responsibility to herself, requiring her presence in the world at least a while longer. A contest with death, however, is not always a death wish. For Asha it was a chance to again be the girl she had grown up as.

She unstrapped Tapti's saddle and bridle, dropped them to the ground, hugged the mare, and slapped her on her way.

Tapti did not move.

"You," Asha said, "are a deeply annoying animal. But I love you anyway."

She went about the rest of her preparations. Having given up her sari weeks before in favor of Ilarô's thermal pants and sweater, she now re-rolled the ends of the legs, which had always been a bit too long for her, to keep from tripping. She gripped the chandava leaf by its hemp fronds, raised her air-sail overhead, ran at the gorge, and jumped.

For the first few seconds it worked: she went gliding along her inertial path, dropping down intentionally to meet the far side of the gorge, slightly lower than the side she had leapt from. Her heart was racing, though when she looked into the depth of the valley below, she was thrilled. Only the sound of her leaf tearing marred the moment. Luckily the tear wasn't running from the leaf's edge toward the center; it was contained at the mid-section, in a two-inch slit. Enough to cause Asha to veer, but she was only seconds from reaching the other side: from here a bit of luck would see her through.

The leaf ripped in two. Asha screamed as she plunged, but by inches she had just cleared the gorge itself, so it was now a question not of dropping to certain death a thousand feet down, but of whether she would snap a limb or smash her backbone in slapping the ground thirty feet below. In the penultimate moment, she thought she might manage to land on her feet and skid to a stop; then a gush of air flipped her upside down and she hit the rocky terrain hard, slicing her arm. A bloody ribbon eventuated from shoulder to elbow, but in applying pressure to stanch it, Asha only felt success.

Across the gorge Tapti whinnied for attention. Asha waved back. The mare hesitated, then bolted.

From here Asha would have to go on foot. This meant a hike from the base of the range to its middle plateau, seven thousand feet up, scooping at the occasional snow-patch along the way for water and slurping protein-glue out of flowers for food …

By the fourth morning of this last leg of her yaatra, Asha had cleared a peak and come within sight of the destination of these several months. Rising out of a summit in the middle distance was an astounding edifice: the sky-lodge of the Shaasakon, nine stories high, built of petrified wood and sealed in pearly resin, its central and highest portion carved out of the mountain's own violet rock, the whole of it topped by a platinum roof and a dozen platinum towers, a palace large enough to house the population of a small city within its eight thousand rooms: Aakaash-Nivaas.

Asha went forward slowly, making the trip in twenty-four hours instead of half the time, as she could have done now that she was so much more fit than before she started. But she thought she should arrive in the morning, with a full day in front of her to explain herself. The appearance of night visitors, especially unexpected ones, is invariably a grandiose moment, and Asha felt cured of all that by this time. She wanted a minimum of grandeur from now on, and as much simplicity as she could get, proving the old adage that a long walk may be the best medicine, after all.

vi

To enter Aakaash-Nivaas, a visitor passed through no triumphal arch, no colossal gateway, no series of imposing passages, but a plain wooden door, left unlocked, attended by no sentry. Asha sent her mental compliments to the ancient architect who had built it this way and to all the kings of history who had decided to leave well enough alone.

She stepped through and was into another world. Here was wealth articulated as beauty beyond anything she had ever seen. She crossed a colonnade lined with pear trees whose branches radiated like human arms balancing golden balls from shoulder to palm; she went through a greenhouse of wildflowers in ascending shades of blue from robin's-egg to sapphire; she passed a shadow-checked cloister tiled in brushed silver and a courtyard walled in alternating panels of iridescent feldspar, polished agate, and vivid malachite.

And everywhere she turned: water gardens. Streamlets ran through channels wedged into slate floors; waters jetted in spirals and drained through stone grilles; fountains of green stone were a constant motif.

After a quarter hour's wandering, Asha had crossed paths with no guard or guide, no other person at all. Anyone else would have felt herself a trespasser; Asha's delightfully imagining mind translated the sensation into a unique spirit of welcome, as though she were exploring a palace lent by friends who were away for a while and wanted someone they knew to come keep an eye on the place until they returned.

When she reached the end of what she would later understand to be the sky-lodge's so-called *outer* galleries, she came into a wing built of the same violet rock as the exterior central portion of the structure, so she knew she was near the heart of the palace. Ahead of her stood a set of high platinum doors, perhaps twenty feet tall. She reached out to touch the bifurcated metal knob between them when a young padaadhikaaree, younger than Asha herself, came running from the other end of the hall to intercept her. (The melodic ring to it notwithstanding, "padaadhikaaree" simply meant "functionary" in Bhaashan.)

He whispered a greeting that was polite enough, though he was patently alarmed at the sight of an unknown visitor. Asha greeted him with a synonym of his courtesy, minus the alarm.

Looking her over with an incredulous eye, the young man said:

"I'm sorry, but you do realize it's the sky-lodge of the Shaasak you've come to."

Asha replied with a question:

"Could you tell me please if the samgha is in session?" She had used the ancient term for a gathering of the Shaasak's court, or perhaps more accurately translated, the Shaasak's community.

"They are, yes. Thank you for asking. Perhaps you might like to leave now that you know it." He was still whispering, as if to compel

Asha to do the same. He gestured in the direction of the nearest exit. Asha turned to see what he was pointing at, turned back to look at him, and brushed back the lock of blond hair that had fallen over his eyes when he came running through the hall. This unsettled him. Asha used the moment to state her purpose:

"I'm here to consult the Shaasak."

Her young judge studied her to be sure he wasn't making some terrible error. "I doubt that's possible just now."

"You've just said he was in session."

"If I might expand upon my answer: yes, the Shaasak, at this moment, is in the middle of his daily *sitting*. Members of the samgha are always welcome, but not after the meditation begins. I would be required to turn away the Jaanam herself if she came late. When the sitting is over, the daily session begins, though we usually have advance word of anyone out of the ordinary planning to attend. Since you weren't able to let us know beforehand, you might like to come back some other time, sending us a note with several weeks' warning, so we can be sure to work out a space for you."

"I'd like to see the Shaasak today," Asha said calmly.

"There's very little chance of that happening."

"Would you be kind enough to look into the possibility?"

The young man made no move to comply. He wasn't offensive, he was even endearingly dutiful, though Asha kept thinking how we warp ourselves by intentionally narrowing our minds for all our little jobs. Life, her father used to tell her, is a broad pursuit, and for the first moment ever, Asha grasped by way of comparison the advantages of having been raised a generalist.

"You can't know how grateful I'd be," she said, "if you would relate to the Shaasak or some appropriate other person that the Vikaantee Asha of Palace Isha asks to see him. I've come down from the far north for that reason."

The padaadhikaaree suppressed an outburst of doubt. It wasn't his right to be insolent, but it *was* his responsibility to discourage frivolous applicants to the Shaasak's daily sessions. Only those visitors of a certain obvious derivation or a distinct seriousness of purpose were supposed to be let through. To this young man's eye, Asha, in her state of physical disarray—and, given this new claim of status as Vikaantee, very likely psychological disarray as well—was an unlikely candidate on both counts. Still, it confused him that she didn't much sound like a liar.

"I'm sorry, the Vikaantee 'Asha,' did you say?"

"Yes."

"Of Palace 'Isha?'"

"Yes."

"I'm not familiar with that particular palace."

"It's some distance."

"So far I'd never have heard of it?"

"The scope of your education is not a subject I can speak to."

She had said this last thing not cuttingly, but straightforwardly. The young man bristled all the same. His resistance, which had seemed on the point of breaking down, firmed up again.

"I see. The Vikaantee Asha then." He tumbled into open skepticism. "*Born* Vikaantee?" Presumably he now meant to debunk Asha's story by picking apart its details. He was quite unprepared for what happened next, when Asha answered him by saying:

"Born Raajakumaaree."

A spray of adrenalin soured the young man's chest, racing down legs to toes and up through his neck to the tongue. In the interest of those listening to our story who lack an ear for linguistics and haven't yet guessed at the etymologies in play or their implications, to be Raajakumaaree, or in the masculine case, Raajakumaar, was to come out of the same lineage, however distantly, as the founders of the raajy themselves. In other words, Asha had just claimed to be the Shaasak's cousin. If a lie, it was so outrageous to utter in the

Shaasak's own house—and on strictly legal terms, so perjurious, since all official speech within Aakaash-Nivaas was governed by the same requirement of truth-telling as that enforced in any court of law—that the perjurer risked everything. An unlikely deception. Besides, impersonations were not common crimes in the raajy. If this girl was Vikaantee and the padaadhikaaree disobeyed her, he was already in enough trouble; if she was Raajakumaaree and he disobeyed her, he was finished. But it was impossible imagining any Raajakumaaree looking like this. Let's not forget that Asha had been weathered by the extreme conditions of her yaatra: she was no picture of privilege. By admitting a fraud or an insane person into the Shaasak's daily session, the padaadhikaaree would be failing at his most basic assignment; though in turning back someone who deserved entry by birth as well as by merit, he wouldn't be doing himself any favors either.

Sensing how hard it was for him to make up his mind about her, Asha took another tack:

"If it helps you at all, you might tell the Shaasak that I was a friend of his geetakaar."

The padaadhikaaree's face brightened. "You know Ilarô?"

"I knew him."

Again the young man's suspicions surged. "Anyone could say that."

Asha reached beneath the collar of her shirt and unclasped Ilarô's choker of shaanadaar diamonds.

"The Shaasak, I think, will recognize these."

This did it. Convinced now that Asha was someone of importance, whether or not she was exactly who she claimed, the padaadhikaaree took possession of the necklace and disappeared through a sliding panel in the wall.

Asha was left to wait. After a bit, her thoughts ran to Omala, whom, we'll recall, she believed to be dead. Omala, in fact, was not

only not dead, she was nearly well again. After months in a thera-
peutic coma induced by the waters of her remedy pool, her lungs
had been mended, her liver fixed, and the damage to her circulatory
system repaired. For several days now she had been intermittently
conscious and in the last several hours had begun to sense an extra
strength coming into her, beyond the threshold of mere recuperation.
Lying in the bubbling nutrients of her hyper-bath, she cogitated
on this new development of health piled on health—and concluded
that the remedy pool's intense liquids were super-oxygenating her
blood and their microbial symbionts triggering steroid production
in her tissues. It gave her an idea. After the long soak to save her
life, if she remained here just the right amount more, she could leave
this remedy pool with a physical power significantly exceeding her
body's natural capacity. Not that it would last, only until the steroids
broke down and flushed themselves out, days at most, but if the
timing worked, and with a little luck, it might be enough for what
she had in mind.

So the fascinating antilogy persists that although Omala's
yaatra had been static, and without any bodily effort whatsoever,
it was all about physical repair, whereas Asha's recent travels, so
defined by locomotion and largely composed of physical feats, had
all concerned the trials of the mind. She had hardly noticed the
cuts and bruises along the way; her attention had been on the older
injuries, the ones she still carried in her head and which she would
only ever displace by means of the love she let in to muscle them
out. For her knowledge of this possibility, and this process, she now
silently praised Ilarô, finding that, contrary to so many of the old
tales, the more she let herself adore him, even in death, the stronger
she became. True love, she concluded, had never made any woman
weak—that inanity of a thousand minor poets.

The platinum doors to the Shaasak's throne room, his White
Chamber to use the formal term, jiggled at their lock from the in-

side, drawing Asha back to her present situation. The doors opened heavily on their braces: the young padaadhikaaree was there signaling Asha with a finger to step in. She went forward in her detached state, the best way to meet a king.

For all the cozy patios and intimate breezeways behind her, this throne-room was a major chamber, built not so much to ignite the senses as to arrest them. It was a perfect circle with a circumference nearly a thousand feet around, walls lacquered shiny white, its roof a glass dome, a hundred feet high. Wooden benches curled around its rim in concentric rows, each several feet higher than the one below, filled now with members of the samgha: householders, practitioners, visitors, petitioners, and dignitaries, all dressed in shades of ivory or pale yellow, either the style here or the protocol, Asha didn't know which.

At the center of this mammoth hoop of a room, on the floor, upon a shimmering violet mat and cushioned by the downy fill of lime-colored silk pillows sat the Silent Shaasak and his wife, the Jaanam. Asha approached them with all the poise that was left in her. There was no sound in the room as five hundred eyes followed her progress along the chamber's diameter from fringe to nucleus. Partly the silence was due to what had already been announced, that a young woman presenting herself as Raajakumaaree-born and in possession of the shaanadaar diamonds of the royal geetakaar had arrived to see the Shaasak; partly it was in reaction to how Asha looked. For us, knowing the cause of her appearance and having adjusted to it in stages along the way, it was easy to forget the shocking impression she gave, but to those seeing Asha for the first time, she seemed a wild woman. Look at her now: her skin browned by the hot suns of the interior, her arms toned, wearing a man's pants and his dust-caked thermal coat, her hair a storm of knots.

She arrived at the Shaasak's violet mat, lowered herself to her knees, and sat with her legs to the side, following the Jaanam's example.

The Shaasak was a gaunt man of seventy-five; his wife, also thin, though not bony to the degree of her husband, was maybe a decade younger. Both were dressed in dark purple sarongs and matching jackets of raw silk, and each wore a bracelet of shaanadaar diamonds of their own: black, spheric gemstones perfectly matched in size and quality to the stones on Ilarô's choker. Even now the Shaasak was rolling the diamond beads around his left wrist between the fingers of his right hand. The action was discreet, though Asha noticed it right away.

The Jaanam spoke first:

"We hear you've come quite some way to see us, Asha."

"I have, Mahodaya." Asha was using the polite form of address for speaking to the Jaanam in person. "Palace Isha sits at the far northern tip of the raajy, just below the polar caps."

"That is, indeed, a distance." The Jaanam's tone was neither haughty nor friendly, but pointedly neutral. A dignified woman with wavy white hair which she wore short, again very like her husband, she seemed cold to the tidbit of geography that Asha had offered, though it should have been the obvious entry point to any discussion of Asha's background, so much contested only minutes earlier. The Jaanam's reaction was less the result of general incuriosity than her desire to hear about something more specific on an urgent basis. Her next remark made this apparent:

"And we understand you've had some contact with our great friend." She glanced at the shaanadaar choker on the mat beside her husband.

"Yes, Mahodaya."

Just when the question of whether the Jaanam would be the only one to speak entered Asha's mind, the Shaasak addressed her directly, his voice warm but firm:

"Tell us, how *is* Ilarô? It's been too long since we've heard his voice."

During the long days of her yaatra, Asha had imagined this moment many times, anticipating the shock that her answer would cause, trying to come up with a way to say it that would lessen its ugliness. She realized now before the words left her mouth that she had underestimated what their effect would be by a terrible factor.

"Mahima, Ilarô is dead."

She clenched her fists on instinct, as if expecting a reaction to come at her in physical form—though for a long moment there was no reaction at all. We tend to think of speech and the understanding of speech as an instantaneous exchange, a self-executing miracle of transmission and recipience; but the way we express a thought through structured sounds and the way those sounds are perceived and interpreted is no less extraordinary for being not so much miraculous as mechanical—or at least anatomical. A speaker's vocal cords, together with the tongue, jaw, and lips, produce utterances in the form of vibrations, which a listener's organs of hearing detect and transduce to the brain via a labyrinth of bones, tissues, and cavities. The brain's job is the big one, converting these electrical impulses into units of meaning; yet sometimes the information received is so hideous, so startling, like a snake shooting up from a flower bed to bite your face, that the end product, namely comprehension, is momentarily delayed, the cerebrum needing an extra second or so to check its work. This accounts for the pause following Asha's statement during which the White Chamber was silent …

… and before the room erupted:

A dozen women broke into ululation.

An old man fainted on a middle bench and fell to a lower one, gashing his cheek.

The children in the room, horrified by what was happening to the adults around them, started to cry.

The daily session was cancelled, the Shaasak helped up from his mat by the Jaanam and an attendant. They quickly retreated from the room. Such an exit may sound impulsive, but the rule of correct speech in the presence of a Shaasak was so long ingrained in the cultural as well as the legal life of the raajy, and so infrequently transgressed, that Asha's announcement of Ilarô's death had been accepted as fact on the spot. The details would always be there for the visiting, but the blow could only come once. There was no question of the Shaasak remaining in the room.

An attendant came out from the corridor that the Shaasak and his wife had gone into, to usher Asha away from the chaos. The Shaasak would speak to her as soon as he was able, for now she was asked to settle in and wait. She was conducted through a glass-encased breezeway toward another wing of the palace, then down a hallway hacked out of the mountain's stony center into a bright suite of rooms overlooking the green waves of the Malachite Sea, a thousand feet straight down the cliff. For the next three days this would be Asha's home, or, depending upon one's interpretation of circumstances, her jail cell.

Meanwhile all regular activity at the sky-lodge ceased. Every window in the palace—nearly eleven thousand—was painted with a black stripe of mourning. Once or twice a year, as a sign of honor following the death of some prominent person, the Shaasak's session with the samgha was cancelled for a day; it would be ten weeks before his court resumed its full schedule this time. Asha knew none of this. In the aftermath of her White Chamber appearance, and for the three days that followed, all she knew about the ways of this place was that she was here now under a kind of room-arrest, left by herself except for the attendants who brought meals and refreshments and the housekeeper who came in the morning to make up her bed and in the evening to turn her bed down. The Shaasak did not send for her. No members of the permanent population of the palace came to introduce themselves, apart from the brief visit of the royal tailor who took her measurements, asked her to specify her taste in color and cut of sari, and returned later that day for a fitting before sending a package the same night containing a new wardrobe. The Shaasak's private secretary did forward a note by messenger inquiring after the disposition of Ilarô's body, to which Asha replied by note that the body had been cremated some months earlier. But other than this, there were no communications at all, not even a request for more detailed information on the manner of Ilarô's death.

To pass the time, Asha read what was on her room's bookshelf, including a famous collection of verse for children by the Jaanam's own great-grandmother. *Birds I Have Known* was still a favorite of young readers throughout the raajy, though the author had not otherwise been in the business of juvenile literature and as a composer of metrically sophisticated odes had ranked as one of the chief poets of her day. Asha hadn't picked up "The Bird Book," as it was commonly called, in years; but revisiting the charms of its rhymes distracted her from her troubles for an hour or so.

> *The Myna Bird will squawk the loudest*
> *His splendid crest makes him the proudest*
> *But when he eats he's not so snooty*
> *A bug will do—or something fruity*

Reading the slim volume again it occurred to Asha how confidently children know their own minds. You can't fool them into liking a story or a song or even a poem, no matter who else says what about it: either it works for them or it doesn't. Unlike their parents of course, who suffer all manner of confusion about what distinguishes the truly awful from the really good.

Apart from reading, Asha spent most of these three days on her balcony high above the Malachite Sea, watching the sun polish the waves and the moon tug at the tides. At first she had no notion that she had been placed in a suite of rooms in the same section of the palace as Ilarô's, or that her view was not only similar to his, but identical. Her bedroom and his shared a wall: at night she lay her head on a pillow separated only by a foot of rock from the pillow on which Ilarô had laid his. In the middle of her third night here she woke up with a sudden awareness of the contiguity. She would never be able to say how she had felt it, but there was no doubt in her mind. Such are the mysteries of tattvameemaansa, so easy to miss, so simple to disbelieve. Asha was in a mood to believe everything.

She rose from her bed and made her way out of the room by spraying a phosphorescent perfume ahead of her, because she had left her lamp in the bathroom and the atomizer of fragrance was on her nightstand. So it was through a mist of fragrant pink light that she tiptoed down the hallway. At the next suite of rooms, after tapping to be sure it was empty, she let herself in.

She saw right away that this was where Ilarô had lived: the plain gleam of the apartment and its indifference to luxury matched all his descriptions. Also the seven heptachords hanging on the wall gave their clue. The windows and doors onto the balcony had been left open, so Asha went out to stand where Ilarô would have stood in the middle of his nights here, and here, gently, she came upon a silvery figure. This was no ghost though, but a man of flesh and blood, leaning against the balcony's railing, gazing at the same starlit sea that Ilarô would have gazed at, and standing in Ilarô's same place: the Shaasak.

He turned to acknowledge her, gestured for her to join him, and returned to the view. Asha stepped forward and settled in beside him. The two sea-gazers stood this way for some time, looking without speaking, listening to the waves churn the coast, a breeze on their cheeks and the taste of salt on their tongues. After a while, the Shaasak, this most powerful of persons, this ruler of a raajy and prince of a lineage that dilated time itself for an unbroken vision into history, turned to go, though not before saying:

"Don't stay *too* long, Asha. We can't have you surviving your travels only to catch cold in your bare feet and end up dead of lung fever. We have, I think, a great many things to discuss."

vii

Ilarô's Memento of the Dead took place in the Shaasak's private solarium, a glass dome on a bluff, ventilated with sea breezes and scented by the plumeria growing wild alongside these cliffs. This was the first occasion at the sky-lodge, after the initial episode in the White Chamber, in which Asha had been in the company of more than one other person at a time. A thousand were in attendance today. Given the outburst of emotion that Asha had witnessed three days earlier, she imagined the service would contain hours of testimonials, followed perhaps by a passage read by the Jaanam out of the long poem of the Zaabta of Souls and capped by a eulogium that the Shaasak himself would deliver: the prashansa bhaashan. Instead it was a silent ceremony. A thousand sat for an hour without speaking, then a thousand dispersed.

Before the service had begun, and frankly once or twice while it was in progress, Asha had been glanced at pleasantly by a young woman a few years older than herself, seated two rows ahead and looking back over her shoulder. Afterwards, in the procession along the cliff's edge to the palace, the young woman caught up to Asha and introduced herself: she was the royal midwife. Her soft features and the large curls of auburn hair splashing the top of her cinnamon-colored sari with its black stripe of mourning put Asha at ease. Also Asha couldn't help being impressed by her age: not only was she beautiful, not only composed, but this young woman was *accomplished*. To hold a position like hers in the house of the Silent Shaasak and not yet have turned thirty? She must have been someone extraordinary, even among midwives, the most revered women in the realm. These practitioners were said to possess such honed powers of sympathy and insight that they could perceive a new life taking shape in a womb from the second week of gestation—at fifty feet! Asha wondered how they could tell. By some touchless transmission? Was there electromagnetism involved, out of the gathering cells of the fetal brain and into the receiving mind of the midwife? Or could a pregnancy be detected by some particulate transference, by sniffing out the subtle variation in hormones relative to all the other estrogens in a room? Or even by some more lyrical assessment, something faintly musical in the voice of the expectant—or unsuspecting—mother? Someday, Asha thought, she might like to look into these questions more deeply, even find out whether she had any talent in this direction herself. If not as a mother, then as a midwife perhaps she could make her mark. This presupposed that she had any future ahead of her at all, far from certain, however much she was trying to believe in it. The truth was more brutal: Asha might still be stopped. Not by Cabaan, at least not directly. But a snake can bite you and then slither off: its venom is still inching toward your heart. Asha knew what poison she carried inside of herself, even here, as far from home as she would ever go. So her recent improvement notwithstanding, it was faith, not yet health, that was guiding her, faith that was holding at bay her old doubts about her place in the world, faith that had taken shape under ideal conditions, during the emptiness of a yaatra. Now that worldly events were about to impinge upon her again and test the strength of her corrections, we'll see how well she holds up.

But first let's return to a bit of unfinished business between Asha and the royal midwife, Amaravati. During their few minutes together in the procession between the Shaasak's solarium and his White Chamber, the midwife wished to discuss Ilarô. This was natural enough, having just come from his Memento of the Dead. Asha told her what she could about him, and in exchange Amaravati mentioned things about Ilarô's life that she imagined Asha might like to hear. Among these were points of praise, large and small. For instance: the Shaasak, she said, had the habit of delaying major decisions of state until after Ilarô could sing for him.

"To calm his mind?" Asha asked.

"To carry him *beyond* mind," Amaravati replied.

"Is that true?" Asha was eager to hear the compliment said again. "His influence on the Shaasak was really that great?"

"I wouldn't say it was so surprising of an Ekko Jagaaya."

Asha stopped in her tracks, forcing the midwife to turn back to see the full effect of her remark.

"You didn't know?" Amaravati said. "No, I suppose you wouldn't have. Ilarô wouldn't have brought it up."

Asha was no student of philology, but even she knew the basic derivations: "Ekko Jagaaya," in the parent language of Bhaashan, meant "an awakened one." *An* Ekko Jagaaya appeared as seldom as once in ten generations, and even then quietly. This was the opposite of hereditary rank. An Ekko Jagaaya's stature exceeded the ancestral, exceeded even the genetic. His arrival in the world, or hers, could not be predicted, and his powers of clarity and compassion were considered, at least by those who studied such things, to be a sliver of the divine.

With this unbelievable piece of news, Asha began recalibrating the whole of her experience with Ilarô, to which her reaction was something you might not expect: she was furious. But there isn't time just now to say why. The procession had arrived at the White Chamber, where a special session was about to begin. Today it was all about Asha.

Amaravati embraced her new friend, holding her tight for a long moment to express support for what was to come. The gesture took Asha slightly by surprise, given the many forces of mind already working on her, together with all the stimuli of the crowd taking their seats in the White Chamber's vast circularity. Nevertheless she smiled her appreciation once released from the midwife's arms. Then she crossed the chamber and reached her position before the Shaasak and Jaanam on their violet mats at the center of the great round room. Few had withdrawn during the walk from the Shaasak's solarium; nearly all those who had been at Ilarô's silent Memento of the Dead were here as well, to attend its counterpart in words. This meant that the attentions of some thousand people were now hardening concentrically around Asha. It wasn't hostility they were projecting, more extreme curiosity. They wanted answers, all the same.

Amaravati caught Asha's eye again, offering a smile of encouragement, even though Asha, who by the way was refreshed in appearance after three days of foaming baths and wearing a finely cut sari of raw black silk, did not seem intimidated. In itself this was a suggestion of something resilient in her, something substantial even, though it would be up to Asha herself to furnish the proof.

The Jaanam addressed her first, apparently the custom. While the Shaasak sat tranquilly beside her, his wife said:

"Now, Asha. Tell us all exactly who you are."

Life offers many occasions to keep quiet. At other times, when circumstances require us to explain ourselves, concision is the key. Then comes a moment to hold nothing back. Asha had learned at least one thing for certain from Ilarô: we are beings made to speak to one another—and some of us to sing. Asha spoke. This was no ungoverned flood of talk, but a methodical, almost medical account of who she was and what she had done. She left out nothing that she could think of, reversing the false picture of things that she had grown used to giving, describing instead as straightforwardly as she was able the disorder of function in herself that had led to her presence in this White Chamber and proving that, every so often, clarity is achieved not by brevity, but by length.

The mesmerized samgha could have listened twice as long.
Many wished to hear it all again from start to finish, though some
were too shaken to have endured any part another time, because to
explain who Asha was meant explaining where she had come from:
her mother and father, her father's botanical art, his stewardship of
Palace Isha; the arrival of Cabaan and Cabaan's violence; her own
addictions, her davaphilia—her *drug*-taking; Ilarô's appearance in
her life, their love together, his murder. The men and women in the
White Chamber also thought they could perceive in Asha's voice
and her ways of describing people and events many of Ilarô's own
turns of phrase. It was true: Asha had picked up Ilarô's rhythms, and
they were beautiful to hear even as echoes.

To the Shaasak it seemed that a daughter had rocketed out
of the death of his son. Not his son by genetic reckoning, but from
a connection no less strong. Twice while listening to Asha's story,
he wept. Nearly two hours after she began, when Asha completed
her long answer to the Jaanam's short question, the Silent Shaasak
rose to his feet from the violet mat that was his throne and softly
thundered these seven words:

"Come near to me, my ancient cousin."

Off every bench in the room members of the samgha dropped
to their knees, the rocking of wooden seats against stone floor
producing a rare din in a chamber famed for quietude. When the
Shaasak stood in veneration of another person, especially someone
he evidently believed to be a relation, others knelt. And while the
rule of correct speech in the presence of *any* Shaasak lent credence on
purely legal grounds to what Asha had reported, it was also true that
the Jaanam had sent the royal chronologist to Asha's apartment that
same morning for an hour-long visit. It hadn't *quite* been an interro-
gation, simply the Jaanam's own way to verify the truth of who Asha
was—or wasn't. The chronologist—in Asha's view a suspiciously
young man for a scholar of history and genealogy, someone suppos-

edly expert in tracing the raajy's complicated lines of descent—had come armed with a portfolio containing birth announcements and death records on the families of the far north. He posed a series of questions to Asha concerning the names and occupations not only of her parents and grandparents, but significant ancestors and their notable achievements going back two centuries, confirming by virtue of her replies what the Shaasak himself, through very different means, was sure of by the time Asha finished speaking in the White Chamber: she was who she said.

The Shaasak stepped forward to take her in his arms, and to the credit of almost all present—some thousand souls, as mentioned—they were glad for him. They knew that the Shaasak's discovery of Asha would not mean his forgetting of *them*. They were happy for this man who led more than ruled, whom they loved, and who deserved any gift that mattered to him. They had learned from him as a group what Ilarô had learned as his private pupil before re-inspiring his teacher with the very same lesson: more for others did not mean less for oneself.

But let's not give a false impression of Aakaash-Nivaas as a social utopia. Here, as everywhere, human beings suffered. They struggled. They made decisions using the poorest of reasoning. They deluded themselves with praise for the things they had done completely wrong. They were imperfect. They grappled with desire and aversion. They contemplated theft and betrayal, they fought back urges to wound and even to kill one another. The seat of the raajy was no house of fantasy, but a true place where actual people lived. From our own vantage point, however—that is, from the vantage point of our own suffering, and compared to how ignorant we have again become of any systematic means by which to address our suffering—there *was* one fantastic-seeming element of residence in the sky-lodge that distinguished life there from life in so many houses and cities across time and space: those who inhabited the eight thousand rooms of this palace followed the Shaasak's example, as the Shaasak followed the example of a line of teachers before him, of sitting in daily meditation, of putting to work that most fundamental of practices on which the fate of the world itself might even, ultimately, turn. And by means of this practice—which is not at all a technique for thinking great thoughts as so many misconceive, but for thinking no thoughts whatsoever, for gently guiding and re-guiding the mind toward a field of pure, formless concentration, where illusions dissolve and wholeness transpires—by means of meditation, the inhabitants of Aakaash-Nivaas had discovered and were daily reminded of an exceedingly powerful truth: their emotions were not their realities.

All who lived in the raajy, under the Shaasak's reign and by extension his character, were beneficiaries of his commitment to these explorations of the science of consciousness: the "supreme science" to give it its full due, or the "brahma-vidya" as the Shaasak himself referred to it, having reached back through many cycles of bygone time to pluck the phrase out of the germinal language of the sages. It was the very science by which members of the samgha transformed themselves into pilots of the mind who, after learning that they could mentally separate themselves from their emotions, acquired the skill to step back from any impulse, even envy, even hatred. This was really the power to neutralize fear itself, since fear is envy and hatred and every other impulse of destruction called by its rudimentary name. And how is it that these meditators were able to neutralize fear in this way? By recognizing it as merely the shadow and light of the phenomenal plane. The Shaasak's guided meditations had proven the world and all its forces to be frequently dangerous but never malicious, making fear an expensive reaction to waste on an enemy who simply was not there.

The residents of Aakaash-Nivaas lived their daily lives too on either side of these voyages of the mind, and certainly they lived normal, *material* lives. They bathed and dressed, fed themselves, wrote letters, cut their hair, raised families, and ran the business of the raajy. But for an hour a day in the Shaasak's White Chamber, they sought to slip away from their clutching minds and step into the limitlessness of the unconscious, beyond the claims of time. Not all of them found it so easy to do, and only once in ten generations was a natural adept born, like Ilarô. More frequently but still seldom was an adept made during his or her own lifetime, the Shaasak being the closest example in the current epoch. In truth many members of the samgha were not very good at all at what the Shaasak was teaching them, but this was a culture of practice that he was elaborating, whether its duration should be long or brief, not a hierarchy of performance. The children in particular were naturals at meditation—they had so much less than their parents to un-learn; but even the fully formed adults who came to reside in the sky-lodge after half a lifetime in some less lofty municipality and found themselves struggling with this revived practice out of the ancient ways, even the diplomats from distant city-states who presumably were used to every kind of exotic solemnity and yet found this ritual a pointless soporific the first few times they tried it, even the merchant princes who came to the palace to make headway on tariff issues or to petition for an extension of some commercial prerogative and found the daily sittings, which they attended out of courtesy, a bafflingly unproductive event, even the patricians who arrived for a month's stay on matters of social intercourse with the Shaasak, privately imagining themselves above any such endeavor as group meditation, which, it should be noted, they were never required nor even encouraged to attend, even those who found the stillness of the exercise pure torture, eventually, if they kept at it long enough, were faced with its startling benefit. All these skeptics were, in the final moment, amazed at what their guided meditations revealed: a fundamental truth had been locked inside of them all along, a truth so crucial that some primal power had coded

it backwards and forwards along every chain of chemical information in their bodies, embossed it on the hardness of their very bones
and suffused it through the wetness of their brains, encrypted it in
every instinct and spelled it out in every cell, a truth both quantum
in arrangement and galactic in consequence, a truth that pervaded
the gossamer of consciousness and projected itself out into the stuff
of all life and all existence everywhere, and not of existence as it must
someday become, but as it was today, this minute, this very second,
a truth that was simple yet total: love was the first law and the last.
Love was the first law and the last.

This is where things *really* got interesting. To quote from the
famous interstitial in the long poem of the Zaabta of Souls:

> *Love is the jot and yet love is the giant*
> *Love is on no earthly edict reliant*

In other couplets too intricate in Bhaashan to make rhyme in
modern translation and still keep semantically intact (a process that
always seems to blunt the original in any case), it goes on to explain
that:

> *as molten metal can be poured any which way to shape*
> *whatever physical structure is envisioned, so can love be made*
> *with the fashioning mind into any other attitude, and from*
> *any attitude, any reality. And the source will never run dry!*

The long poem of the Zaabta, and the inner explorations of
the Shaasak in turn, debunked scarcity, proving sufficiency. Rules
of supply and demand were discredited here; economic doctrines
obliterated. Here the only resource that mattered was self-generat-
ing, self-replenishing, endless. Love was the first law and the last.
Why this truth of both the metaphysical *and* physical universe was
not taught to every child from birth was a mystery greater than the

marvel of the law itself. And yet Asha, the least likely of seers, had perceived it already, perceived it while *deprived* of love for five long years. Even then she had sensed that love was ineradicable, that *it* was the sole reality and hatred merely the twitch of fear performing its shadow-dance in the corner of love's vivid field. During the tribulation of these five years Asha had divined it was love alone that was still making her heart pump, her lungs breathe, her limbs move, her eyes see and cry. How could the Shaasak not have adored her as a daughter the instant he realized who she was? She was the daughter any father would have prayed for.

viii

Over the next nine days the Shaasak and his guest were constantly together. In the mornings they could be seen on the high path over the Malachite Sea, the Shaasak a gaunt dash of violet beside Asha in her new silver-mesh sari, which the Jaanam had sent as a special gift. Often they walked the Shaasak's field of ziqqurats, those mounds of blue grass shaped by the Shaasak's gardeners into their concentric square-on-square stacks. In the afternoons, when light poured into the sky-lodge like honey off the sun, they strolled the colonnade of pear trees and circled the black reflecting pool made from crushed tons of onyx. The Shaasak took Asha through the palace's cultural galleries too: the map room with its collection of charts and logbooks from the ships of the aboriginal mariners; the small museum of natural history, featuring the fossils and skeletons of creatures that had gone extinct from the world—and a new exhibit of butterflies under glass, so implausibly patterned with stripes, dots, and spirals that their didactic panels described each gorgeous insect as if it were an intentional work of art; the display room of ancient glassware: vases and vials, cage cups and cameo-etched vessels, glass tesserae for mosaics, gold glass medallions portraitizing families

from the distant past, a three-thousand-year-old cinerary urn, several
of its pieces still iridescing the color of a pink pearl or a peacock's
neck; a corridor of dioramas of the raajy's anterior tribes, including
a full-sized clan of lifelike hemolactics; and the ever-popular hall of
astropoetics.

But most of all Asha loved the secret gardens, flowering to life
where you least expected: through a back door in a kitchen pantry;
down a sliding pole under a bed; up through a ladder in the ceiling
of your bathroom. You might be deep inside the palace and with
one small turn find yourself in a water garden whose streamlets ran
through stone funnels in the floor in such a way and with such a
mix of tones from liquids rushing at different speeds as to play you
a musical work composed specifically for the space in which you
stood.

In the evenings, before dinner, Asha and the Shaasak strolled
the palace's lunar garden, where the beaming moon caused fronds
of photoreactive plants to wiggle like silvery fingers. It was also here
that, at other hours on her own, Asha sat on a bench scanning the
sky for its rarities, like the occasional, faint spot of light opposite the
sun's invisible nighttime position, called a "countershine," believed to
be a solar reflection in the dust that lay above the envelope of gases
surrounding the earth; and the even rarer lunar halo, by-product of a
night sky replete with ice crystals.

After dinner, Asha and the Shaasak often sat fireside in the
latter's private reading room, a cozy annex to the main library at
the sky-lodge. Asha had been tickled to find that both in the range
and depth of its holdings the library was notably less splendid than
the athainaaium at Palace Isha—and indeed the Shaasak himself,
a true bibliophile, openly lamented the gaps in the royal collection,
particularly its dearth of original editions of the poets and epicists of
antiquity. Also his reading room was a bit dark. Watching him squint
at a page as he read aloud to her, Asha promised to send a hundred

cords of whitewood, whose white fires were easier on the eyes for nighttime reading, though the wood itself was all but impossible to find outside the far north.

But more than the joys of a room full of books, more than the mystery-nooks and hidden chambers that the sky-lodge contained, more than its musical water gardens, its alcoves paneled in precious metals and minerals, more than its galleries of pear trees, more even than any of the terraces and overlooks ringing the great palace itself, Asha felt drawn to, and with the Shaasak daily paced, the cliff-walk above the Malachite Sea. They discussed no philosophies along this lonely lane nor any profound states of being, they simply appraised the waves and the wildflowers. Where the cliff-walk ended, they would take a seat for a quarter hour on the Shaasak's favorite bench, and here each day he asked Asha for more information than had been offered in her White Chamber talk. First he asked her to describe day by day the course of her yaatra. He liked hearing about Asha the autodidact, about how she had learned to do the things that no one had taught her. Next he wished to hear more about the careers of her parents. Penultimately he requested a more detailed history on her childhood at Palace Isha; and then, lastly, he wished to be given a supplement on how things had gone wrong between Asha and her husband. With a refined turn of phrase he hoped it was not unreasonable of him to ask about the discrepancy of thought between bride and groom ignored at the time of the marriage, given the sequence of events that had been its disastrous result.

Sometimes they stayed together in the White Chamber after the day's sitting, members of the samgha glancing back as they exited through the room's high platinum doors, left open whenever the space was not in official use. After a few days they realized that the Shaasak and Asha were not always speaking to each other, but continuing to meditate together. Having heard her account of her life, they knew that only months earlier, and for several years before that, Asha had been a davaphile for whom pure concentration was beyond reach, and that, to put a point on it, before coming to Aakaash-Nivaas she had never meditated a single time in her life. So to see her practicing now, knee to knee with the Silent Shaasak no less, made her come alive to them in a hundred different ways, not least as the love that Ilarô had died for.

Often the Jaanam came in to sit with them too. She was warmer than she had seemed to Asha at first, less self-absorbed; really she was just extraordinarily busy. An engineer by training, and perhaps the best-educated person in the raajy, she oversaw the building program of a kingdom. Her taste was refined yet experimental. She could improve any architect's conception with six strokes of her pen. "We're designing buildings to last centuries," she would often remind her drafters, "it's my job to make sure they're not out of date in a decade."

One night after dinner, when the Jaanam was called away to deal with the collapse of a bridge under construction, Asha was sent for, to keep the Shaasak company in his wife's absence. They sat together under the starry dome of his solarium. After a while the Shaasak took a necklace of shaanadaar diamonds from his pocket: Ilarô's choker. The gems shone like a string of black moons, and with sudden embarrassment Asha realized that the Shaasak was giving them to her.

"Oh, Mahima, no, I couldn't possibly!"

"Couldn't you?" The Shaasak was as unused to his gifts being declined as Asha was to declining gifts. "And why not?"

"Because I always meant for you to have this necklace *back* again!"

"Except it wasn't mine to *take* back. It belonged to Ilarô."

"But they're *shaanadaar* diamonds! *You're* the only one who's supposed to wear shaanadaar diamonds!"

"The custom, Asha, and it's no more than that, a custom, not a law, is that only the Shaasak may wear them, or whomsoever he gives them to. These diamonds I gave to Ilarô, not on loan, but forever, to do with as he liked, and now they belong to you, whom Ilarô gave them to in turn."

Unsure just what she wanted out of the moment, Asha switched tracks:

"Is the legend true, Mahima? If you crush a shaanadaar diamond, will it actually release a strand of trapped starlight back into the sky?"

"I couldn't say. I'm unaware of anyone ever having crushed one to find out. I suppose because the loss would be prohibitive."

"But were you never tempted yourself? Even with one little stone? If anyone could afford it, it's you."

Of all the many ways in which the Shaasak might have deflected such a question on the grounds that it was unsuitable to allude to his wealth, or even answered it vaguely, to be polite while revealing little, what he said next was nothing that any partner in conversation would have been in a position to guess:

"Well, Asha, since you bring it up, I'll tell you this … when I was a boy, at the age of nine, I was something of a would-be physicist *and* an aspiring metaphysician. I made it my business to conduct any number of experiments of my own design involving the use of photoscopes and macroscopes, magnifying glasses and the leaves of rare plants, matchsticks, chemistry kits, frog's blood, and formulae said to harness the power of ghosts—all in search of the ever-elusive nexus between science and tattvameemaansa. And one night in particular, when the rest of the world was in bed beginning to dream, I slipped down to the tool room, then up to the roof beneath a sky graced by no moon but alive with the flurries of the cosmos. There I intended to conduct the experiment of all experiments, the components of which were a pair of pliers, a shaanadaar bracelet acquired earlier in the day from my mother's jewel drawer, and my own observing self. Sadly, the experiment's outcome was neither to confirm nor disprove the shaanadaar legend, but rather to learn that, *at* the age of nine, and my zeal for unlocking the mysteries of existence notwithstanding, while I may have possessed a certain youthful strength of mind, I lacked the corporeal force required to test the premise in question. The diamonds simply would not crack. The following morning, while my parents were in their solarium for breakfast, I managed to spirit the bracelet back into its drawer in my mother's dressing room, a lucky thing for me since by pure coincidence she appeared later that day wearing it to complement a black-and-white sari at a lunchtime recital of madhuratshruti, performed by the cohort of young geetakaaron who lived with us at the sky-lodge in those days, a recital at which I myself sat glumly ignoring the music and in a state of not inconsiderable disappointment at the failure of my effort to conjure and document one of the more fabled phenomena in nature, though at least I'd left no one the wiser about my mischief or its non-result. And in the sixty-six years *since* then, not a living soul has once posed a question that's disposed me to share the details of the night I tried to send starlight back to the stars—until now."

Asha bit her lip in delight, so charming the Shaasak that it felt to him, with perfect illogic, as if his experiment of sixty-six years earlier had been a fated prelude to this very conversation.

"Now back to the matter at hand," he said in mock sternness, "which is you taking rightful possession of *these* diamonds."

He tried again to give Asha the choker, though she still resisted: "I couldn't, I *couldn't*. It's a treasure!"

"People are treasures, my dear, never objects, which are only ever things."

Asha fought on, but the Shaasak was the Shaasak and he was going to have his way. "You can do with it as you wish," he said. "Put it on and never take it off, vault it up until the end of time, auction it off to the highest bidder." He gestured for Asha to lower her head; reluctantly she obeyed. The Shaasak placed the choker around her neck and fastened its hidden clasp.

When Asha lifted her head again, she was beaming. "Thank you, Mahima," she whispered. In response to her quick turnaround, not to mention the white burst of her smile, the Shaasak allowed himself a moment's fatherly pleasure. He knew it was no greed for jewels that had convinced her, but simply her love of Ilarô, who had worn these black spherules around his own neck for six years, and he was sure that Asha would have been just as glad to have back any trinket of wooden beads that had been the geetakaar's.

Asha lowered her head again: she was crying now. The Shaasak held out his arms and gathered her up, letting her sob against him and onto his sarong. He took love and gave love with dignity, but generously, and he knew that love could be a mess. He had no children of his own to ease through moments like these, only twin nephews who were too emphatically manly at their peculiar age of fifteen to require his affection. He admired them anyway, though he seldom saw them: they lived at too great a distance from Aakaash-Nivaas, in the desert-palace of their father, the Shaasak's brother, three hundred miles to the south. Here in his own home, which he hadn't left in a decade, the Shaasak was always looking to offer whatever he could to those young persons with whom he came into contact. He was a man who rose up in life each time he gave something of himself away, a good thing in a king. Asha, he felt, needed him now.

It was not the Shaasak, however, but his wife who finally brought a more practical attention to bear on the question of what Asha would need in the longer term. At breakfast the next morning, seated on a newly built balcony jutting out atop wolfram-wood pylons a full thirty feet from the end of the sky-lodge proper and over the sea—land brazenly annexed out of the air itself—the Jaanam, after briefing her husband on the bridge calamity of the previous night, turned the discussion to Asha's plans. But first a word about the matter of the bridge: the collapse of this half-finished structure only two miles from the sky-lodge had been the result of a midday tremor, though a minor one in this land of seismic liveliness, yet had still meant death for three men working its span.

"Never another plain wooden bridge as long as I'm alive!" the Jaanam vowed. "I don't care if wolfram-wood *does* cost twenty times as much! If we can't get all we need, then we'll do without new bridges altogether! We can all walk the long way around every river in the raajy!"

We might like to keep the content of this principled eruption in mind, as Asha would; its recollection should prove of value sooner rather than later. But now to the breakfast that followed it: the Shaasak ate his yoghurt, the Jaanam her grilled bread and bean curd, both sipped pomegranate juice, and Asha spooned at a melon. Then the Jaanam made reference to their guest's longer-term needs, raising the question of what length of time Asha planned to stay with them.

"Asha must stay as long as she likes," the Shaasak said.

"Of course she must, Suravaraman—as this was the Shaasak's given name—and we'd be glad if she stayed for months. I only wonder if that's the best we can do for her. After all, she didn't come here for a holiday."

"She came here to deliver difficult news."

"She came here, I think, to ask a favor."

The Shaasak swiveled to Asha and saw in her eyes it was true. Asha gave no indication of being embarrassed at whatever she had in mind, though she was apparently still in the grip of some strong reluctance to mention it. The Shaasak knew what to do. Using a small trick of liberation, and speaking in jurisprudential phraseology that he was devising on the spot, he offered Asha official exemption and personal forgiveness in advance for anything she cared to ask him within the next sixty seconds, no matter how shocking or presumptuous, warning her to speak quickly though, because once her minute was up, the normal rules of conduct would again apply. Asha laid her business on the table in a twentieth of the time allotted to her:

"Mahima, I want a divorce."

The Jaanam nodded in satisfaction at having guessed correctly. The Shaasak's reaction could not be read. A lighthearted maneuver had been used by him to prod Asha into declaring herself; no light-hearted reply would follow her declaration. Divorce, in a land of lifetime marriage, was a serious matter. They had all learned enough from Asha to understand the troubles at Palace Isha and to appre-ciate this was no frivolous request she was making, and it was clear that something would have to be done about Cabaan in any case. Still, divorce as such did not exist. The Shaasak had his powers and could do as he wished, but the raajy's jurisprudence was not to be bypassed lightly. Asha might have done better by petitioning for an annulment, no simple thing either but at least an action with a basis in the civil code. In fact an annulment had been her original idea in setting out for Aakaash-Nivaas. This had changed during her yaatra. Day by day, she had begun to question what an annulment would truly mean, until one morning she had woken up beneath Tapti's long shadow knowing she could not abide any royally sanctioned fantasy of the marriage never having happened. Let it have hap-pened. Let it have happened exactly the way she had lived it. But also let it end.

"A divorce," the Shaasak said. He was supposing out loud more than objecting.

"A divorce," the Jaanam articulated more pointedly, and speak-ing to Asha, "runs counter to the law of the land." With masterful neutrality, the envy of every ambassador at the sky-lodge, she turned to the Shaasak and added: "Of course, even the land changes over time. We add and subtract to it ourselves, every day of the year." She rose from the breakfast table, kissed her husband on his cheek, whispered into his ear her parting love for him the way he liked (the Shaasak was as much a man as a monarch and said so often)—and went off to begin her morning.

Gesturing for an attendant to come close, the Shaasak canceled his appointments for the day. "We'll have no interruptions," he told Asha, "and by dinnertime, we'll have all this settled, one way or another."

✢ ✢ ✢

They spent the day in what the Shaasak referred to as "Ilarô's garden." Odd, Asha thought, for an indoor space that contained no plants whatsoever: not an orchid, not a succulent, not even a tamaatar vine. It was ten walls of polished stone rising into a green sky—an impression of light off the Malachite Sea—and a fountain burbling through the centuries. A hypaethral retreat at the center of the palace's layered hulk.

The Shaasak and Jaanam cared little for material things, a quality they had transferred to Ilarô, who had grown up under their roof and absorbed their moral as well as aesthetic influence. This didn't stop them from encouraging a love of beauty among their subjects: in painting, in sculpture, in architecture. And as for the art of the garden, they were its great patrons. A battalion of horticulturalists lived and worked among the several thousand permanent residents of the sky-lodge, maintaining the palace's flower gardens and rock gardens, its sunken gardens and hothouses, its adjacent arboretum, its paths lined with wildflowers, its herbarium. They also kept up its illusion of floral adventitiousness. You could turn any corner of the hundred thousand here and stumble onto a seemingly forgotten niche of marigolds in bloom; you could come to a low, wrought-platinum portal at the end of a breezeway, bend down and climb through, and find yourself in a moss-covered courtyard so soft to the step that you yearned to lie down and curl up not on its weathered benches but right there on the ground. Hummingbirds thrummed the air in these spaces, high-speed sprites from all nine of the hummingbird clades: topazes and hermits, mangoes and mountaingems, brilliants, bees, emeralds, showy-crested and giants: nectar-robbers darting from blossom to blossom. Even when you missed spotting them, you could hear the music of their wingbeats, or as Asha remembered Omala once explaining it, "the oscillations and harmonics generated by the rapid downstrokes and upstrokes of their unique means of flight." To bring them into the palace's interior gardens, they were lured using sugar cubes infused with pear juice, hidden in the planters lining the hallways. Equally by design among botanical matters at the sky-lodge was the aromatic air of the place: each day before breakfast and again after dinner, gardeners carrying soft wands walked the palace stroking the branches of citronella and eucalyptus, releasing fragrance from foliage.

But Ilarô's garden was bare as a cave. Sitting in it now, listening to the Shaasak speak, Asha guessed why: the acoustics. This must have been the spot where Ilarô gave his recitals. Its ten stone walls and stone floor, its lack of adornment, its rooflessness all made for a clarity of sound unique among the palace's eight thousand rooms, concentrating the mind on what was *heard* here. Asha was about to ask if this was right when six dark spots appeared on the floor, a cluster of shadows moving in formation from right to left across the room.

She and the Shaasak looked up: in the decagon of green where a ceiling would ordinarily have been they saw six gubbaare passing beneath the sun. These were no sailboats of the sky for a passenger or two, they were immense objects: long rather than round and moving without sails of any kind, entirely propeller-driven.

"Our new fleet," the Shaasak said. "Under construction for two years and ready at last."

Asha wasn't sure if it was satisfaction at progress or regret of the same that she was hearing in the Shaasak's voice as he described the feat of engineering that had produced these impressive craft, including the design of each ship's large underside compartment, roomy enough for a crew of twelve. On the other hand she now had her answer as to why *Omala's* little gubbaara had cost so much. On top of the small fortune the sky-wrights of the south regularly asked in payment for their work, they had charged that exorbitant premium for taking the job because they were already busy building this fleet for the Shaasak!

Each airship overhead and its shadow underfoot passed out of sight in exact pairs, like entangled particles synchronizing their actions at a distance. Of course it was not an example of that mysterious principle of nonlocality in which objects may mirror each other's behavior even from as far apart as opposite sides of the universe—a principle that still fascinates and eludes us today, six millennia after the morning that Asha and the Shaasak sat together in Ilarô's garden; it was instead simply the play of light upon the world as we classically experience it. All the same, in the moment Asha intuited something of the higher principle. It even occurred to her that two *people* might correlate nonlocally. She raised her hand to the sky, knowing the Shaasak would think she was waving to the crews of the gubbaare, though really she was waving to the other end of the cosmos, where she imagined the dead might reside, and wondering if Ilarô's hand might not be rising identically at that far edge of the stars. Had she been a trained vigyaanik she might even have tried putting her intuition of entanglement into words, and from words into formulae. But the moment passed, and the insight evanesced.

Asha and her host returned to a previous state of contemplation. For a while after this the Shaasak brought up impersonal topics: the once-a-century hailstorm that had cracked window panes and shredded palm fronds a week before Asha's arrival … the growing number of young people riding the waves of the Malachite Sea on their surfplanks—until Asha realized that what he was doing, in his invisible way, rather than plunging them directly into the question of the divorce, was giving her the chance to take over and guide the conversation there herself. As a matter of fact, she did have something else in mind that she wanted to touch on first. Since the Shaasak hadn't been unwilling to discuss any other aspect of Ilarô's life over the past several days, Asha felt comfortable now bringing up the circumstances of his death, which were still confusing to her. Cabaan had supplied the particulars over dinner at Palace Isha, a week afterwards. In the mind-pause of the nepentee then, Asha could only hear without comprehending what was said to her, including how, in the final moment, Ilarô had given in to Cabaan, or, to use Cabaan's word, "surrendered." A point that she had chosen not to include in her White Chamber talk.

"But if Ilarô *did* surrender, Mahima, what does that mean? Or was it only Cabaan misconstruing something very different that actually happened?"

"No, Asha. Probably not."

Even here, in the safety of the Shaasak's house, Asha felt the sting of reality on her fingertips each time she reached out to shape a fantasy of the world.

"Give me what you hold dearest ..." the Shaasak recited from that beloved passage in the long poem of the Zaabta, "... the results of such giving are infinite."

"Are you saying, Mahima, that what Ilarô held dearest was his life, which he gave up because he knew it would defeat Cabaan in some infinite sense?"

"I'm saying that what he gave up, Asha, was *you*."

Neither of them spoke for a time; until:

"Mahima, tell me something else please. Is it true that Ilarô was Ekko Jagaaya?"

The Shaasak nodded—and Asha's face flushed with rage. It was a possession: she struck the Shaasak on his shoulder with her open hand. "But how could you have let him leave then?" she said. "How could you have let such a person out into all the dangers of the world?" She pounded the Shaasak's shoulder over and over, unable to bear her losses: the blessings of her childhood, her father and mother, Omala, and now Ilarô, which not all the Shaasak's lessons or the truth of his sittings or his beautiful recitation of a moment ago were enough to make up for.

The Shaasak, who had never been touched unbidden in all his seventy-five years, much less struck, at this moment decided he would do anything for Asha that she asked.

"An Ekko Jagaaya!" Asha cried out. "Once every ten generations! Mahima, how could you have let him *leave*?"

"How could I have forced him to stay? He was a geetakaar. It was his pleasure to sing for people. He was not my prisoner."

Asha wept—and coughed—and then sneezed twice, which sent a hot itch down her forearms, her body speaking the disarray of her emotions.

"I'd have given up even *knowing* him," she insisted, "if that would have kept him here—and alive!"

The Shaasak smiled hearing this, which to Asha seemed an appalling reaction, until she realized just what she had said.

Lunch arrived. Asha wiped her tears and blew her nose. Neither she nor the Shaasak had much of an appetite, but they both ate to keep up their strength, the Shaasak because he was old and had a great deal still to do in the world, Asha because she was young and had such a long way to go. When their plates were taken away, Asha burst out laughing in strange spurts and gulps, the way it happens after a shock.

"Breathe deeply," the Shaasak said.

Asha breathed deeply. Glancing down afterwards, she saw a

line of ants crossing the garden's stone floor.

"Mahima, you have ants."

The Shaasak sighed. "We have ants. Though at least we don't have termites, a larger problem for a wooden house on a cliff." He watched the march of insects across the garden. "We leave strips of papaya hidden in the corners, to give them what they want and still keep the fruit on the trees for ourselves. It's not a clean victory, but it's a successful coexistence."

A breeze ran down from the sky and circled the garden's ten walls, cooling Asha's forehead. She relaxed her mind too. The hiatus was brief: she felt the moment coming to advance her plan. Since working out a way forward was the day's agenda, she felt not quite so guilty about her plotting as she might have otherwise; nevertheless it may be surprising to hear that in her approach Asha was about to take inspiration not from Ilarô, not from her parents, not from the Shaasak himself or even from the Jaanam, but from Cabaan. He *was* extremely skillful at identifying what motivated the people he came in contact with: you don't make yourself rich at fifteen without that kind of talent—or that kind of technique. So why *not* lay claim to Cabaan's practicality? If ever there was a moment to try it, Asha told herself, this was it. Right now.

"Mahima, when I asked you to put an end to my marriage, I had it in mind not just to beg a favor, but to offer you something in return."

The Shaasak seemed amused. "My dear, is it your wish to negotiate with me?"

"Would you mind that, Mahima?"

"Not at all. It happens to be something I'm used to."

"Then may I?"

"If you like."

Asha forced down the urge to vomit. It was less the pressure of preparing to bargain with a king that was turning her stomach than the terror at what she had to bargain with. She didn't have too little to offer, but too much. "Give it up!" her father had urged in the dream of the moon-viewing pavilion. "Give it all up!" But now that the moment was here, it required a strength of mind that Asha was unused to relying on, let alone revealing.

She began so earnestly that the Shaasak had to hold in a smile:

"Mahima, I understand that the law does not provide for divorce, and that, while the prerogative is yours to dissolve a marriage if you feel such an action is right, setting the law aside to do this is not something you can easily allow."

Not for nothing was the Silent Shaasak so named. Most assumed the sobriquet to be a reference to his wordless voyages of the mind, but those closest to him knew it derived from how little he liked the constant discharge of opinions that was a symptom of the untreated human condition. He tended to listen to the preambles of supplicants without replying in word, gesture, or expression.

"I also know," Asha said, "that during the Age of the Builders, the law itself was an instrument of each Shaasak's personal authority, and that grants of land, agricultural concessions, titles, even the right to marry or adopt or in rare cases divorce were, at a certain level of consequence, transactional. Payments were made by petitioners to the public purse in name, though in effect to the Shaasakon themselves. In this way the kings of antiquity amassed their private wealth, however much or little of it was spent on the good of the raajy from reign to reign."

"Happily, Asha, such a state of affairs has long since passed. Today we govern from Aakaash-Nivaas in a more transparent and, I should hope, more consistent manner."

"Yes, but it wasn't *all* bad, was it Mahima? If both parties to an exchange are clear-minded about their purpose, and if no one else is disadvantaged as a result, mightn't the old way of doing things be a useful basis for decision-making in an otherwise intricate circumstance?"

The Shaasak gave no reply, so Asha nerved herself for what she had to do next. "I realize what a serious request a divorce petition is," she said, "but a divorce, Mahima, is without doubt or alternative what I'm in need of. In exchange … I offer you Palace Isha."

She leaned back a little, on reflex. Her heart was disconcerting her with its absurd palpitations, but she felt that she had more or less maintained an outward composure proportional to the moment.

The Shaasak practiced a reticence that was lengthy even for him. In doing so he was honoring the magnitude of Asha's proposal, though from Asha's point of view he seemed to be conjuring a vision of her home, his gaze moving along its line of domes and spheres, its crescents and minarets, its forests and surrounding mountains, taking all of it in, judging its merits and flaws, assessing its cost of upkeep and its worldly worth.

"Palace Isha," he said, as if to summarize the offer.

"Yes, Mahima. For reasons I've explained, I've ceded its surrounding lands to Cabaan, but the residence itself and all it contains still belong to me. The palace is no minor edifice. And its contents include an athainaaium which, if it's not impertinent of me to say, would fill every gap in your collection here at the sky-lodge and make your library the finest in the raajy."

"You would trade away your father's house, Asha?"

"My father resides in my memory now, Mahima. He is indestructible there."

It was a good answer. Impressed, the Shaasak seemed to be considering the proposal. After a time he said, "Asha, I thank you for your offer and I'll answer you in the following way. Please remove your necklace."

Asha took the necklace off and handed it over, wondering if her audacity had been too much after all.

"There are a hundred and twelve shaanadaar diamonds in the world," the Shaasak said. "Previously there were a hundred and twenty-two, but my great-aunt misplaced a pair of earrings. They all derive from a single mine in the eastern desert that collapsed in my grandparents' day. So there will be no more stones like these. There will be others, rare in their own way, but never any more with these same qualities. They're rather like a beautiful family whose line, after a long appearance in the world, is nearing an end. Because one by one, over time, each diamond on my bracelet and on the bracelet of the Jaanam, each diamond on your choker, on the chokers worn by my nephews and on the ring worn by their father, will be damaged or lost or destroyed, until, finally, none will remain. Now, Asha, take back your necklace and put it on again."

Asha did as she was told.

"Do you follow the arithmetic of it?" the Shaasak said.

"I think so, Mahima."

"Good. Then I'll add only this: due to their flawlessness no less than their scarcity, the eighteen diamonds you now wear are worth as much as Palace Isha itself, all its domes, gardens, and books, every stone and step it's built of, and very likely a trunkful of platinum into the bargain."

Asha felt the stones on her choker, which until now had been as light on the skin as they were smooth, suddenly push down into the back of her neck and press up into the circle of her throat— which was odder than you know, since she had never had an adverse reaction to expensive jewelry in all her life. She straightened herself up again, and this is what happened, unexpectedly, next: out of the continuum of imagination sprang a new plan. Asha's heart jumped at the thought of it, but she breathed deeply to regulate herself.

"I understand, Mahima. If you'd needed money, you could have simply kept the choker in the first place. But you don't need what Palace Isha is worth. It only amounts to a fraction of the wealth that's already yours, which is more than enough."

"That's right, Asha."

"You don't desire another palace."

"No, Asha."

"You're not anxious for more houses or gardens."

"I'm not."

"Needing less is better than wanting more in any case."

"Just so."

"And yet, Mahima, what about wolfram-wood? Do you also have enough of that too?"

She startled him. The Silent Shaasak had been startled by a girl of twenty-two.

"Go on," he said.

Asha took her chance. For some time now she had been listening closely when discussion at the sky-lodge turned to that vital commodity which, of all the many substances that the earth supplies, Asha herself happened to know something more about than the average individual: wolfram-wood. There was simply not enough to go around of this strongest, lightest, most reliable of all building materials. From Cabaan Asha knew its value in the marketplace, from the Jaanam she knew its scarcity as against its importance, from the Shaasak she had learned it was the critical component in his new fleet of airships. Asha knew that wolfram-wood could make the safest bridges, the longest aqueducts, and could even be used to retrofit quake-damaged structures against the threat of future calamity; she knew that, when fashioned into the implements of agriculture, wolfram-wood could lighten loads and double yields, that in the breadth of its applications it could advance, improve—and here was the indispensable thing— *save* human life. Most of all, on the subject of wolfram-wood, Asha had in her possession a fact unknown to all the official planners at the sky-lodge, unknown to the Jaanam and her engineers, unknown to the Silent Shaasak himself: there was more to be had than anyone guessed. Cabaan had been undersupplying the market to drive up the price. He had told her so, proud of his scheme and pleased with his secret. It was a secret she was about to give up.

"As I've described, Mahima, Palace Isha supplies more wolfram-wood than any other producer in the hemisphere. Our official estimate says that we can turn out a thousand maatras a year. Our official estimate is a lie. We have twenty times the pure wolfram beneath our feet than my husband has allowed to be known. From which our kuroop trees can produce at least ten times more wolfram-wood per year than he's said."

The shock to Asha's interlocutor upon hearing this could only have been profound. He showed not a single sign of it, merely gesturing for Asha to continue.

"Cabaan hides the true numbers to inflate the price. He styles himself a one-man kaartel. We're too far for the Jaanam's engineers to visit. They've had to take Cabaan at his word, or more precisely the word of his go-betweens, whom he has deceived. And his go-betweens, unwittingly, have deceived *you*. But if my marriage contract were voided, authority over Palace Isha and the populace of our northern annex would revert to *me*. Cabaan would still own the haiktars I've given him along with the kuroops he's planted on them, but he would have no further power over our *people*. The staff of the household, Cabaan's labor force of aapravaaseen who reside on the premises, every living soul between the glaciers and the mountains, "between ice and alp" as we say, would turn to *me* for direction. Cabaan's enterprise relies on the people who make it run. If I were to stop them from running it, all commercial activity at Palace Isha would come to a halt. Cabaan would have no choice but to negotiate with me for what I want—and what I want is to improve by ten times the flow of wolfram-wood to Aakaash-Nivaas."

The Shaasak nodded without conveying any sentiment. Only after a daunting pause did he speak again, though not to reply to Asha directly, and in a voice revealing to Asha the first hint of weariness—or possibly even frailty—that she had perceived in her host in all the days she had spent with him. He said:

"Your husband, the Vikaant Cabaan, stands accused of crimes for which he must answer. We will send a marshal-at-arms to Palace Isha to see to this—and adjudicate."

Leaning forward, Asha took gentle hold of the Shaasak's hand.

"No, Mahima, I'm terribly sorry, but that's something *I* can't allow. I was the one who invited Cabaan into my parents' house, I am responsible for what has happened there, and I am the one who must right what's gone wrong. I don't wish to contradict you, but this is a decision that *I've* made. It must be me who sees to Cabaan. I once said as much to Ilarô out of guilt—I say it now out of responsibility."

How brave Asha was becoming, the Shaasak thought. How strong she already was in her mind!

"So, Mahima, what do *you* say? May I give you what you require in exchange for what I need? Wolfram-wood for a divorce? I feel certain that the Jaanam, for one, would approve."

The Shaasak might have turned against Asha for these machinations; but as much as he loved the life of the mind, he loved the world too, and he knew that the world was where they lived. Asha had amazed him. Through her trials and pains, her disappointments and even her betrayals, she had shed her naïveté, but kept her hope. He was in awe of her even as he declared:

"We help one another because this is the purpose of our birth, Asha, not on the expectation of favors returned. You will have what you have asked, and I will take nothing in exchange. Your marriage to Cabaan will be dissolved."

ix

The day before Asha's departure she received a note from the royal midwife. Amaravati hoped that Asha's many sessions with the Shaasak, which had become an enduring topic of interest among the residents of the sky-lodge, had gone well, and asked that Asha remember not to leave without seeing her. It was the implication of the word "remember" that piqued Asha, since she hadn't made any plan to visit Amaravati in the first place. But the request sounded friendly enough, so after breakfast Asha made her way to the north side of the palace.

Amaravati's suite of rooms included a greenhouse and adjacent studio where she grew the plants, algae, fungi, and foodstuffs needed to craft her tinctures and treatments, liniments, balms, and embrocations, her oils and acids (both amino and essential fatty), her extracts, physics, antidotes, and correctives. After giving Asha a tour of the workspace, the midwife selected from her shelves three vials of dark liquid made, she seemed to enjoy explaining, from plants and fruits rich in beneficial phytochemicals: beets, blackberries, cherries, cabbage. The scientific term that Amaravati mentioned was "anthocyanidins." She enumerated for her visitor their anti-inflammatory properties as well as their salutary effect on circulation, prescribing them for Asha twice a day, immediately upon waking and again before bed.

Asha, with gratitude, declined.

"Well, I wouldn't try to be *too* self-sufficient," Amaravati warned pleasantly.

"How do you mean?" Asha had no idea what Amaravati was talking about and was even a little bothered by this unbalanced conversation.

"I mean I can see you're in good health, but when pregnant and entering the second term, even the hardiest woman on earth can't expect not to need a *little* supplemental nutrition."

"*Preg*nant!" Asha laughed. "What could I ever have said to make you think I was *preg*nant?"

A peep of alarm slipped from Amaravati. "Asha, you can't possibly be unaware that you're in your fifteenth week."

"Well, that's beyond absurd."

Amaravati held her tongue; but her eyes gave her away.

"Amaravati, *stop* it!" Asha still thought the midwife was making a type of odd joke.

"But surely you've realized something was happening to you," Amaravati said. "You won't have had your maahavaaree in months."

"Which has happened to me half a dozen times in my life! Whenever my appetite goes! I was in the desert eating *leaves* for weeks on end! Of course my maahavaaree stopped!"

"You've been here eating properly long enough for your cycle to start up again—if not for the pregnancy."

A great weight clamped onto Asha. It felt to her as if she were no longer standing on the earth, but on some giant world with triple the earth's gravity, leaving her heart and lungs too weak to do their work. She tried taking short, controlled breaths to counter it, but hyperventilated and had to sit down to keep from passing out.

Amaravati brought a cold compress, dabbing it against Asha's temples with Asha whispering dismally:

"You can't be right."

But Amaravati knew what she knew. The common belief that royal midwives possessed such honed powers of perception that they could make out a newly pregnant woman at fifty feet was more than an exaggeration, if not quite a myth. With respect to exactly *how* they detected the pregnant woman's status, the truth was less esoteric than receiving electromagnetic signals from the fetus, less animalian than sniffing estrogen in the air, but perhaps more sensitive than either. It was the power of sound. Amaravati had been trained to hear a fetal heartbeat, and let's recall that after Ilarô's Memento of the Dead, in the White Chamber just before Asha's long talk to the samgha, the midwife had embraced Asha, holding her tight for a long moment. With her ear to Asha's body, Amaravati had known about the pregnancy from that moment.

"Amaravati, are you absolutely sure? Sure beyond even the smallest doubt?"

"As I've said, you're in your fifteenth week."

"But how can I—

By accident Asha bit her tongue so hard that she screamed as if stabbed. She shot up from her chair, spoke something unintelligible, and ran from the room.

Back in her own suite, she threw herself onto the bed and pressed her face into a pillow. The old reflex to escape was still with her; but weaned from every substance to achieve it, sleep was the only choice.

It didn't work the way it used to. She found herself in a nightmare, running across the backlands at Palace Isha, which you simply did not do anymore, not since Cabaan's glazery had filled the air with its static charge that ignited quick-moving skin. Asha's arms and legs burst into flame. She raced for the river, but it was on fire too. So she stood there, burning without dying, until—

—she wrenched herself awake with a supreme exertion, like kicking your way out of a sealed coffin.

An hour later the Shaasak spotted her pacing a secluded stretch of the cliff-walk beneath his solarium. Coming close, he saw that her eyes were bloodshot, her face puffed from tears.

"Asha, what's happened?"

"Nothing, Mahima. Everything's fine."

That she was pregnant with a child whose father she couldn't be sure of was something she could not bring herself to say. Under the mindlessness of the nepentee she might have forgotten once or twice to prepare herself against conception before the yaun sambandh with Cabaan; or in the days just prior to the nepentee, during her brief time with Ilarô, the sheer transports of joy might have caused her to slip in her precautions. She simply did not know. How she would endure the uncertainty of it for the next many months was unimaginable. Even after giving birth, it might not be clear. If the child happened to resemble her rather than the father, favoring *her* complexion, at the chromatic midpoint between Ilarô and Cabaan, they might not be sure for some years to come. They might *never* be sure.

This would complicate everything, it might bind her to Cabaan forever; it would, at minimum, throw into question the timing of the divorce. She couldn't tell the Shaasak. Instead she fell backwards in her thoughts.

"Mahima, am I not possibly rushing things by leaving so soon? I think you were right, maybe I *should* stay a while longer. Just for a year or so. If you wouldn't mind."

Uncertain which piece of her upcoming ordeal Asha was suddenly afraid of, it was apparent to the Shaasak that she wanted to stay here less than she wanted not to go home. The idea of keeping her at the sky-lodge, not as a replacement for Ilarô, as he had first imagined, but for the joy she gave in her own right, was unappealing if it came at Asha's own expense. She would have to leave, as planned. He told her so in his own way:

"Either we face our fate, Asha, however awkwardly, or we perish avoiding it."

"But Mahima, my fate is too unfair!"

These final bursts out of Asha's girlhood shouldn't have been as charming as they were, but the Shaasak knew they were almost at an end, and they already had their nostalgic tinge. "Ancient cousin," he said, "unlike most, though not unlike myself, you have more than your own fate to contend with."

Asha lowered her voice to confess:

"Mahima, I'm afraid I may never become the person I want to be—or even the person I *need* to be."

"We become like that which we hold in our minds. That is the everlasting secret."

With this, his greatest transmission, the Shaasak left Asha alone to find her courage. She sat breathing salty gusts off the water below while the Shaasak's wisdom fixed itself in her memory: a lucky thing for Asha, since these were the last words that she would ever hear him speak.

x

Six airships hovered over the lime-frosted waves of the Malachite Sea: Asha's convoy. This was the official debut of the Shaasak's new fleet. If the still untested speed of these gubbaare confirmed the hopes of their builders, the distance to Palace Isha would be crossed in a matter of days instead of the months it had taken Asha to come the other way on foot. Proving it would mean a new age of air travel: the wolfram-wood frameworks of these craft made them light, swift, and efficient in the energy they required for propulsion; their silk skins had been braced with wolfram-wood to make them strong against the shredding winds that would have torn apart any of the older gubbaare attempting to traverse the wasteland separating the raajy's north from its south.

Some hundred residents of the sky-lodge had come to the mooring platform to see Asha off, but it was the absence of the senior resident of the palace that was the conspicuous thing: the Shaasak did not make an appearance. His note to Asha from earlier in the day had referred to a sudden matter preventing him from dividing his attention, the implication being a sudden matter of state. Asha knew it was a sudden matter of heart: the Shaasak did not have it in him to watch her go. She didn't mind; she preferred keeping him alive in her imagination instead of freezing him in her memory, the way such leave-takings will do. Anyway, the Jaanam had come in her husband's place, to honor the moment with parting good wishes of a formal variety, though she had an unofficial aside to offer as well:

"You're a better person than *I* am, Asha. If I'd been in your position, I don't know that I'd have come here asking for a divorce from my husband, I tend to think I'd have asked for a death decree."

She added a few last words of encouragement that Asha could take with her into this next phase of her yaatra, but didn't scruple to conclude:

"And once you're done putting things right for yourself at home, remember us here at Aakaash-Nivaas—and send me every maatra of wolfram-wood that you can grow."

Asha stepped into the air-raft waiting to lift her to her ship, but a familiar voice flew across the bluff to stop her:

"Asha, wait!"

Amaravati came running from a beach-level egress of the palace. Asha hopped down out of her raft, already three feet off the ground, to meet the midwife by the mooring station, where they could have a semi-private word together.

Amaravati was out of breath. Her hair, recently dyed, was clipped in a black bouquet behind her head, and her white sari was sprayed with blood.

"I would've come earlier but I've had a woman laboring all morning. We just caught triplets!"

This made a mixed impression on Asha due to her own situation, though she managed to congratulate Amaravati graciously enough. Amaravati was already onto another subject:

"Asha, I can't say how sorry I am about what happened yesterday."

"No, no, I'm the one who's sorry." Asha dropped her voice to a whisper, though the wind would have kept those nearby from overhearing. "But you have to appreciate how shocked I was. Finding out I'm pregnant, not knowing whether it's Cabaan's or Ilarô's, it's all been too much."

Amaravati twisted her face into a pretty puzzle. "Not knowing?" she laughed. "Who said anything about not knowing?"

"I'm sorry?"

"If *you* didn't know, why didn't you simply ask?"

Asha's sleepless night and all her tribulations had exhausted
her of any power to work out what Amaravati was telling her. The
midwife had to declare it out loud:

"Asha, it's not Cabaan's. You're carrying the child of our greatest geetakaar. You're going to be the mother of Ilarô's son."

The pilot of the air-raft called over to the two women, saying
he should deflate the raft's lifting bag if they were going to be delayed much longer.

"Just one moment please!" Asha called back.

She turned to the midwife again. "Amaravati, is what you've
just told me information or intuition?"

"I wouldn't have said it if I weren't sure."

"But *how?*

It would have taken hours, not seconds, to reply to Asha's
question in such a way as to fully illuminate the science as well as
the mystery of the answer; but Amaravati, used to working under
pressure, managed to convey the essence of it in a few phrases.

Asha understood. She kissed the midwife's cheek, stepped over
and into the air-raft, and was lifted into the sky.

xi

The fleet moved in formation out to sea, a bit of spectacle to
show off the gubbaare for those watching on the ground and from
the many balconies of the sky-lodge before the ships curved back
and crossed over the violet mount that shadowed the palace. They
were headed for the interior.

On the bridge of the lead ship, Asha stood beside the fleet

commander, looking down at the haven of rock and wood that had sheltered her these several weeks. She felt as if a clawed hand gripping her brain had let go in the moment of hearing Amaravati's news. And though there hadn't been time at the mooring station for Asha herself to learn in any detail about how Amaravati and her sisters in midwifery knew what they knew, nothing prevents the setting forth here of what she would eventually learn:

As has been mentioned, Amaravati could detect a fetal heartbeat without the aid of any listening device, she could hear the mother's own circulatory throb alongside the uterine pulse, two hearts syncopating within a single body, the one pumping life into the womb, the other echoing life back out. The music of it was gorgeous to the raajy's women-healers. They had a special appreciation for the biology of rhythms and tones: in ancient days, these wise-women-to-be had been schooled side by side with geetakaaron-in-training, boys and girls studying the primal sound of creation and how it had split into every thing and then every person in the universe. Midwives and geetakaaron had been cognate across the divide of sex during the first years of this vanished discipline, until they branched off in their separate directions. Where geetakaaron became shapers of sound, midwives became interpreters; where geetakaaron used sound to inspire and sometimes help conceive life, midwives used sound to guide life into the world. The ancient predecessors of Ilarô and Amaravati had been instructed in methods of vocalizing tones so potent they could create physical effects in their listeners.

These are the quantum events referred to earlier in our story. Here then are the facts: geetakaaron had once been able to shape moods in an audience not only by poetry and melody, but through a bio-sonar that altered the brain chemistry of those within range. Midwives had possessed their powers too: at one time they could induce labor when necessary with a sharply sung burst of notes—or stop labor by projecting a sonic wall around the birth canal if the child was coming prematurely, until tinctures could be prepared to keep the gestation going longer, when every extra day in the womb made a difference. Even in Asha's epoch, a thousand years after these skills had largely died out, a geetakaar who knew something of the old methods could still wrap his listeners in penetrating bands of sound that excited neurons while inspiring emotions, lifting body as well as mind to ecstatic states. Midwives too could be found who still knew how to sing in such a way as to release the neurotransmitters that modulate mood and relax the body of a woman in labor. These techniques were no longer taught—there wasn't anyone left to teach them—but is not the best definition of genius a person who can work out what she most needs to know? Ilarô, when he wished, had been able to sing or even speak his spell of sound, casting waves of pure power. Amaravati could make you feel better merely by humming at you. It shouldn't be surprising that these two had found their first romance together as teenagers living under the roof of the Shaasak.

Amaravati had perceived Asha's pregnancy as easily as seeing that her eyes were brown. That the father was Ilarô had also been obvious to her. She had known Ilarô well, she had known the signature of his heartbeat because she had listened to it for years. To those who studied the sound-splittings of creation, every heartbeat was as distinctive as any voice, and the signature of Ilarô's heart had been reborn in the heartbeat of his child, albeit with its maternal grace note: this is how Amaravati had made out the paternity. The sex of the child had been determined by a less esoteric method. Recall for a moment Amaravati dabbing Asha's forehead with a cold compress after Asha had hyperventilated on learning she was pregnant. Minutes later Amaravati had placed the compress in a shallow pan and covered it with the liquified contents of a beaker of carotene extract. Its white cloth had turned rust-colored where drops of Asha's perspiration had touched it, indicating a boy. Proof of gender by hormonal induction.

Had Amaravati come along on the flight to Palace Isha, she and Asha would have had fascinating talks. But Asha was on her own again. By now the fleet was beyond sight of the sky-lodge, though the Malachite Sea itself, which had preceded by a billion years the palace built on its cliffs, still threw its jade shine into the sky. Asha, standing in an aft gallery of her ship, witnessed the dimming of this last link to the house of the Shaasak until the light off those distant waves flickered out against the horizon.

For the next three days the gubbaare made an elegant flock in the skies of the interior. The fleet commander was also chief engineer of this new class of airship, and out of him tumbled, with Asha for an audience, endless technical details about the construction and specifications of his craft. He also liked pointing out the views, though not he nor any other person had seen the raajy's interior from above before now. Taking in the miniature canyons and oases below, Asha's mind ran ahead to the landscapes of their destination—the woodlands and the dells, the ice and the alp—and she wondered if they would make the crossing before Cabaan finished his dam. He would be close to it by now, nearly done diverting the river and clearing the last suitable tracts around the palace for a monoculture of kuroops. The western woods would be choked, but Cabaan would have his yield.

At Asha's request, the fleet commander gave permission for the gubbaare to accelerate to their maximum speed. During the night, pilots steered the flying ships by starlight while captains and crew, and Asha in a rare room for one, slept in their compact berths, in quarters built adjacent to each gubbaara's engine-room and within the bone-warming throw of heat off each furnace. But on their fourth night of transit, the turbulence at two thousand feet was severe, even worse when they dropped down by half, so the commander, confident of his ships' sturdiness though unprepared to risk catastrophe to prove it, ordered them down onto a flat-topped hill. They would wait out the squall.

Here the commander took the opportunity to deliver to Asha, as instructed to do at an appropriate moment of his choosing before arrival at Palace Isha, a packet containing three items:

The first was the instrument of divorce, which Asha knew had been entrusted to him before their departure.

The second was a volume of poetry by the Jaanam's great-grandmother, looking less than priceless in its cloth binding, with ragged edges and a cover crisped by the sun, though the flyleaf was inscribed with the affections of the Jaanam herself, which was very nice.

The third item in the packet was a royal pramaanpatr of stunning content: Asha was Raajakumaaree again. She hadn't even been sure that a marriage-voided title *could* be restored, and asking the Shaasak about it had seemed unbecoming, though his signature on the document via blood-thimble left no doubt about its validity.

An hour later, after the winds had died down and the fleet lifted off again, Asha found herself drifting over the moonlit curve of the earth. If she had been given the choice to stay here, above the land but below the stars, living permanently in the sky during the pause of night, when the rest of the world lay asleep and nothing could be expected of her, she might have said yes. But a breathing space between past and future is brief for a reason—and Asha's short fantasy of avoidance was less a relapse than a revelation …

She realized what the pramaanpatr meant. At first she had thought it was the Shaasak's parting gift to her, a reward for the work she had already done. Now she knew it was a shove to start the work she would have to do next.

xii

"Life," goes a minor canto in the long poem of the Zaabta, "gives us less than we hope for but more than we expect." Bear this in mind as you adjust yourself to an acute disappointment: Asha did not arrive at Palace Isha in time to stop Cabaan from completing his dam. On her nine-day return journey by air from the sky-lodge, she had described for the curious fleet commander and his crew the glacial flats and alpine crests of the far north, and the silver-white sheen of the western woods. The commander called her to come look as they neared their destination, but in sight of a palette of colors unlike anything Asha had mentioned. These forests were blue! It wouldn't take long to see that Cabaan's dam had not only robbed the land of its natural water supply, but released jets of boiling wolfram up from the lithosphere and into the root systems across an area surpassing two thousand haiktars. Excepting the unique kuroop, wolfram was deadly to the botany here. Even worse, geysers of mercury were now spewing over the surface, coating bark and leaf alike. The otherworldly beauty of these blue woods was not what it seemed: this was the hue of poison. While Asha had been away learning to offer herself a degree of the compassion that she offered every other person of her acquaintance, her husband had been subtracting compassion from the world around him in such prodigious amounts that without some countervailing infusion, death would soon end every sentence that began with the words, "At Palace Isha …"

The world may rise up to beat back the evil it creates, but seldom as fast as we'd like. Cabaan's dam had been working for sixteen days. Waters had been diverted and wolfram-rich land exposed for the largest tract of kuroop trees anywhere on earth. Only the nursery finally running out of seedlings brought the frenzy of planting to a halt. It wasn't that Asha had lingered at Aakaash-Nivaas a week or a day or even an hour too long to change the course of events at home: she could never have gotten back in time. Cabaan had been too efficient. He was, let it not be forgotten, exceptional at his job.

xiii

An air-raft came down from the fleet. Of the original group of ships, two had been forced to turn back midway, the first due to a defect in its steering system, the second after an outbreak of ptomaine from a batch of tainted lentil cakes impaired the crew. So now it was a group of four hovering above Palace Isha. The air-raft bearing its trio of passengers did not touch down in the gardens fronting the great series of domes and spheres that formed the ancient house, descending instead through a vapor into the backlands.

Cabaan was nowhere in sight. His planters and pruners, however, put down their loppers and shears; while his score of managers, who had been staring anxiously at the imposing ships overhead, felt secretions greasing their bodies. These were not foreigners like the laboring aapravaaseen, but men of the raajy who had aligned themselves with their employer not out of desperation, but from desire. Desire to be powerful, desire to be respected, desire to become rich. They had assumed there would be time enough in life to profit from the suffering they had inflicted on themselves by working here; now, all at once, they sensed a great rotation happening, and they felt the rewards that they had counted on abruptly circling out of reach. Many were dismayed, but at least a few of them, despite heavy investments in their own misery, were ready to cut their losses and get out.

The air-raft landed. For the staff of the household, who had been watching from windows along the domes of the palace and run downstairs and onto the backlands to see up-close, the reality of Palace Isha's one daughter coming back to them was incredible. Her hair was cropped at the ears where in their memories it fell below her shoulders. The sari she wore was made from a golden mesh that wound around a sleeker form than they recalled. Her bearing had changed too: she stepped out from the air-raft and onto the cracked ground of the backlands not only with her mother's famous poise, but her father's quiet conviction. She seemed to those watching her, as if through a mysterious forward-remembering, to be the Asha they had always expected. Even the aapravaaseen, who had presumed without information to the contrary that Asha had either fled or died, were astonished. These men from across the raajy's western border—their hands scarred by kuroop thorns and their skin stinging with wolfram, toiling in a foreign land for just enough money to send home and keep their families afloat—even they still had hope in their hearts for what this return might mean.

Out from the air-raft to stand on either side of Asha came the fleet commander and an officer of the sky-lodge, the Shaasak's message-bearer-cum-proxy, his "sandeshavaahak" and "pratinidhi," to give the translations in ever lyrical Bhaashan. (Because who can resist knowing such words that sound like tiny songs in themselves?) A marshal-at-arms had been excluded from the contingent that had set out to bring Asha home, at Asha's insistence; but even she hadn't been able to argue against including this gentleman whose sole assignment was to communicate to the people of Palace Isha the legality of what was now what—then leave the rest to her.

He spoke through a vocal-cone, identifying himself and offering for inspection his medallion of office before ordering all work in the backlands to cease and the Vikaant Cabaan to present himself for a process of adjudication that Asha would oversee. Cabaan failed to appear, but a manager rushed out from the glazery, not having heard the message-bearer's pronouncement and demanding to know on whose authority planting and pruning had stopped.

With the turn of a knob on his vocal-cone, the message-bearer projected a reiteration across the length of the backlands:

"YOU ARE
COMMANDED
BY
WRIT
OF
SURAVARAMAN
SHAASAK!

I AM SENT
FROM
AAKAASH-NIVAAS
AS
MESSAGE-BEARER
AND
PROXY!

ALL WORK
MUST NOW CEASE
AND
THE VIKAANT CABAAN
IS TO
PRESENT HIMSELF!

THESE ARE
THE WORDS
OF
THE
SHAASAK!"

The combative manager resisted no further, even as a commotion broke out across the backlands. Asha took possession of the vocal-cone and did her best to put aapravaaseen and managers at ease. She and Cabaan would speak shortly, she promised, and the state of confusion at Palace Isha would come to an end.

xiv

One hour and forty minutes later, Cabaan arrived along with the messenger sent to find him, having charged back from a technical scout in the northern woods, where core samples had brought up wolfram-manganese composites and preparations were underway for a test-planting of kuroops. He marched into the Gathering Dome to find its seven thousand square feet packed with aapravaaseen, managers, staff of the household, friends, neighbors, and persons unknown to him: the fleet commander, the crew of the remaining gubbaare, and the Shaasak's message-bearer.

Asha herself was seated by a window speaking with Jothi-Anandan when a voice called affably through the vast room:

"Asha! I can hardly believe my eyes! So it's true, you've come back to us after all!"

Though his tone was charming, the effect of Cabaan's words was another matter. Jothi-Anandan leapt off his window seat and hovered protectively near Asha while others bit their lips and clenched their fists in what was a response without conscious thought to the stimulus of Cabaan's voice.

"It's been so nice not having you here," he said, sounding perfectly sincere. "You may remember me telling you that I disliked the house empty. Well, I'm embarrassed to say I've changed my mind!"

He was keeping his distance as he spoke, studying Asha from the doorway. Her new look had made an impression, though the gold mesh of her sari was what had really caught his eye.

"You look well, Asha. Where have you been?"

"To a place of not even one time more."

The obscurity of the reply provoked him, though he didn't know why. He drove his mind at Asha from across the room, demanding an explanation, but receiving none. Not even someone as repellant of awareness as Cabaan could have failed to see that this was not the Asha of the last five years, though to what extent the difference would matter to him he still was unable to imagine.

Asha chose her moment to speak again:

"I'd like to say something now about the White Forest, my father's botanical masterpiece that you've—

"Your father's *master*piece?" Cabaan howled. "Are we back to that already? Referring to your father in the reverent tones due a great man? Be*lieve* me, Asha, your father was no—

"You did not know my father," Asha said, cutting him off, "and it consoles me to remember that he did not know *you*."

Even her manner of speaking to Cabaan was new. Whether it was an affectation or some true change he couldn't tell, though in a single terrible instant he realized that he liked her better this way.

"You've been to the sky-lodge," he guessed.

Asha produced the instrument of divorce. It was passed by many hands to Cabaan, who read it slowly. He looked up at Asha and said in his lighthearted way:

"It seems our marriage has run its course. Well, I hope it won't upset you hearing this, but I have to tell you, I'm relieved. All the more convenient now when I boot you out for good."

For the first time Cabaan's habit of speaking ugly words with a cheerful air provoked no reaction in Asha whatsoever. Not so for others in the room. Asha could feel the anxiety radiating from brains and glands, the collective response of hundreds of nervous systems, agitating the very particles of the air. To mitigate the effect, she proposed to Cabaan that they step away for a private word. He agreed without saying so, walking directly to a door that led to the dome's antechamber. Asha followed and entered, closing the door behind her.

A small room of bright white marble, the antechamber happened to be where the mosaic-style portrait of Asha that her mother had painted was hung. *Asha At Twenty-Two.* Surprised to see it hadn't been taken down in her absence, Asha only in this moment realized that she had reached the age envisioned by her mother in the image, gazing at it just long enough for Cabaan to notice.

She turned to him:

"I want you to know that I invited the others in to keep them calm, by letting them witness events for themselves instead of hearing what's happened secondhand and not being sure. I didn't bring them in to shame you."

"You don't have the power to shame me, Asha."

Now it was Asha's turn to study Cabaan. A beam through the antechamber's high, oval window was firing his hair to the hot shine of precious metals. He seemed to have grown taller and stronger than Asha remembered him, and this in someone who was already the tallest and strongest among them. His heterochromia iridis was accentuated by reflections off the white of the marble, making his mismatched eyes, the one violet, the other pale blue, even more striking than usual; and the color on his face from a morning in the sun had conferred a radiance that any artist would have been lucky to capture. He was—Asha finally saw it—staggeringly handsome. But the outer Cabaan and the inner had diverged completely. How very unexpected, she thought: for such a long time she had imagined that *she* would be the one to split apart.

An urge came over her to tell him everything: all about the months of her yaatra and her weeks at the sky-lodge, explaining at length and for as long as it took what she had realized about him—about *them*—during her time away. She even started to compose in her mind a few words to broach the subject—until she stopped herself. She could see in the way he was staring blankly at her that he was right: she had no power to affect him, no matter what words she used or how much she tried to explain. So she made a simple statement of fact instead:

"It's time for you to leave my house, Cabaan. You don't belong here anymore."

She braced herself for a storm of abuse. But Cabaan said

nothing. His blank expression did not change. Asha thought for an instant that he might even be happy to go, that being divorced might free him too, in his own way.

He took a breath, let it out as if in vague regret, and turned away.

Asha watched him step over to her portrait on the wall and take it down. The thought that flashed through her mind was that he wanted this memento of her to bring with him to his next home. All but confirming it, he turned back and smiled gently at her. Then he placed the portrait flat on the floor, unbuckled his belt, opened his pants, and began relieving himself.

He urinated in circles onto the small canvas, burning into paint and cloth. His thick stream in contact with its target produced a sound among that particular class of noises instinctively vile to the ear, though the odor of saffron that his urine released into the room, reminiscent of metallic honey, was not wholly unpleasant. When he was done, he shook himself clean, closed up his pants, buckled his belt, and blew Asha a kiss.

He looked down at the portrait again. Asha's painted face, made of delicate pigments, had not withstood the salt and acid from his body. The dozens of precise brushstrokes that Asha's mother had labored over, the tiny squares of ruby and gold, dark purple and pitch black adding up to her daughter's image, had run to the edges of the frame. But Asha was not her image. When Cabaan looked up at her once more, he saw that she had remained as she was: intact.

She turned and left the room.

He followed.

They came into the Gathering Dome, moving back to opposite sides of its great space, with hundreds between them.

"My former wife," Cabaan declared to the crowd at full volume, "the Vikaantee Asha, has chosen to make her next—

—"She is *not* Vikaantee!"

Heads swiveled to find who had spoken. It was little Jothi-Anandan. He was clutching the Shaasak's pramaanpatr, which Asha had left on a window sill when she left the room for the antechamber. "She is *not* Vikaantee!" he called out again to Cabaan. "She is Raajakumaaree!"

He turned to Asha beside him and offered a toothy grimace. "Sorry, Raajakumaaree. I got bored waiting for you, so I read it."

With her gaze Asha told him that she did not mind, while the attention of others in the room shifted again to Cabaan. He was forced to leave his side of the dome to approach Jothi-Anandan.

He took the pramaanpatr from the boy's outstretched hand. No one spoke while he studied it: not Asha, not Jothi-Anandan, not any of the hundreds of laborers, managers, staff of the household, friends, or neighbors. It was a long interval for such a short document, during which many in the room who had held their breath when Cabaan had begun reading had to exhale, inhale, and hold their breath several times over.

At last Cabaan looked up. With a dullness in his voice that had not been heard from him before, he told Asha:

"The wolfram-wood is still mine. The land we grow it on is mine. You signed it away. The Shaasak has restored you Raajakumaaree, but even he can't give you back what's no longer yours. He can't overturn the law. You and I entered into a series of legal transactions. You signed your land away, Asha."

"Which you can easily sign back again."

"And why would I ever do that?"

"For your liberty. Some months ago, you confessed to me a murder of premeditation. Our marriage contract is void, so I am now the authority in these lands on matters of justice, and it falls to me to adjudicate your crime. I've taken nine days to make my deliberations, and the sentence I've settled on is lifetime imprisonment. Or, if you wish, exile—though only in exchange for every haiktar that you own."

Asha was speaking formally, in a voice to settle rather than inflame. It worked on everyone except Cabaan, who reverting to form seemed about to laugh.

"I expect it won't surprise you to hear," he said, "that as amused as I am to see you've taken my advice at long last and learned to negotiate, in this case I'm going to decline your terms outright. No, Asha: I'm *not* going to give you back your haiktars, I'm *not* going to surrender my land to suit your whim, I'm *not* going to put at risk my wolfram-wood enterprise, which operates *on* my land, and I'm certainly *not* going to defer to—pardon me for being the one to have to tell you this—your implausible 'authority.'"

"Then it's prison for you," Asha said. "You'll spend the rest of your days a very impressive landowner living in a ten-foot-square stone box."

He lunged at her. His huge hands were around her neck in a second, and not all the jumble of women and men who leapt in to help could get him off. He was strangling her. He would have killed her too, but exactly now, and with the kind of timing that once in a while life truly delivers, a bandook was fired inside the dome. Cabaan jerked around in reaction along with everyone else, his hands flying off Asha involuntarily.

Bandooken were rare in the raajy, even rarer outside a forest, meaning the shock of an indoor discharge was real, made more shocking by the woman holding the weapon: Omala.

"I'm told Ilarô died to stop you, Cabaan. I've stayed alive to finish the job."

Omala's glance shifted to Asha, each cousin silently shouting her joy at finding the other among the living. Then Omala laid her firearm on a table, crossed to Cabaan, and struck him in the stomach. Remember this: she was stronger than *he* was now, at least temporarily, braced by the steroids of the remedy pool. Where her fist made contact, she burst a blood vessel in his stomach, not only provoking but actually hurting him. No one had done this to Cabaan since he was ten years old.

With no inhibitions left in him to hold him back, he attacked Omala intending to kill her for good this time. His first blow landed on her neck.

She suffered it without crying out—and struck back. Her brutality surprised him, giving her the advantage she needed. She pinned him to the floor, kneed his cheek into a square of cold slate, snatched a wolfram-wood dagger from the air—tossed to her by one of Cabaan's managers—and raised it up to stab Cabaan dead.

"Omala, stop!" Asha shouted. "That's enough!"

Crackling with adrenaline, Omala wasn't ready to give in. "Asha, he tried to kill me! He must've thought he *did* kill me! Is this not a fair reply?!"

"Cousin, put the knife down!"

In her whole life Asha had never commanded another person in this manner; yet she was unwavering:

"Put the knife *down*!"

Omala let a bloody dribble of spit fall from her mouth onto Cabaan's lip. Only after it ran down his cheek to his collar did she comply with Asha's order, setting the knife on the floor. Cabaan squirmed, testing her hold on him, but she was still pinning him down with knees on wrists; and her dagger might easily be snatched back up and plunged into his throat.

Asha called over to them:

"Come here, Cabaan."

Omala released him: he sprang to his feet. Omala stood too, picking up her weapon and placing it on the same table with her bandook, far from Cabaan's reach.

After wiping Omala's spit off his neck, Cabaan crossed to Asha. She set down a document for him to sign: an agreement written up on the last morning of her nine days in the air, offering exile in exchange for land. While he read, Asha motioned to Jothi-Anandan, who retrieved a small box from the window sill and brought it to her.

She held it out for Cabaan. He reached to take it, his resting expression—vacant yet oppugnant—unaltered. Flicking it open, he extracted the blood-thimble it contained and jammed it onto his index finger, puncturing himself without wincing, indeed without any contraction whatsoever of the bands and bundles of fibrous tissue beneath the skin of the face that produce signals of emotion.

He signed the document in his own gore.

"Vikaant Cabaan," Asha said, "I banish you from Palace Isha in the name of my honored father. I banish you in the name of my beloved mother. I banish you in the names of all those who lived in and around this house before you came to be among us and all those who will live on here after you go. I banish you in the name of the geetakaar Ilarô, and I banish you in the name of the child growing to life inside my womb, whose father you are not."

There was no sound in the dome, not a cough, not a breath, as Asha concluded:

"The Zaabta of Souls will record that at a place called Palace Isha, for a time there lived a man named Cabaan who did not care for the people around him—so they learned to care for themselves. Vikaant Cabaan, you are from this moment a banned person. You will leave here and you will never return."

Cabaan tried one last time to negate her with his gaze—in vain.

So, finally, he turned to go. All eyes were on him as he made his way to the door … as his arm left the side of his body … as he whipped Omala's bandook off the table that she had laid it on, as he pivoted, aimed for Asha, and fired. Asha and her unborn child would have died in the moment that followed, except that Jothi-Anandan, ahead of everyone, was already in motion. He stepped in front of Asha to let Cabaan's wolfram bullet strike him down instead.

Darting in, Omala slapped the bandook from Cabaan's hand before he could fire again. But Cabaan kept his eye on Asha. In this single act he had triply condemned himself. He had tried to kill Asha, not only attempted murder but the attempted assassination of a Raajakumaaree, a cousin of the Shaasak and born out of his same line. This was more than a capital offense, it was an aggravated crime which in ancient days had been punishable by evisceration of the still living offender. Secondly, and even worse in the eyes of the law, Cabaan was guilty of assault against an expectant mother, discussed in all the commentaries on the long poem of the Zaabta as an offense more heinous than regicide, because who knew what gifts a child would bring with it into the world, who knew what child might *save* the world, or at least show the world the way? This was an act of barbarity considered to have passed beyond the ways of men. Except, it now seemed, by Cabaan. Lastly, he would in minutes be guilty of hatya—or as we would say it today, inadvertent killing. Jothi-Anandan wasn't dead yet, though he was about to be. But here was his secret: he didn't mind. A boy in body, he had in him the instinct of a sage: he had guessed at, and now knew for sure, the joy of sacrifice.

The reaction in the room was less serene. Giribandhava ran in and dropped down beside his bleeding friend. Asha was already on her knees next to the boy, though it was clear to everyone that his wound would take his life.

As if slipping into a warm sleep, he whispered:

"I want to die outside."

Giribandhava tried lifting him, but needed Asha's help. Together they carried him out, passing and ignoring Cabaan. Hundreds filed out after them, leaving a dozen or so—and Omala.

She and Cabaan fixed on each other. Omala went for her dagger just as Cabaan, seemingly blocked from the door by three of the aapravaaseen, punched through them and bolted.

Omala flung the knife—but missed. The new bulk of her muscles had spoiled her aim. She snatched her bandook off the table and ran after Cabaan, chasing him into the back channels of the house and up a nearly vertical set of stairs onto the long roof, that stony field held high by a tetrad of colossal orbs. Cabaan was far enough ahead to conceal himself behind a row of chandava trees, their vegetation heavy with the season. Meanwhile, on the grass below, Asha and Giribandhava had laid down Jothi-Anandan as gently as they could. Asha held the dying boy's hand; Giribandhava was crying; but Jothi-Anandan was unafraid of what was happening to him. He smiled one last time … and was gone.

A shot sounded on the roof. Cabaan could be seen darting between chandava trees in their wooden planters, Omala pursuing, her bandook outstretched.

Cabaan leapt behind the last tree in the row, but there found himself trapped. Omala tried drawing him out:

"I knew you were a monster! I never guessed you were a coward!"

This had its intended effect. Cabaan stepped out to face her.

"You've gained weight, Omala. You look worse alive than you did dead."

"Do you understand what a waste you were?"

"Don't dare speak of me in the past tense, you intolerable kutiya."

"Ah. That's the real you, isn't it. Foul mind, foul life. I did warn you that you'd become yourself in the end. And that's exactly what you've done."

"You can't kill me."

Omala raised her bandook. "And why not?"

"Because you're only a—

She fired at his mouth, as if to shut him up once and for all—but her bullet only grazed his cheek.

Tearing a leaf off the chandava tree behind him, he whipped

it over his head, gripping each end. Asha and Giribandhava below had a clear view of him as he leapt off the roof and began a floating descent. For a long moment, they could do nothing from below, nor could Omala do anything from above. She couldn't fire at him for fear of missing and hitting someone on the ground. His inertial path was taking him directly toward a covered jackal-trap, where he would land easily and either flee if he wished or stay to torment them further.

But Giribandhava knew how to stop him. Wiping away a tear, he left his dead friend in Asha's arms, crossed to the trap, and slid back its cover of whitewood.

Still a hundred feet off the ground, Cabaan grasped his reversal of fortune: the jackal-trap's wolfram-wood stakes rising up from the base of its pit were now his inescapable target. He barked at Giribandhava, ordering him to slide the cover back, but Giribandhava shook his head. At fifty feet, Cabaan began to beg. Asha couldn't bear it. In her mind she told him to close his eyes and give in. He did the opposite, thrashing arms and legs as if to swim even by inches in any other direction—to no result.

Stories abound of lives flashing before eyes in the moments preceding death. A complete life history, so it's said, unscrolls from start to finish in seconds, during which the unhappiness that a person about to die may have caused others through his selfishness or his indifference, whether knowingly or not, in ways large, small, forgotten, or never noticed, is made plain—as, alternatively, is the joy that a different person on the verge of departing may have brought into the world during her time incarnate. Whether the phenomenon is real or fanciful, what can be said for certain is that the urge to imagine it is a way to reflect on what separates us from those creatures of the earth that live only by instinct, organisms without the ability to make conscious decisions about how to conduct themselves or the faculty to review and assess their past actions. What can also be said for certain is that Cabaan, falling from the height of Palace Isha, had no mnemonic experience of any sort. No unveiling of what had been hidden or forgotten or never understood. No revelation. No triumph over himself.

He shouted a last time for Giribandhava to slide the cover back …

… and Giribandhava stepped away.

Cabaan balled himself up, but the wolfram-wood stake that he fell onto straightened him out in an instant of agony, impaling him from his foot up through his groin and straight out his head, splitting his skull. Chunks of his brain fell into the pit like the droppings of an animal.

Asha looked away. There were hundreds around her, but no one gasped or cried out or even spoke. The way it had gone here once before, though for every different reason in the world, only the breeze against the trees made any sound. Giribandhava stepped forward and slid the plank of whitewood back over the jackal-trap, entombing Cabaan.

After a minute, Asha knelt on the unexpected grave. No one could tell what she was thinking. Then she started to cry. At first Giribandhava and Omala—who had run down from the roof by now—and everyone else watching her were shocked. They didn't understand how she could weep for Cabaan, how she could feel sympathy or even pity for this beast. But Asha knew that although Cabaan's sins hadn't been theirs, who could deny that sins had been committed in the world they had made together?

So here it was. We've had many fits and starts along the way to Asha's transformation, but now, at last, it came: everything that she felt flowed from her, all her versions of love, which had already raised her up in life and would soon raise others alongside her. The tears that she cried now on Cabaan's grave might even, in time, wrench the world itself back on track, for they were tears that contained in them more power than the explosion of a star, more potency than the droplet from a remedy pool, enough power even to cure the universe! In Asha's tears were no mere salt and water, but all the chemicals of forgiveness.

She wiped her cheek, and though it may sound strange, though it may even seem incomprehensible, these were the words that she spoke:

"I'm sorry, Cabaan. I'm so very sorry."

Those within earshot were stunned. Disbelieving what they heard, they repeated it to the people behind them, who passed it along in turn. In this way it took only moments for the hundreds present to know what Asha had said. But no one could comprehend it, they couldn't grasp what Asha meant by it, they were still many steps behind her as she declared out loud her regret at not having known how to help Cabaan, as she asked him to forgive her, promising that she would forgive him too in time, that in time they would all forgive each other.

Then the hundreds around her began to catch up. They were starting to make out what she was doing, starting to feel what she meant, and they let themselves be lifted up by it, above their pain and even above their hatred.

Asha's mercy flowed wide. And in this moment, and for this act, she became a woman of greatness.

PART THREE

i

ORANGE CLOUDS lurched across a bruised sky. It was the morning after Asha had come home, and at Palace Isha no one was anywhere.

An irregular wind blew. The whitewood of Cabaan's grave flickered light and dark. On the other side of the ancient house, the backlands stood unworked, its planters and pruners absent, its managers elsewhere, its thousand rows of kuroop trees unattended. The following day was no different. If you hadn't known better, you would have thought the place abandoned.

But on the third morning after Asha's return, it was time to come out again. Together with a small investigating party, Asha toured a terrain flashing on and off from sunshine shooting down between high, scudding clouds. Having readied herself for the worst, the further she went beyond and around the backlands, the more she was encouraged, finding the state of things not so bad as it might have been. For instance: the western woods were in distress, though not, it seemed, fatally. Bizarre, Asha thought, to appreciate the merits of torture over murder, but life plays tricks with our expectations, and she was ready to take the good out of the bad. When the day's tour was done, she asked Omala, who had led the investigation, to give an analysis from the scientific point of view. The land, Omala believed, would recover; the wildlife too. Though how many seasons it would take was beyond knowing.

The question of general recuperation in and around Palace Isha would now be set aside for several days, because it was time for Jothi-Anandan's Memento of the Dead. Asha devoted herself to the arrangements. During her stay at the sky-lodge, she had picked up something of the spare tastes of the Shaasak and Jaanam, and of Ilarô too. Their taste for understatement, their taste for restraint. But with respect to Jothi-Anandan's last rites, Asha went her own way. His departure from this earth was to be nothing less than the funeral of a prince. Silks were dyed iridescent green using the oil of rare polar mollusks collected on the banks of the glacial lakes: the sparkling banners made from these fabrics were flown atop poles around the boundary of the palace. Enough gold foil was pounded out to make sixty lanterns, now strung in rows across the grounds, because this Memento of the Dead was planned for midnight.

A funeral pyre of whitewood was built on a low platform. There the body, draped from hip bone to hip bone in purple linen but with legs and chest left bare, was laid on a bed of white petals: Asha had ordered every rose in her gardens used for the purpose. Not a single flower was left on the trees; but just as the dictates of physics tell us that energy can neither be created nor destroyed, only transformed or transposed, no beauty was lost in the making of Jothi-Anandan's floral mound, only shifted from one place to the next.

Asha delivered the prashansa bhaashan before three hundred mourners. She began with a story of Jothi-Anandan jumping off the roof of Palace Isha, holding a chandava leaf overhead, gliding down and alighting squarely on a blue napkin that he had placed on the ground as his target. More fluke than physics, she said, but that was Jothi-Anandan: the boy who made luck do his bidding. She ended with an account of Jothi not only living but dying in joy. It would have been easier for her to sink into heartbreak, so we can be sure that she believed what she said.

When the eulogium was done, it was time to light the pyre. Asha did not give the signal, but stood where she was, rolling her fingers along her choker of shaanadaar diamonds. She had imagined wearing Ilarô's necklace until the day she gave it to their son. She had watched in her mind as it traveled down the chain of generations. She had pictured it worn by her descendants—her descendants with Ilarô!—in fifty years, in a hundred years, in a thousand. Instead she knew now it belonged to Jothi-Anandan. Her own unborn son, and her son's children to come, would owe Jothi their place in the world. Despite everything, she began to weep, hoping Jothi might know that this necklace of shaanadaar diamonds, worth more than Palace Isha itself, was still worth less than *him*.

She turned to Giribandhava:

"Bring me please the Vikaant's wolfram-crush. You'll find it on the table in his dressing room."

He flew to do it. Let's use the time before he returns to comment on Asha's willingness to refer to Cabaan in this way. For the rest of her life she would never flinch from mentioning her former husband. When the occasion required, she would speak of him openly and evenly. You might ask how such a thing could be possible after the harm he had caused her; but while Asha had always and would forever flame up against wrong done to others, for herself she chose not to mind. This was her existence: privilege and suffering, fairness and cruelty, trial and error—ordeal and acceptance.

In her life's first role, Asha had grown up a happy child. In her second, as Cabaan's wife, she had drifted from herself: with her dava and her nepentee she had tried to escape the truth of what was changing around her. Now, in her third role, as a student of reality, she had begun to put into practice the Shaasak's lessons. But the one lesson that she had gone to the sky-lodge having already mastered, that she had held within herself from the start, was the lesson that still counted most. Even while others in the Shaasak's circle strove to become voyagers of the inner world, to reach the place that Ilarô had reached and come back to them to sing about—all those dimensions of love beyond body—Asha had already been there and back. She had seen that love was the buzz in every atom, that it flowed from every direction, that it was the voice of the primal mastermind who will keep speaking to us until the end of time. The Shaasak and his samgha meditated with dedication to arrive at this place of under-standing, to hold onto what they learned there, and to remember once they returned that they must only give up all their opinions on inadequacy and failure and defeat to know how love truly worked. Asha was ahead of them. The Silent Shaasak had taken her in and advised her in a way worthy of the prince of an age; but Asha, in turn, had given this prince the proof of everything he believed. Even now she confirmed it by refusing to banish Cabaan from her mind or her speech—or even from her heart.

Giribandhava came running back from the house with the requested wolfram-crush, Cabaan's favorite tool, used for cracking apart bits of ore in which wolfram naturally occurred. Asha placed her necklace between the levers of the device and one by one pulver-ized each of its priceless beads … until she no longer held a strand of shaanadaar diamonds but a handful of shaanadaar diamond dust, already starting to luminesce in her palm. Sprinkling the crystalline powder over Jothi-Anandan's face and arms and bare chest, she watched as, on contact, his skin began to glow, and then to shine, emitting a radiance that no doubt came from science but hardly ended there, corresponding with the night sky by returning starlight to the stars.

"Goodbye, Jothi. You were a gentle soul."

His corpse shimmered with black diamond light. So the ancient legend was no myth, though many were startled by what Asha had done to prove it. Was it right, they wondered, for her to give up her greatest asset in this way, considering the uncertainties of the future and the many needs that might arise in the days and years ahead for such a treasure as a strand of shaanadaar diamonds? Because who knew when the moment would come in which jewels like these could change everything?

Asha knew. Her yaatra had made it all clear to her. The moment, she realized, was now. Anyway, were not diamonds as precious as these, so precious that no one could afford them, ultimately worthless in the material sense? You could trade them for no object of equal value because no object of equal value existed—and their price in cash could never be met. Asha, it seems, was beginning to develop her own set of views on that branch of knowledge concerned with the production, consumption, and exchange of wealth. So let others wonder if she had done right by crushing her shaanadaar necklace into dust—for her part she was thinking of the long poem of the Zaabta. "Give up your riches for riches," went the line from its invocation. Asha considered herself no philosopher, but even she knew a good tip for living when she heard one.

Out from Jothi-Anandan's pyre beamed the strong signal of his life. Asha stepped back and allowed the fire to be lit. It was a sacred night at Palace Isha as the blaze of cremation rose to the height of the treetops. Watching it, Asha gave thanks out loud to Jothi-Anandan one last time. There had not been a thanksgiving like this at Palace Isha for many years.

ii

The White Forest of Asha's childhood, her father's greatest work, which Cabaan had uprooted for a field of kuroops, would never be remade, nor would Palace Isha ever return to the way it had been. But some scars age well. It would take six years after the last kuroop tree was dug up for the backlands to heal completely, though small improvements began to take shape almost right away.

In the first weeks after Asha's return, she was often in the backlands, hands gloved, pulling up kuroop roots, carefully disposing of thorns, and burying the skeletons of birds that had tried to fly here before bursting into flame. But once the aapravaaseen working alongside her gathered the courage to tell *her* what to do, they insisted she stop. Gloved or not, the risk of wolfram poisoning was too great for a mother-to-be. She was paying them three times what Cabaan had paid, they reminded her: she should go inside and let them do the work she was spending her money on.

Asha did as they asked, persuaded less by the pecuniary argument than out of concern for her coming child. Which is not to say that money matters were irrelevant to the state of things at Palace Isha. By this time it had been discovered that Cabaan had died richer than anyone had imagined. Having exploited the connection between the wolfram and the kuroop not only to an efficient but a relentless degree, he had been rewarded accordingly. Not even Asha had guessed at the sum reported to her by the auditor brought in to assess Palace Isha's finances. But the instrument of divorce had inadvertently severed her right to the money. She had not been Cabaan's wife at the time of his death, so neither was she his beneficiary. His fortune, squeezed out of her land, went to his distant cousin, in a far province. Asha did not contest the legality of it. She would start again, on her own. She knew that as a consequence of this decision she would never be as rich as Cabaan had been, and nothing close to as rich as he would have become had he lived to carry on his activities for any length of time; but she had always needed less than Cabaan had supposed and now was ready to prove it. Of course, she could have been rich beyond measure had she been willing to capitalize on the wolfram still in the ground and the capacity of the kuroop to soak it up. It should surprise no one that she resisted the very concept of profit-taking.

There was, however, a complication: the Jaanam. Asha was thinking of the men killed on that collapsed bridge under construction near the sky-lodge and how the Jaanam believed that a wolfram-wood framework would have saved them. Night after night she considered the matter, reclining on her father's bench in his moon-viewing pavilion, watching the heavens wax and wane. After a month of it, she launched herself out of her seat one night and shot to the door. She dashed across the grounds, toward the thousand cobalt moons in the panes of the rotunda.

Inside she found Omala at her workbench, inserting a stick of wood into a beaker of foamy pink liquid. She watched her cousin gyrate the beaker for half a minute before asking:

"How did you occupy your mind, lying in the remedy pool all that time?"

"I wasn't conscious for most of it. But when I was, I conducted various socha prayog."

"And remind me what that means again?"

"It's the ancient phrase for 'thought experiments.'"

"Ah."

Another silence followed as Omala continued her work. Finally Asha came around to her quandary:

"Before I left the sky-lodge, the Jaanam asked me to keep sending wolfram-wood. How can I do that without picking up in some way where Cabaan left off?"

Omala gave a death stare in reply; but Asha carried on:

"The kuroops are nearly all dug up from the backlands, but

what do you think of trying a hydroponic garden in one of the old domes? Cabaan mentioned the idea once, growing kuroops in giant trays of solution made of dissolved wolfram and duck manure. He never got around to it, but might it be a less baneful way to produce a crop? Is it something I should look into?"

"Certainly nothing you do should *ever* resemble any action or idea of that revolting despot." (On the subject of her late cousin-in-law, Omala had proved less forgiving than others in their community.)

Undeterred, Asha asked her question again, though wording it differently and leaving out any mention of Cabaan. This time Omala didn't bother answering at all. She put down her beaker of pink liquid, apparently having soaked the stick it contained to her satisfaction. She reached into it, drew the stick out, shook it clean of clinging liquid, and held it out for Asha.

"Snap this please."

"What is it?"

"Just a bit of pine. Snap it in two."

Asha took the stick between thumb and forefinger in both hands and applied force—but it wouldn't snap.

"Try harder," Omala said.

Asha tried harder, then as hard as she could. It was only a twig that should have broken easily, but it wouldn't even crack. "It's hard as metal!" she said.

With a jolt she realized what this was. Gulping and gasping in quick succession, a bit of saliva went down her windpipe. Omala had to bring a glass of water to help her stop coughing. After regaining her composure, Asha said:

"Is it really possible? You've found a way to make pine as strong as a kuroop?"

"Yes and no."

"Explain to me the 'yes' part."

"Well: the kuroop's mechanism for absorbing wolfram into its biomolecule was not, as it happens, indecipherable. It turns out Cabaan never tried. Though, if we're being fair, neither did anyone else."

"Until you."

"Let's say until 'us.'"

"Us? *I* certainly had nothing to do with this."

"You were the inspiration."

"I don't see how that's possible, Omala."

Omala rolled her eyes in mock irritation.

"Anyway," Asha said, "wolfram is still part of the equation, yes? It's wolfram you've somehow put into this stick?"

"In a manner of speaking."

"So how is it different than the way Cabaan worked it, other than it being a less grotesque tree?"

"This stick is not pure pinewood. It's a hybrid. That's the 'no' part."

"I see."

The cousins held each other's gaze ... until Asha gave in:

"Omala, you know perfectly well I don't see at *all*! Please tell me this instant how this works!"

Omala allowed herself a prideful smile.

"Your beautiful pine trees, dear cousin—

—"My father's pine trees," Asha interrupted.

"The pine trees of Palace *Isha* ... have been cross-bred with Palace Isha's kuroops. The best characteristics of both were compatible. I've simply done some microscopic matchmaking. The hybrid has the look and scent of pine, and yet it can soak up wolfram like a kuroop, making possible its conversion to a metallic strength. Yes, it's twenty percent heavier than wolfram-wood, but no thorns, no poison, no pain."

"O*mala*!" For a moment Asha was at a loss for words. All she could think to say was:

"How is this not the most astounding news in the history of our lives?!"

Omala gave a bow of appreciation, though an afterthought was already troubling Asha:

"But what about the glazing process? Is it not still toxic? And electrically charged? Will birds not still burst into flame flying through our fields?"

"Not toxic. Not electrically charged. No birds in flames."

Asha bit her lip. "But how did you do it?" she whispered, as if afraid to hear the answer.

"I skipped the glazing altogether."

"You skipped the *glaz*ing? But then how did you finish the process?"

"Come back to me at midnight—and then, Raajakumaaree, you shall see."

iii

Under a Flower Moon of May, so-called for the abundant blooms of the month beaming their colors up to the heavens in reply to the full lunar light, Asha left the athainaaium, where she had spent the evening reading a book on household management, and crossed to the rotunda.

Omala was waiting for her outside, smoking a spearmint pipe. She gestured for Asha to follow. They walked on together without speaking, coming to a small field that had been cleared in a grove behind the lake. Asha hadn't visited the spot in several years and was surprised to see how Omala had transformed it into some sort of agricultural experiment. Half a dozen saplings were growing here, presumably the pine-kuroop hybrids. But the really intriguing part was what stood over each tree: a large glass lens atop a bamboo pole.

"Between deep sleeps in the remedy pool," Omala said, "I had time to think about how satisfactory my fist felt connecting to Cabaan's jaw before he left me for dead, with my wolfram ring cutting all the way to his chin bone."

Asha winced, though Omala wasn't trying to be obnoxious, merely informative.

"Which made me think of living tissue," Omala continued, "which made me think of skin as an organ, which made me think of the bark on a tree, which made me think of leaves, which obviously made me think of the green pigment in a leaf that absorbs light, which made me think of the sun, which made me think of the moon. And then it occurred to me: moonbeams."

Not wishing to disappoint, Asha had to confess that she simply wasn't following.

"I've ground these lenses to harness the electromagnetism of moonlight in a way of particular interest to us, "Omala said. "The beams catalyze the wolfram in the hybrid's biomolecules, priming the wood for hardening. Of course it doesn't *complete* the process, because we still need to saw the wood into planks. *After* that, to finish what we've started and lock in the transformation, we soak the wood in—now try to keep an open mind … mango juice."

"*Mango* juice?"

"Mango juice."

Asha looked a touch crazed at hearing this. "So the pink liquid in the beaker was *mango?*"

"Who would've guessed? It does the job as well as the glazery did—only benignly. No outgassing involved."

"But why does *mango* work?"

"It's the phytochemicals in the pulp. Triterpene. A class of chemical compound made of three terpene units—or six isoprene units if you like. Hydrocarbons, of course."

Asha was reeling at all this, but tried to keep up as Omala

elaborated, her voice sparking with the joy of discovery:

"The specific triterpene we care about, and that the pink mangoes of Palace Isha happen to produce, is squalene. Precursor to all steroids. Which, in combination with the mango's polyphenols, particularly gallic acid, caffeic acid, catechins, tannins, and especially mangiferin, a xanthonoid unique to mango fruit, did the trick."

"Did the trick of …"

"Hardening the hybrid to uncuttability. Obviating the glazing. Saving the birds."

"But how did you even think to *try* mango?"

"Honestly, it wasn't my first idea. You should see the list of produce I went through. Nothing worked. Then I recalled a chat I'd had with your former husband about the one fruit he loathed: pink mango. It's painfully unscientific, but I just had a feeling. So I put it to the test."

"Forgive me, but didn't you tell me not two hours ago that nothing I do should ever resemble any action or idea of Cabaan's? Why doesn't the same hold for *you*?"

"It most certainly *does* hold for me. I haven't done a *thing* that resembles any idea of Cabaan's. That's exactly the point: he steered clear of mango, I went straight for it. And aren't you glad I did?"

Asha looked stunned and even a little horrified that such a brilliant solution had gone un-guessed-at and un-looked-for, for so long.

"It can't be as easy as that," she said.

"It can be and is."

"I don't be*lieve* it!"

She did believe it though, because she had seen for herself it was true: if the evil visited upon us was a puzzle never to be solved, the good things that happened made perfect sense. What an absolute wonder was the world!

iv

On a balcony of the Middle Dome, Asha sat contemplating the backlands. The kuroops were gone. Cabaan's glazery had been dismantled and its pieces carted off. The vapors had dissipated, so the blue of the sky, an effect of the atmosphere scattering shorter more than longer wavelengths of sunlight—to go by Omala's not entirely comprehensible explanation—was again the gift of looking up. No less important was that a bird could fly here now without bursting into flame; and a person, if she wished, could run from house to river with no risk of setting herself on fire.

The aapravaaseen were gone too. Asha had sent them back across the raajy's western border, though not before ordering her great-grandmother's deepaadhaar—that ten-foot-tall candelabrum of solid platinum designed to light the Middle Dome's enormous dining room—melted down for them. Each man was given six platinum ingots to take home, a fortune apiece where they came from, enough to buy land and livestock, start and run businesses, support children and parents. Asha had been appalled to learn that a single object in her house equaled money enough to so change the lives of a hundred families: she wondered why she hadn't thought to melt down the deepaadhaar years ago in secret and send Cabaan's men home in the middle of the night while he slept.

She stayed where she was for another hour, studying the backlands, imagining the ways she might re-landscape, picturing what to plant here:

A eucalyptus forest?

A checkerboard of silver birch and pear trees?

A spice and herb farm, with plots of turmeric, ginger, curry leaf, cinnamon, and spearmint?

Or why not make the location available to young botanical artists and offer them funds to practice their art on the property?

Then it came to her: ornamental grasses. A sea of color, texture, motion, and sound, ever-changing with the wind and the light.

It would take several years to achieve, since the nutrients of the terrain had been leached away. Composting would replenish the land eventually, and a simplicity of design would suit it. And young botanical artists could still be given the flats between the far riverbank and the foothills—plus the money to create something new there.

Each day, looking out from this same balcony, Asha watched her plan sharpen from thought to form and form to fruition. These were the years in which her son grew too, becoming a double of Ilarô to look at, so it will be strange to hear that in a way of special relevance, he and his father could not have been less alike: the son had no musical talent. He possessed neither singing voice nor any aptitude with musical instruments; nor did he take after his grand-parents: he showed no inclination toward either the fine or botanical arts, failing to manifest any potential for painting or sylviculture.

On the other hand, he was an athletic child: a famously fast swimmer, a natural horseman, a chandava-leaf jumper without peer. He could run further and leap higher than any boy his age, though in this department he seemed to be taking after no one except himself. This is the extent to which he was distinct from the pair that had given him life, but there were similarities too. Like his father, he was calm by nature—a great gift, Asha believed. Like his mother, he was generous with his affection, and for this Asha often knelt in her bedroom at night and wept. She wept because she could see that her son would restore the goodness of his grandparents' house. She wept because her son was a kind boy who would become a kind man. She wept because her son could not abide cruelty: Asha had many times already seen him reach out to put a stop to—and even personally absorb—some instance of callousness that he encountered. He could ease the suffering of others, or at least their passing pains, with his laugh or his kiss. He had a temperament even more charming than his father's—and in his presence he made every person his equal. Not to mention his endless supply of jokes! Where he learned them all, his riddles and puns and funny stories, Asha never knew, though she guessed his source was a shelf in the athainaaium. The ancient library of Palace Isha must also have been where his recent curiosity about tattvameemaansa had been sparked, an unexpected development that pleased Asha in a way she could never have explained.

Watching him any number of times from the window of her favorite minaret, while on the grounds below he alternately amused and inspired friends and gardeners, visitors and staff of the household, Asha recalled a lesson from her days among the samgha of the Shaasak's White Chamber: in dire times all the world's evil may rival all of its good, so that the act of a single person, in the end, can mean everything. As it goes in the long poem of the Zaabta, even an eyelash off a compassionate being weighs enough to tip the scales of humanity. Asha quietly came to believe that her child was a contribution in the right direction and that in raising him she had finally done something of consequence. Those who knew her would have taken issue with the word "finally" in that sentiment, but on the subject of herself Asha remained modest in the extreme. Ah, well. It didn't stop her from pressing on.

Which brings us to the question of the rest of Asha's life. She might easily have married again in the time that remained to her after her return from Aakaash-Nivaas. Once or twice a man did come into her life whom she thought for a while she might love as a husband, because not all her tribulations had subtracted from her the desire or even the readiness to know and be known in this way. But of the few pleasant romances that filled out her years, none inclined her to make it a permanent arrangement.

Now a word on the Shaasak and Jaanam. Asha kept up a correspondence with them for nine years after her time at the sky-lodge, receiving a last letter from the Shaasak the same week he died at the age of eighty-four. The Jaanam continued to write after her husband's passing, though her letters were mostly about wolfram-pine. And though the supply of it that Asha was able to send was a boon to the raajy, it was not limitless. Over time Omala's lenses began to crack with the nightly frost, proving more difficult to repair, let alone build in quantity, than had been hoped. Without their steady magnification of the rays of the beaming moon upon each hybrid tree, Palace Isha could not produce wolfram-pine in a world-changing amount. Three hundred maatras in a good year, but never anything close to a thousand. The Jaanam had to set her priorities accordingly. Quake-proof bridges were first on the list to be built from this extraordinary timber. Gubbaare, by comparison, were not a truly vital use for the new wood, so sky-travel to the far north, which had only just begun, soon ceased. Crossings overland did increase slightly through the years, though never enough to alter the interplay between regions. The raajy's polar fringe and the white domes of Palace Isha remained distant to the rest of the realm.

On the death of Suravaraman Shaasak, his brother, Gajvadan, inherited the seat of state, and on the death of Gajvadan Shaasak, Suravaraman's nephew. As leaders of a realm these new Shaasakon were worthy men, though as guides through the inner dimensions they lacked their predecessor's fluency with the ancient techniques. So the Silent Shaasak's epoch passed, and the raajy settled into steady if unimaginative rule. At Palace Isha the effects were hardly felt one way or the other: they were simply too far away. Yet Palace Isha itself, which is to say the people who lived there, thrived. A general health returned to the region, lasting for many generations.

In the third year after Asha came home, Omala met, and to the delight of the community married, a vigyaanik from the raajy's southern borderlands who had come north to pursue his theory that the force of gravity varied with latitude. After the wedding he chose to stay on permanently at Palace Isha, moving into the rotunda with Omala rather than pressing her to return with him to his family home twelve hundred miles to the south. He and Omala went on to conceive many of the scientific marvels of the day, and it was to the pair of them that the electromagnetic spectrum yielded a handful of nature's most astonishing secrets. Asha's name was about to become something mythological, a name beyond time; but it was the name of her cousin, Omala, that fixed itself in history as the maker of an eon.

As for Palace Isha proper, Asha stopped spending her money on it. She needed what resources she had left to keep her people alive and well, and to invest in ways to provide for their children and grandchildren. So she let the gardens fronting the house go wild, and many felt they became even more beautiful than when they had been tended. The great house too, as whole domes were closed off and locked up for good, went from palace to beautiful ruin. This was typical of Asha's doings: she never led an army into battle, she never conquered the glacial peaks, she never wrote a seminal tome or cracked an atom, but she cared for the people around her. For this the Zaabta of Souls would list her, simply:

Asha of the Air
Princess of Palace Isha
A blessèd one.

After her return from the sky-lodge she lived just short of eighteen years more, until at the age of thirty-nine, without warning, a tumor took shape in her throat that no doctor could remove or remedy pool dissolve. It spread with violent speed to her lungs. She died in less than a month, her every beauty intact.

From across the far north admirers and well-wishers arrived at Palace Isha to pay their respects. Asha's son, the only child in the long story of the raajy born to a Raajakumaaree and an Ekko Jagaaya, gave the prashansa bhaashan at his mother's Memento of the Dead, starlight falling on him like tears from the face of the cosmos. But these were tears of gladness, not of grief. Because when it is said, as it is said in every age after the passing of some great soul, "there will never be another one like him" or "no life as beautiful as hers will come our way again," they are always mistaken. Do you understand?

Do you understand?

PART FOUR

AT NIGHT I often slide open the glass roof of my study and lift my eyes into the glow of space. I like to follow the astral paths and imagine where they lead. The lights of the galaxy are enticing—it's easy to see why we craved interstellar travel for so long, though personally I think less about going up to the stars than down to the earth. Now that I know my daughter has been dreaming earthward too, I might make the trip with her someday soon. There are no prohibitions against such outings. The dangers that sent us into the sky four millennia ago have long since passed: the magma-storms bursting up from an agitated planetary core, the fire-waves, the sulfuric winds. History was full of expectations that the earth would finally be threatened from space, by a monstrous asteroid or a gamma-ray burst or even by the arrival of some bloodthirsty super-race, but the Age of Magma proved the point that trouble usually begins closer to home. The earth's eruptions incinerated cities of millions without warning and went on scorching and crisping the earth for seven hundred years. It was safer in the sky. By the time the world calmed itself and grew blue and green again, we had been settled for centuries into our floating abodes. And so we stayed.

Here we have given back many of our technologies into the arms of time. We prefer relying on fewer devices than we used to. Yes, we enjoy our megascopes to peer to the expansion edge of spacetime; we maintain our particle-spinners for the lift to keep our cities hovering and the energy to keep our homes warm. But in general we have simple tastes and, truthfully, simple lives: we read, we teach, we raise our children. We are both a more advanced and a less complicated people than we used to be, though we still have the old problems of learning to be kind and struggling to be wise. Always an effort, but as my mother used to remind me: whatever you fill your head with, that's what you become. It was a lesson she liked to say she had learned from Asha, whom you may have guessed by now she believed to be her ancestor and the progenitor of our line. It's true, there are a few vaulted-up scraps of ancient data, recorded on magnetized candle near the end of the Age of the Poets, that support the connection between Asha and ourselves, or at least support the theory. With a bit of imagination you could devise a family tree that makes it work on paper. I've done it myself, amateur historian and translator of long-ago languages that I am. But it's nothing you could prove. And really, six thousand years later, it may be a nice thing to dream about, though beyond that I'm not sure it matters.

Anyway ... I'm thinking that for my daughter's birthday I might arrange a lander to take us down to the earthtop, so we can see firsthand the turquoise world beneath our silver cities, where no one goes. We'll find a eucalyptus forest and breathe its spicy air. We'll pick a bouquet of wildflowers. We'll lie on the grass listening to the wind. Asha will like that. And yes, I mean the Asha who is, of course, my daughter. The second "Asha of the Air," if you will. It was my mother's dying wish that her granddaughter should have this name, which is intriguing when you know that my mother passed away a decade before

I met my wife and twelve years before Asha was born. But my mother was a gardener of the mind: she liked to plant seeds.

I think I do too.

❖

❖

❖

Let's return then, in the moments before we part company, to a day three months before the original Asha's Memento of the Dead. In the Gathering Dome of Palace Isha, on a summer's evening, a young geetakaar is singing, a girl geetakaar, something new in the cultural life of the raajy. Asha's son, seventeen years of age, sits at the front of the room, host of the event; while in the back Asha stands listening to the song, until suddenly, and for no reason we can see, her hand flies to her throat, where she feels Ilarô's diamond necklace, though of course the necklace isn't there.

Stepping out of the room, she slips away. Soon she's riding her new mare past Palace Isha's boundary and into the western woods. She canters along a route familiar to followers of her story, arriving at the Dell of the Geetakaar, as Omala renamed it on one of her cartographical renovations of the area several years before.

At the stone temple we know, unvisited in many years, Asha dismounts. She walks this other home of hers that she made so briefly with Ilarô, all that time ago. Its corners shimmer in the twilight and a warm breeze flows along its roofless room.

Asha fills a cracked vase with wildflowers. She sits on a toppled column, but finds herself overcome with a need to close her eyes, so she moves across to the stone altar and lies down on top. She sleeps for an hour, until she feels someone standing over her, someone watching the constellations and their stories curl out from her very body and rise into the night sky. Gasping herself awake, she finds herself quite alone—and laughs.

After a minute, she swivels her legs off the altar, but where her foot lands against a jutting slab, she scrapes an ankle. It's a lucky thing: in bending down to wipe away the blood, her eye lands on the metallic tip of an ivory tube caught in a niche beneath the stone and reflecting starlight. A candle. A *magnetized* candle, from the bundle that Ilarô recorded on in the days before his death, and which Asha believed she had taken away with her and used up during her long yaatra to the sky-lodge. But this candle evidently remained; and now Asha remembers why: it isn't from the bundle of twelve at all, it's the partially used candle that had already been in the ebony box when Asha borrowed the device from Omala's laboratory, it's the candle that she discarded in place of a fresh one when showing Ilarô how to work his gift. She must not have noticed it in gathering up the others, nearly eighteen years before. A candle of Ilarô's. And it's opaque! But is it possible that Ilarô recorded on it? Or would it be a chance recording of Omala's? Was it just an assortment of Omala's notes? Or would Ilarô have recorded over this half candle too?

With a pounding heart, Asha dashes to her mare, finds a box of matches in her satchel, and dashes back to install herself beneath the temple's altar, safe there from the wind. She strikes her match, lights the candle, and listens as Ilarô begins speaking to her, having been with her in frozen time only an hour earlier. And then, for Asha, he sings!

Asha's life—can you see it now?—was like our lives: chaos, intuition, sacrifice, horror, holiness. Hard to say in the end whether Asha herself was fact or myth, but it's clear her love was real. Though perhaps the last word on who she was should come from what the geetakaaron themselves had to say about her, because in the years and then the centuries after she lived, they spoke and sang of her often. If you too had lived during that distant age and wandered some night into the range of a geetakaar's voice, if you had given yourself over to a spell of sound, this is what you might have heard:

"Listen if you like and I'll tell you the tale of Asha, of who she began as and who she became, of how she died in her mind and restored herself to life. Asha's time on earth was short, yet her achievement was complete. And though her tale contains extreme sorrows alongside its many tender themes, remember: all of these will fit together before we're done."

❖ ❖ ❖

❖